THE TRUTHS WE SEEK

USA *TODAY* BESTSELLING AUTHOR

LILY WILDHART

In the words of Mother …

Who you are is not where you've been.

ONE

MEYER
ELEVEN MONTHS AGO

My phone buzzes across my desk for the third time in a row while I look at the accounts for the club and try not to launch my computer across the room. I fucking hate doing the books, but I also don't trust anyone enough to let them handle it and not screw us over.

Sighing as I scrub a hand down my face, realizing I'm not going to be able to focus on the spreadsheet in front of me until I get more caffeine in my system, I close the document and take a deep breath. I flip my phone over when the buzzing stops and notice Tommy's name on the screen. That's unusual, we're not due to check in for a few weeks.

It starts to buzz again, so I swipe across the screen to answer. "Four fucking tries. Good thing nobody's dying, Kid."

A laugh escapes me. Not many people would dare call me "Kid", let alone speak to me like that. "Oh, people are dying, just no one we give a fuck about. What's up, Old Man?"

He guffaws down the line. "I swear to God, if you little shits don't stop calling me old…" He pauses and I can't help but wonder who else he's talking about, but before I can ask, he starts to speak again. "I need a favor."

My forehead creases as I frown. Tommy never asks for anything. Hasn't for a long time. He hates owing people, despite the fact that he'll literally bend over backwards for the people he cares about. Not that he cares about many people; I can probably count them on one hand.

Which means whatever this is, it's important, meaning it's enough to make me nervous.

"What's up?"

"The girl I told you about that I've been helping?"

"I remember," I confirm. He's mentioned her a few times. Hasn't gone into the deep details, but for Tommy to go out of his way for her the way he has means there's something about her that's special. "What about her?"

"I need you to put her somewhere safe. I've tried doing it her way, the small-town way, but you and I both know that disappearing in a small town is never going to last long. She needs resources I don't have—"

"But I do. Who exactly is she running from?" I ask,

curious.

"Her ex."

"Husband?"

"No, just a piece of shit that roped her in and beat her until she didn't think she deserved any better." My jaw clenches at his words. There are few worse cowards in the world than the ones who beat women to make themselves feel like men. "He nearly killed her, but she woke up. She ran. Except he's a cop."

"Fuck," I say with a sigh. That explains why it's been such a thing moving her. "I can help. Send me her file, and don't pretend you don't have one. I'll put a plan together. How long do we have?"

"She got his little package today so she'll be on the move tomorrow. I'll be sending her your way. She'll get there late tomorrow night, I imagine."

"Plenty of time," I respond with a laugh.

"Telling me you're not up to the challenge, Kid?" I can hear the bullshit grin in his voice and I shake my head.

"Fuck you, Old Man. Why aren't we just handling the ex?" I ask, curious. Seems a much simpler solution.

"One, he's a cop, likely to bring too much heat. Two, she doesn't want it. Says she doesn't want to be that person. She has a lot of demons she's running from, I think not killing him keeps some of them at bay."

I nod, not that he can see it. It makes sense in a fucked

up kind of way, but I've never been one to disobey a lady's wishes…well, not unless I have to anyway. "Send me her details. I'll get it sorted out and let you know the plan asap."

"You're a good kid," he says, and I laugh again. "Catch you later. Say hi to Angie for me."

I shake my head as he ends the call. I am not saying hello to my mother for him. He can deal with that shit show on his own. The trapped girl, I'll help, but his weird love triangle shit, whatever it is, with my mom? Not a chance.

My email from Tommy pings a second later. I click on the notification and download the document he sent. Without even reading, I hit print. This blue light shit is giving me a headache, I need paper.

God, I sound like my mom. I'm getting fucking old.

The machine whirrs, printing off page after page, and my curiosity piques further. How does one girl require so much information?

I grab my phone and send Harper a message asking her to bring me up a cup of coffee. I really need to get an espresso machine in here. I have the bar, but it's too early for whiskey. Her snarky response makes me laugh, but I know she'll bring me the coffee whether she bitches about it or not.

The printer stops as the door to my office opens. Harper struts in, face like thunder, but a cup of coffee in her hand.

"Coffee," she snarks, putting the cup on the desk, then stands, arms folded, hip cocked, glaring at me. "Anything else you need, Your Highness?"

"A back rub wouldn't go amiss," I tease, smirking at her. She rolls her eyes and huffs.

"Sometimes I wonder why I'm so attached to you assholes."

I grin wide at her as I grab the coffee and lean back in my chair. "You love us. We're amazing. You'd be bored without us."

"Uh-huh. Seriously though, anything else before I go back and finish the stock count?"

I shake my head before taking a sip of the apparently-scalding-hot coffee. "Nope," I hiss, blowing out air to try and cool my burned tongue. "You're an asshole."

"You asked for coffee," she says with a shrug before turning on her ridiculously high stiletto heels and leaving my office, slamming the door behind her.

I close my eyes, pinching the bridge of my nose and taking a deep breath, reminding myself that women are necessary for this business to work. Harper is a good worker, she's loyal, and she'd never betray us. Even if she does bitch and moan all fucking day long.

I trust her. That's rare in my world.

The door opens again and I open my eyes, about to ask Harper what sassery it is she forgot to spew at me before, but lock eyes with Hunter instead.

The smiling blond jerk strolls into my office like he doesn't have a care in the world and drops into the chair opposite my desk. God knows I love him like a brother, but if he puts his feet up on my desk one more time, I'll cut the fucking things off.

It's like he can see my train of thought because he leans back, stares at me, smirks, then winks and leans forward rather than kicking his feet up.

See? Jerk.

"What's got you so cheery?" I ask, despite knowing he's just a cheerful bastard ninety-eight percent of the time.

"Just got my dick sucked, I am living the good life. Who knew being single was so good?"

I drop the smile on my face and deadpan. "No one. The girls sucking your dick want more from you and you're going to have to deal with the fallout of it soon enough."

"You're a stick in the mud. I know that you haven't stayed celibate since—"

"Don't start with me, Hunter." I get up and head to the printer, hitting reprint before dropping the giant stack of paper in his lap. "Not today. Read up."

"What's this?" he asks, his face turning serious as he leans forward and flicks through the pages. "Quinn

Summers, twenty-seven, nearly twenty-eight. She's stunning, but why am I reading what looks like a personnel file?"

"Tommy needs our help." I tell him as I replay the quick version of my call with Tommy before picking up the re-printed file and starting to read myself.

By the time I'm finished, my headache is worse from the tension in my jaw alone and I want to take out this sorry excuse of a human.

"Why aren't we just dealing with the ex?" Hunter asks, his expression not far from mine. I tell him what Tommy told me and he rolls his eyes. "That's bullshit."

"I agree, but for now, we're going to help her hide. We didn't fill the bar position yet, right?"

He shakes his head. "No, why?"

"She looks like she'll fit in here. We can put her in the tower, you've still got your place there. You can keep an eye on her."

"That I can," he says with a wink.

"Don't be a dick, and stop thinking with yours."

"She's hot, and reading these journal entries Tommy somehow got—totally not asking if she gave them up willingly—I feel like I know her already. The struggle, the sadness, the darkness, but the light that shines through anyway."

I nod, agreeing, trying to tell myself that I can't be half

in love with someone from reading about them alone. Life doesn't happen like that. But reading about her, the notes in here from Tommy, the extensive medical records, the pictures, some of the therapy notes—though they're sparse, and that's being generous—it's like I've seen something that I know lives inside of me.

Our stories might be different, but I understand that darkness. The feeling of a tainted soul. The thought that you'll never be good enough, questioning your worth, smiling, despite the fact that inside, you're falling apart.

Something in that, in her words, in her eyes in the many pictures in here…something in all of that feels like a jigsaw piece connecting with an empty space in my soul.

I sound like a fucking crazy person, even if it is just inside my own head.

"But I'll keep my dick in my pants and I'll watch out for her. Does Rory know yet?"

"Does Rory know what?" I look up as the door to my office opens again as the man in question enters the room. Hunter turns and gives him the file he has in his hand.

"This," Hunter says as Rory takes the papers and moves to lean against the wall.

"Who is she?" Rory asks, and I find myself repeating the conversation with Tommy again. I watch him as he reads her files and I know the minute he reads the line I did, the one that made me connect with her.

'I've never thought of myself as a monster, but I continue to find myself surrounded by them. So maybe I am a monster, just one who doesn't see it. Maybe I deserve this life, the punishments I receive, because I am a monster too. Except I'm the worst kind, because I don't even see it.'

"When does she arrive?" he asks, looking me dead in the eye.

"Tomorrow," I tell him and he nods.

"Dario has been dealt with for now, but we need to keep an eye on him. I'll watch for her tomorrow. Did Tommy say how she's coming into town?"

"Not yet."

"Let me know and I'll be there to make sure she isn't followed." He pushes off the wall, drops the papers onto my desk, and leaves.

And just like that, I already know that this girl might be coming to us as a favor, but she's going to be so much more than that.

So much more.

TWO

MEYER
NOW

The fake laugh falls from my lips at the senator's terrible joke and never have I ever been more thankful for my phone ringing. "Excuse me a second, gentlemen."

I pull my phone from my pocket, stepping away from the group, my eyes scanning the room for Quinn. I can't see her, but then, I don't see the other two either.

Hunter probably has her pinned against a wall somewhere.

I laugh at the errant thought as I answer the phone. "Two seconds," I say as I head out the back of the hall into the crisp air of the evening, the noise of the room disappearing in an instant. "Hello?"

"Hello, is this Mr. Marino?"

A shiver runs down my spine and I stand a little taller. "Speaking, who is this?"

"Mr. Marino, my name is Shelley, I'm a nurse here at Shorefront Emergency room. We have you listed as the next of kin for Mr. Tommy Miller. He's being taken into surgery now and we need to go through some details with you."

Wait, what? Shock makes me freeze for half a second before anger and confusion settle inside of me, writhing like two snakes at war. "What do you mean, surgery?"

"I'm sorry, I thought you were contacted. Mr. Miller was shot this evening, he's in critical condition and has just gone down to surgery. As this is a private facility, we wanted to contact you immediately."

"He was shot?" Someone needs to give me more fucking details.

Shit, Quinn. I need to get her and get to Tommy like, now.

"Yes, sir, do you have a minute—"

"Do whatever is needed to keep him alive, money isn't an issue. Keep him alive." I put the phone on speaker and text Rory and Hunter, telling them to meet me at the entrance now.

"We will endeavor to do our best. You should know he had lost a lot of blood before the ambulance got to him—"

"I understand, just do what you need to. I'm on my way." I disconnect the call and head back inside, ignoring the people that call out to me. I head toward the table, finding Rory sitting there, standing as he reads his phone. He looks up, sees me, and nods, pausing until I get there.

"What happened?" he asks as he grabs his jacket off of the back of his chair while I grab Quinn's bag from under her seat.

"Tommy's in the hospital. He was shot. We need to get there, now."

He nods, pulling his phone from his pocket. "David, good, get to Tommy's place. Find out what the fuck is going on and report back."

Without waiting for a response, he ends the call.

"Where the fuck is Hunter?" I grunt as I check my phone again. I told him to meet me at the entrance, so I'm being unreasonable, but I do *not* like not knowing what's going on.

We reach the entrance and find the media presence has all but disappeared, off getting food before people leave, most likely, but Hunter and Quinn aren't here.

Rory checks his phone and pales.

"What the fuck now?"

"It's Quinn. She's not here."

My phone pings the next second and Hunter's name is on the screen.

Hunter:
Help. Bathroom.

My brow furrows, but my feet are moving before I can say a word. I slam the door to the bathroom by the entrance open and the world tilts for a second.

"Fuck! Rory, call an ambulance!"

I rush to Hunter's side, ripping my jacket off and placing it on his body, applying pressure as much as I can. There are too many fucking wounds. Rory enters the room, phone at his ear, and kneels on Hunter's other side, trying to staunch the bleeding that I can't reach.

"Trent. Took her." Hunter splutters, blood trickling from his mouth. "Get her."

THREE

HUNTER

"Oh, Angel, I'll let you devour me good and right, don't you worry. I wouldn't dream of denying you. Now how about you head to the bathroom, the one just as we came in, and wait for me. I won't be long."

Quinn stares at me, wide-eyed, for a heartbeat, a smile playing on my lips as I hold her gaze, wondering if she'll take the challenge.

As she lifts her brownie to her plump lips, I stifle a groan, thinking about them around my cock. She pats at her mouth with a napkin, winks at me, then stands and walks away without a word.

I stare as she sashays away from me, biting my lip as she puts an extra sway in her hips because she knows I'm watching.

Goddamn that ass is biteable. Fuckable. Slapable.

So peachy you could bounce a dime off it.

Keeping my ass in my seat is difficult, but this is part of the game. The anticipation is half of the fun. Even if my dick is hard as a fucking metal pole beneath this table. Not that I care if anyone sees. I know every single man in here tonight has seen her in that dress and pictured himself fucking her.

Unfortunately for them, they'd lose precious limbs if they tried.

Fortunately for me, I get to have her all to myself. Just as soon as these few minutes pass.

I can be a very patient man, but right now, I'm like a kid being told to wait for cake.

I don't fucking want to.

Someone at the table asks me a question but I don't really hear it, continuing to check my phone as the minutes pass slower than time has ever moved.

"Excuse me," I say to the table before standing. I have no idea who was even talking, but I am done waiting around. Without so much as rearranging myself to hide my straining dick, I make my way through the people in the room. Smiling when needed, trying to stop as little as possible, but then my phone rings and I want to throw it.

Except it's Harper. So I can't.

I duck into an alcove and answer the call, exasperation filling my veins like poison. "Someone better be dying, Harper."

"Hello to you fucking too," she drawls and I roll my eyes, pinching the bridge of my nose, trying to keep my calm. I don't have the mindset to deal with her shit at the moment. "The other two aren't answering and we have a problem. Four of the girls have called out sick, they're all from the basement."

Shit.

"Do we have anyone big coming in tonight?" I rack my brain because most of our clients are here tonight anyway.

"I don't think so."

"Then keep numbers reduced down there, we'll just have to take the hit and keep going."

"I could call Elise? See if she has girls who want to come over?"

"The fuck you will," I hiss. "The two clubs don't swap, you know better than that." The chastisement is sharp, but she, more than most, knows exactly why we keep the two separate.

"Fine, fine." She sniffs and I groan. Her manipulative ways might work with Meyer, but I've never liked her much. "We'll just take the hit."

"Suck it up, Harper. Meyer won't think less of his pet, don't worry."

"I am not his pet," she snaps back. "That would be the little blonde bitch you're all drooling over."

Rage floods me and my nostrils flare as I press my lips

together. "Be very careful what you say. Meyer might like you, but he won't think twice about cutting you out if you keep talking shit like that."

"Sorry," she mumbles, and the insincerity is so thick it coats my tongue, but I am over this shit. I have my girl waiting for me and this call has me distracted enough. "I didn't mean it."

"We both know you did. Keep your shitty, jealous opinions to yourself. Do your fucking job and suck it up. I have to go."

I don't wait for an answer before dropping the call. The moment I do, I feel it.

Except I don't get a second to move before I feel the blade on my throat. "You're the pretty one she's been simpering over. Fucking pathetic. She's mine. Always has been, always will be."

I clench my jaw but keep stock still. I can already feel blood trickling down my neck. Having my carotid sliced open really isn't on my fucking yes list for tonight.

"Trent, I assume?" His name tastes like ash on my tongue, but most of my thoughts go to Quinn. "Where is she?"

"Let's go find her, shall we?" His laugh makes his hand shake, the blade cutting my skin a little deeper. The second he relaxes, I'm going to stab him with his own fucking knife then cut his tongue out for daring speak of her after everything he's done.

My mind flits between Quinn and thoughts of torturing him as he leads me across the hall to the bathroom I was supposed to be meeting her in.

"How did you find her?" I ask as he opens the door with a kick.

He laughs again. "Not everyone is as loyal as you think. It only took three of your people giving up details to find you all. One of them was very helpful indeed. It's amazing what money can buy from the scorned."

I grit my teeth as he pushes me forward when I feel something heavy in my back. A knife and a gun. What is this guy, a fucking Boy Scout?

He pushes me forward, the door closing loudly behind us, and that's when I see her.

Slumped in a pile on the floor, bound and unconscious. "What the fuck did you do to her?"

All semblance of reason leaves me and I turn, feeling the blade slide against my skin but not caring. I swing at him, my fist connecting with his jaw before he has a chance to react, and I pounce, using every ounce of my weight and height to beat him into submission.

Except then I feel the air leave my lungs as his blade enters my stomach.

Once.

Twice.

Three times.

Again and again until I fall to my knees.

He laughs, spitting blood on the ground beside me. "Fucking idiot. I should just shoot you and be done with it, but then it's over too quickly. You wouldn't get to watch me take her."

I try to push to my feet but I can feel the energy fading from me. Glancing over at her, shame floods me.

I failed her.

He's going to take her and there's nothing I can do.

My phone buzzes in my pocket but I can't reach for it. Not while he has the gun trained on her.

He hits me in the jaw and I slump to the floor, trying to keep my eyes on her.

Wake up, Quinn.

I reach in my pocket for my phone, trying not to draw his attention. He lifts her from the ground, draping her in his arms like she drank too much. I pull up the message from Meyer, trying to type out anything that will let him know there's a problem, but I can't look at the phone. I just hope something makes sense.

"Oh, I'm going to have fun teaching you not to run from me, Quinn baby." He pauses, looking at me as I finish trying to send the message. He walks back to me, a wide grin on his sadistic face, and I make a vow to Quinn and myself that if I survive these wounds, I'm going to make him hurt. So slowly that he'll beg me for death.

He kicks me in the side and the little breath I have left whooshes from me as he stomps on my head. He laughs again and everything fades to black, his laughter ringing in my ears.

FOUR

RORY

Rage filters through me like ice taking form beneath my skin. I don't think I've ever been so focused, seen so clearly, as I do now.

The paramedics arrive so quickly, I wonder if I spaced out for a second, but as I move out of the way and they start working on Hunter, I realize it's not just me. Meyer looks as shocked as I do, but then, neither of us expected to be covered in blood tonight.

Especially not our brother's.

"His pulse is thready, we need to move him. Now."

I shake my head, trying to shed some of my rage so I can pay attention to what they're saying rather than playing out the scene of how Trent is going to pay for all of this in my head.

"How bad is it?"

The paramedic doesn't answer him, but from the

grimace on the guy's face, I know he doesn't think Hunter is going to make it.

Fuck him and his assessment. He doesn't know the man he's working on. Hunter's will is stronger than almost anyone I know. He'll survive out of sheer stubbornness alone. I'd bet my life on it.

In a blink, Hunter is loaded onto a stretcher, covered in gauze and wires and fuck knows what else and we're following behind as they rush out the front of the building with him.

Flashes go off from the cameras of the media still out here as the paramedics rush Hunter into the back of the ambulance. I stand here, covered in blood, hopeful that my brother will pull through, despite the medical assessment, but my mind is on the girl who stole my soul without even realizing it.

"I'm going to get her. I have her tracker, it won't take me long."

It's then I notice the crowd that has gathered around us. Close enough that they can get a piece of the action, but not so close to appear like the vultures we all know they are.

Meyer looks at me and I see the hurricane of emotions I feel reflected back at me. "Do it, but bring him back alive. He doesn't get a quick death. I'm going to call Mom, get her to go to Tommy, I'll stay with Hunter. Keep me updated."

I nod and take off without another word. It doesn't take me long to run to the stash house, just two blocks from here. I rip off the suit, slide into jeans and a t-shirt, grab my jacket, the keys to the truck I keep here, and check my phone again.

I'm coming, baby girl.

They're still on the move, heading down the 101. I calculate how long it's going to take me to reach them while grabbing two guns from the cabinet and a hunting knife, just in case. Trent might like to know just how skilled I am with a blade, and I'd love nothing more than to show him how to use one properly.

A dark smile plays on my lips while Meyer's request for him to be alive plays in my head.

He can be alive and maimed.

Without another thought, I head out to the truck, bring up the tracker, and start the engine. I'll follow them until he stops, then I'll take them. I won't risk Quinn any more by running them off the road, but there isn't a sliver of doubt in my mind.

I will find them.

I will bring her home.

And he will regret his miserable existence for the rest of what is left of his pathetic life.

Five hours.

That's how long I've been following this asshole who took my girl. He had the hilarious audacity to take her into a fucking cop shop. I barked out a laugh when I saw it after I caught up to them.

Not once has he stopped and I refuse to run them off the road. The highway might not be crazy busy as we drive through the darkness, but I'm not willing to hurt Quinn. The night vision binoculars showed me her slumped form in the back of his car and she hasn't moved the entire time I've been with them.

I refuse to think that she might be dead already. I'd know if she were dead. He wouldn't still have her if she was dead. I might not know much, but I know that.

A motel light flashes in the distance, catching my eye. The sun will be rising soon, so I'm surprised when I see his car blinker turn on before he takes the exit. I stay back, my lights off like they have been for the last few hours, and follow slowly.

He pulls into the lot of the motel, so I continue on a little and pull up on the side of the road. I rush from the car to the parking lot, watching as he walks, so fucking sure of himself, to the small office.

Taking my chance, I creep across the parking lot to the car, trying the handle on the back door.

Of course it's unlocked.

His cockiness will be his undoing, but it works in my favor. Without hesitating, I open the door and take in the sight of Quinn. Her chest rises and falls and it's like I can breathe properly again. I grab Quinn once I realize she's just out cold, her breath on my neck as I hold her giving me relief I didn't know I needed, and rush back to the truck. Once I have her situated on the back seat, I snap a picture of her and send it to Meyer.

Me:

Got Quinn. Dealing with Trent now.

Meyer:

I want him alive.

Me:

I know.

I roll my eyes as I pocket the phone again and head back to the parking lot, just as Trent is leaving the office. Waiting in the shadows, a wide smile on my face, I take great delight as he opens the back door to his car and proceeds to lose his shit, punching through the window.

Waiting until he's facing the other direction, I keep my breath steady, remaining patient as he throws his tantrum. The only thing putting a lock on me right now is the possibility of Quinn waking up alone. I don't know what he gave her, or how much, but I know he gave her something for her to be out the way she is.

It doesn't take long to creep up to where he is, and I take great pleasure in tackling him, wrapping my arm around his neck, and cutting off his oxygen. He fights back, but that was expected. He has no idea who he fucked with, and I've fought worse monsters than him.

"You thought you could take my girl and win?" I mutter as his movements slow. "Stupid, little wannabe. You thought you were a monster? You're about to learn what it's like to play with the real monsters."

His body goes limp and I hold another few seconds just to be sure, ignoring the blood running down my arms from where he scratched at me like a bitch. I check his pulse, just to be sure, then push him off me. Bending down, I lift him over my shoulder and walk him to the truck.

The tailgate drops and I bind his hands and feet, essentially hogtying him. No one said he needs to be comfortable when he wakes up.

Once he's secured, I check his pockets, grab his phone and the door key, then head back to the office, finding a kid no older than seventeen behind the counter. He looks up at me, and fuck knows what I look like, but he about pisses his pants as his eyes go wide and the blood rushes from his face, leaving him looking at me like a pimply ghost.

"You got cameras here?" I ask.

He shakes his head so hard I have to stifle a laugh. Him trying to decapitate himself isn't on the win list today.

"You wouldn't be lying to me, would you?" I quirk a brow and he shakes his head harder. "You going to let me look for myself?"

"S…sure," he stutters and I head behind the counter, check the space, then head into the back office. There's nothing but a decaying sofa back here.

Lovely.

"Thanks, kid. Forget you saw me, yeah? And the guy who was in here before me? He didn't check in, okay? Keep the cash he gave you for yourself." I slide the key across the counter and he gulps as he swallows.

"Yeah, okay. I didn't see anyone."

I smile, but it doesn't seem to make him feel any better. "Good. You don't want me to have to come back here, right?" I glance at his name tag. "Right, Dylan?"

"No, sir."

"Good, have a nice night."

"Yes, sir." he calls out as I push the door open and head back to my truck. I pull my phone from my pocket and dial Tonio. He answers after one ring. I give him the motel address and tell him to take care of the car then hang up without waiting for an answer.

I get back to the truck and check the bed, just in case. Dickhead is still passed out and nicely secure. Quinn is still passed out in the back, so I buckle her in, securing her as best as I can before climbing up front and starting the trip back.

I'm about three quarters of the way home when Tonio messages to let me know that he and Derek handled the car. They weren't moving as slowly as I was following Trent, apparently, or as slow as I am now knowing Quinn is passed out in the back. I want to go faster, get her to Rob to check her over as soon as possible, and get to the hospital to check on Hunter. But one, I know Hunter would want me to make sure she's safe first, and two, I'm not willing to jar her even a little because I have no idea what he gave her. All I have to go on are the three little puncture marks in her neck that I noticed as I buckled her in.

Three fucking doses of whatever he gave her.

I just hope it wasn't too much, but she's breathing, so I remain hopeful and keep my eyes on the road, aware that I've been up for over twenty-four hours. Isn't the first time, probably won't be the last, but I need to stay as focused as I can with the adrenaline slowly leaving me on top of no sleep.

"Rory?" Her voice is little more than a rasp, but I hear

it and pull the car over onto the side of the road. I hop out faster than I should be able to move and have the back door open and her in my arms in a blink.

"I've got you, baby girl." She starts to cry in my arms and I want to rip Trent's throat out. Sobs wrack her body and I hold her tight until she calms.

"What happened?" she asks as her head rests on my chest. I pull back and look down at her, her eyes fluttering closed for a minute before she opens them and focuses on me again.

"Trent drugged you and took you. I got you, you're going to be okay, but whatever he gave you is still in your system. Let's get you up front and head home. You can sleep the rest of the drive back."

She nods, but her head lolls a little, so I grab her by the waist, planting her in my lap before climbing from the truck with my arms tucked beneath her as she nestles against my chest again.

"Thank you for coming for me," she murmurs as she starts to fall asleep again.

I kiss her forehead before opening the passenger door to the truck. I lift her in and secure her seatbelt again. "'I'll always come for you, Quinn. Never doubt that."

"Who knew being kidnapped by you guys would be so good for me?" she jokes, groggily, and I laugh before closing her door.

By the time I'm in the truck and starting the engine, she's asleep again, but at least she seems to be okay other than being drowsy. Before I get back on the road, I call Meyer.

"How is she?" he asks the second he answers.

"She just woke up. She was talking and seems coherent enough, but she's asleep again now. We're about an hour out. How is Hunter?"

"He's out of surgery. They're saying it's still touch and go because he lost so much blood. That even if he wakes up, he might not be the same. He coded on the table twice, so it's a waiting game."

"Any news on Tommy?" I ask, and the silence that greets me is enough.

"He didn't make it," he says anyway, and I let out a soft curse. "It's going to break her."

"She's stronger than you think, but yeah, it's going to tear her up. Was it Trent?" I ask, trying to work out the timelines. Tommy doesn't live that far from here. He moved up here not long after she did, though I don't know if she knows that. He said it was easier for business to be back here and none of us questioned it. Could've been for Angie. Could've been for business. But it was probably to be close to her in case anything happened.

"Still looking into it, but it's too coincidental for me to think he's not at least partially responsible for it."

I clench my jaw as I glance over at Quinn. Just another reason that asshole in the bed of my truck is going to suffer slowly before I grant him the escape of death. "Okay, I'm not going to tell her yet."

"That makes sense. Get her home, Rob will be waiting. I'm going to wait here until there's progress."

"Okay," I say, running a hand down my face. "Once Rob checks her out, you know she's going to want to be there."

"We'll deal with it when we get there. Drive safe with her."

"You know I'd protect her with my life." My words are harsher than I mean them to be, but neither of us has had any sleep and I know he won't take it personally.

"I know. Get home, get some sleep. What are you doing with Trent?" Meyer just about spits his name and it's enough to make me smile.

"I'm going to put him in the hole till I'm ready for him. Tonio and Derek are meeting me back at the house now that they're done with the car."

"Good." I can hear his smile in the word and I know it matches my own. "We'll deal with him later."

He pauses and I hear voices in the background. "I've got to go. Keep me updated."

"You too."

He makes a noise of agreement before the call ends

and I frown at the screen. He'd have told me if it was really bad, so I swallow down the frustration and focus back on the task at hand.

Getting my girl home and getting her dickhead ex to Hell on Earth.

Sounds like a good day.

FIVE

QUINN

Oh, God. Why does my entire body hurt? It feels like I got hit by a semi-truck. I attempt to open my eyes, but even my lids feel like they have weights on them.

A groan spills from my lips as other sounds filter into my consciousness. Beeps, the sound of breathing, the scuff of soft footsteps. My heart rate picks up and my eyes open as panic filters through me. The first thing I notice is the doctor Meyer had me see before. The rest of the room comes into focus from a dim light somewhere and I realize I'm in the hospital.

What the hell?

I try to move and pain shoots through my entire body again, another groan leaving my chapped lips.

"Quinn?" The doc says my name like a question, so I open my mouth to try and speak, but it's like someone poured sand down my throat. A broken croak is all I manage before movement to my left draws my attention.

"Quinn? You're awake?" Rory almost jumps to attention, like he was asleep. He runs a hand down his face, his gaze meeting mine before moving to the doctor's. "What's wrong with her, Rob?"

"Give me a second, Rory. Jeez." Rob moves toward me as I try to tamp down the panic tightening my chest.

What happened to me? Why am I here? Why can't I remember anything?

"Rory?" His name falls from my lips like a prayer and he grips my hand before leaning down and locking his gaze with mine. He cups my cheek gently with his other hand, stroking my face with his thumb.

"It'll be okay, Jellybean. Rob just needs to look you over, and then I promise I'll tell you everything." His voice is low, soft…like he's walking on eggshells, and while his presence calms me, I can *feel* that something fucking awful happened. Not just because I'm lying in a hospital bed, but because he's being…he's not himself. I can't even explain it, but it's like his eyes aren't quite right. There's a sadness in them unlike any I've seen before.

He's always been haunted, but this…this isn't right.

Oh, God.

Something really bad must have happened.

My stomach twists as my brain conjures up every possible worst-case scenario, but I try to keep the whirring thoughts from taking root, locking them in my chest. It grows tighter but Rory squeezes my hand and I'm able to ground myself for a minute.

"Rory—" I start again, but I'm cut off by Rob clearing his throat.

"Can't check her out if I can't get to her, man."

Rory grumbles, but pulls himself back. He doesn't release his grip on my hand, and despite my panic of him not telling me what's going on, I'm grateful, because I think my vise hold on his hand is the only thing that's keeping a full-scale meltdown at bay.

Rob looks me over, blinding me with his little pen light, asking me a dozen questions, but when I tell him it just hurts everywhere, right down to my bones, he frowns. "We should take her to the hospital. I need to run more tests."

His gaze leaves me and moves to Rory, and that's when it occurs to me that the others aren't here. There's no reason they wouldn't be here.

The machine to my left starts beeping louder as panic clamps down on me, choking me, stealing my air. I open my mouth to speak and a squeak falls out.

"Rob," Rory growls, but the doctor is already moving.

"I've got it," Rob says before lifting a syringe and injecting something into the IV I'm hooked up to. "Try to relax, Quinn. This should help, but I need you to take some deep breaths if you can."

He watches me and I try to match the deep breaths he's attempting to instruct me with. After a few minutes, the world doesn't feel quite so fuzzy as whatever he gave me takes hold.

A yawn escapes me and I frown. "What did you give me? I don't want to sleep. I want to remember. I want to know what happened."

My brain feels like it's emptying as exhaustion rocks me. I wanted to ask something.

Something that was important.

Trying to fight whatever he gave me to find my train of thought, I let out a groan of frustration. Then I remember, but the world is growing darker.

"Sleep, Quinn. We can talk when you're better." Rory's voice soothes me and I feel him lift me before, I assume, he crawls into the bed with me and I settle on his chest.

"You shouldn't be on there with her," Rob says, exasperated, and if I had the energy to smile, I would. I swear they bicker like brothers.

Brothers.

Wait.

That's what I wanted to ask about.

I fight the tiredness sweeping over me, but my eyes flutter closed anyway and the words I manage to form end up being little more than a whisper.

"Where is Meyer? Hunter? Why aren't they here?"

The next time I wake up, the beeping sounds are gone. My mouth is dry, my head is fuzzy, and I realize I woke because I'm so hot that I feel like I'm suffocating.

That's when I register the arm around my waist and the radiator-like body nestled against my back like my very own heated blanket. Except if I don't cool down, I'm not just going to be thirsty, I might pass out from dehydration. I move and grimace.

My body is slick with sweat. So freaking gross.

"Are you okay?" Rory's voice is thick with sleep as he tries to tuck me in closer to him, but I'm not sure how that's even possible when our skin feels like it's melded together.

"So hot," I mumble, almost coherently, and he grunts before begrudgingly letting me go. Throwing the blankets from my body, I sit up, pushing my legs over the side of the bed, and give myself a minute as the world spins.

Yeah, being lightheaded is no fun.

"You were cold last night, so I turned the AC off," he tells me as he fumbles in the dark, but the sharp beep once he stills lets me know he's turned it back on.

"Thank you."

Taking a deep breath, I push to my feet and head straight to the bathroom. Closing the door, I flick on the shower, stepping out of my panties and what I'm assuming is Rory's t-shirt, trying not to take note of my reflection and the mottled bruises that cover my skin.

I step beneath the deluge of water, hissing as the hot spray stings against my skin, washing away the gross remnants of the last however many days, scrubbing with Rory's soap until my skin is red raw where it's not a wash of purples and greens.

Pain isn't something new, but I'm glad the water from the shower hides my unwanted tears as they trace silently down my face as memories obliterate my mind.

Trent.

The bathroom.

Expecting Hunter and then my world falling out from beneath my feet when I saw Trent's face instead.

I close my eyes as it all rushes back.

My breath hitches with excitement when the door opens and I stand up straight, glancing in the mirror, ready to see my blond-haired Adonis.

Except what I see turns my blood to ice and I'm frozen in place, despite everything inside of me screaming at me to run.

Trent steps forward, the gun in his hand pressed against

my back, and I want to vomit when he leans forward and sniffs my hair. That's when I notice the blood spatter on his white shirt. He's dressed in a tux, except his tie is loosened around his neck and there's a tear in the shoulder of his jacket.

This can't be happening.

Tommy was supposed to be watching him.

How is he here?

Icy fear trickles down my spine and every part of me that's been training to fight him freezes. I can't fight, I can't run, it's like everything shuts down and I can't even scream.

He runs his nose up my cheek and I gag, swallowing the vomit that rises. He takes the panties from my fingers and presses them against his face as he pushes the gun harder into my back. Glancing at the panties in his hand, his sadistic grin widens. "Oh, Sweetheart, I knew you'd be missing me, but I didn't think it would be this much. It took a lot to get to you, but I made a few new friends who helped. Even if it took spilling a little blood, we both know that wasn't going to keep me from you after all this time."

My heart stutters, because I don't know who he's talking about.

Tommy?

Hunter?

He should be here by now.

Why isn't he here?

He moves slightly and pain splinters through my head. It takes a second to register the sight in the mirror, the gun above my head where he hit me with it. My vision starts to falter and I feel my legs go weak. I try to grip the counter, to stay conscious, to buy time for someone, anyone, to find me. Just something.

But then I see the syringe in his hand and in a blink, a stinging pain explodes in my neck as he plunges it into my flesh. "I imagine after slutting it around like you've been doing, you have a whole host of new things to show me. Now, you sleep. I'll get us out of here before one of your little thugs decides to come and find you. By the time you wake up, we'll be home. You belong to me, Quinn. You should know better, but I'm going to make sure you can never leave me again."

A shiver runs unbidden down my spine, and despite the shower, sweat coats my skin again. I switch the heat to cold, hoping to cool down. To push the memories away. I still don't know what happened after that, but I know it can't be good.

Not from the look Rory gave me yesterday.

Not from the fact that Hunter and Meyer aren't here.

Trent said he spilled blood, but I don't know who he was talking about.

Urgency rises up in me as my stomach twists, and I

launch myself from the shower to the toilet just as the contents of my stomach rise. I throw up until I dry heave, but that doesn't stop the churning feeling inside of me.

I *need* to know what happened.

A knock at the door tells me the sound of the shower didn't overwhelm the noises of my upchucking. "Quinn?"

"I'm fine," I tell him as I move to lean against the wall, the cold from the concrete on my bare skin helping me feel a little better.

"You don't sound fine. Open the door."

I roll my eyes because we both know it isn't locked, but I voice as much anyway. Seconds later, the door opens and Rory appears. He glances down at me before walking across the room, shutting off the shower and grabbing a towel.

"Can you stand?" he asks and I nod, gripping onto the towel rail to help me stand, but I get half way and flop back to the floor.

"Apparently not," I groan as my head swims. He leans down and tucks the towel around my shoulders before lifting me from the floor. Closing my eyes to stop the world tilting again, I rest my head against his shoulder. "I'm getting you wet."

"A little water isn't going to hurt me," he says, and I can hear the undertones of amusement in his voice, despite the concern that's laced there. He sits me down on the edge of the bed, wrapping the towel around me properly, and crouches in front of me. "You feeling better?"

"Not really," I say, shrugging. "But I'll be fine. I need to know what happened, Rory. I remember Trent cornering me…" I trail off as his jaw clenches and take a deep breath. "I remember him injecting me, and then nothing until I woke up here with you and Rob."

He scrubs a hand over the top of his head and down his face before meeting my gaze again. A war of conflict plays out on his face, and I don't like making him uncomfortable, but I need to know.

"I don't know everything, but I'll tell you what I know. But first, I'm getting some water and food in you."

I recognize a diversion tactic when I see one, but I nod because I'd like to not pass out. "Let me get dressed and we'll go eat. But then you talk."

He nods again, not taking his gaze from me. "I promise."

Standing, he moves over to the dresser and grabs a t-shirt before walking back to me. "Put this on. Carlos is home, so I don't want you walking around naked."

I can't help the smirk that pops onto my face, despite everything, as I imagine the scandalized look Carlos would give me if I wandered into his kitchen butt-ass naked.

The amusement passes as I slip the t-shirt on, my body sore as I move, and I'm reminded of reality.

Right.

Trent.

A second later, Rory has a pair of my underwear hanging from his finger and I take them, slipping them on along with a pair of giant socks he hands me. He moves forward and lifts me into his arms, drawing a squeak from me. "I can walk."

"You just nearly fell down trying to stand. I'm not risking it."

I don't bother arguing because I know it's futile before I even start. Instead, I lean my head against his shoulder before he walks us down the spiral staircase, through the living area of his room, then to the kitchen before he sits me on a chair at the dining table.

Carlos starts talking quickly, hands moving as much as his mouth, and despite my Spanish having gotten better, I still have almost no idea what he's saying, other than hearing Meyer's name a few times. Rory calms him across the room as I cradle my head in my hands and close my eyes.

"Drink." I hear and open my eyes. A glass of water, a glass of juice, and a mug of coffee sit in front of me on the table.

"Silent freaking ninja," I mumble before grabbing the glass of water and taking a sip. He shakes his head before walking back to Carlos, their conversation lost to me, but by the time I've finished the water and I'm eyeing up the coffee, Rory sits down beside me as he puts a plate before me and has one for himself.

"Sourdough, avocado, poached eggs, and feta with chili oil. Eat."

I blink at him like he's grown an extra head, but do as he says. We eat in silence, despite how good the food is, and before we finish, Carlos disappears, leaving us alone.

"You promised to tell me what happened," I say quietly as I finish my last mouthful. He finished before I did and has just been watching me eat. It should be weird, but somehow, with him, it's not.

"I did," he says before taking a deep breath. "I can tell you what I know, which isn't much, but I know that Hunter came to find you. He found you with Trent, tried to fight him, and lost." He pauses as I suck in a breath, but I keep quiet, letting him continue. "He suffered multiple stab wounds and was left to bleed out on the floor in the bathroom. Meyer and I found him, got him to a hospital in time, but he was in bad shape. According to Meyer he's still in critical condition, but I'm due an update any time now."

He looks down at the watch on his wrist before glancing back up at me. "Meyer went to the hospital with Hunter, I came after you. Trent isn't as smart as he thought and it didn't take too long. I found you, dealt with him, and brought you back here."

I blink at him, wondering where the rest of the details are, then ask that exact thing. He responds with a shrug before leaning back in his chair. "That's all the details you're missing about what happened to you. At least that I have. What happened before Hunter got there?"

Opening my mouth to speak, I try to find the right words, then shrug. "Trent arrived, threw around some toxic bullshit like always, cornered me, jabbed me, and that's all I remember."

His frustration reflects mine with the lack of details, but if Trent is dealt with, they don't matter. Though… "Do I want to know what 'dealt with Trent' means?"

A sadistic look flickers on his face. "You never have to worry about him ever again. You're safe."

I could ask for more, but I don't know that I want to know. Opening my mouth to say as much, I'm cut off by the ringing of his phone. He pulls it from his pocket and frowns. "It's Meyer, I need to take this."

He answers the phone as I nod. "What's up?"

Standing, he leaves the room as I'm assuming Meyer speaks to him. Frustrated, I let out a sigh and leave the room myself, heading up to my room. When I get up there, I see my bag from the gala lying on the bed. I grab it and check my phone, but it's dead.

Of course it is.

I find my charger and plug my phone in before heading to my closet and dressing, all while trying not to obsess over what's happening with Hunter, and what Rory meant by 'dealt with Trent.' I'm fairly certain I don't want to know, but a small twisted part of me wants to know he suffered.

Suffered for what he did to me.

For what he did to Hunter.

But the other side of me, the more rational side, knows that knowing probably isn't going to help me. Even if it will distract me from the fact that Hunter is in freaking critical condition.

Guilt spikes through me as I pull off Rory's t-shirt, replacing it with a tank to go with a pair of leggings and a hoodie. My body aches too much, so comfort is my only aim right now. I check my phone and it's finally on, but there are no notifications.

Weird.

Instead of obsessing, I sit at my dresser and pull a brush through my now-dry bird's-nest-like hair while trying to let a reasonable enough amount of time pass before I go and find Rory to discover what Meyer told him.

My stomach twists with worry and I chew at my lip.

Checking my phone again, I ignorantly push down my worry at the lack of notifications. Not that there's many people that would check on me, but I haven't heard from

Tommy. My gut tells me it's bad. That there's absolutely no way he wouldn't have gotten in touch, but the rational side of me that is still trying to cling to my sanity isn't allowing me to voice my concerns.

To think about them too hard.

Because if the worst happened to Tommy in all of this…I don't know if I'll survive it. I'm just barely clinging on by sheer force of will. The determination that all of this wasn't for nothing. That Trent can't win.

Rory might not have said what happened to Trent, but he said I was safe and that I wouldn't have to worry about him again, so I have to assume he's dead and gone.

I should feel bad that I'm relieved by the thought, but I don't.

Not after everything I just found out.

Fifteen minutes pass once I finish brushing my hair and my curiosity pushes me from my seat. It doesn't take long to find Rory, but the look on his face makes me pause. He looks like he wants to tear someone in two.

Oh, God.

Hunter.

No. Please no.

Swallowing past the lump that rises in my throat, I call on the shards of courage I have left before I open my mouth. "Is he alive?"

SIX

QUINN

It's been four days since I woke up and I have *finally* convinced Rob and Rory to let me out of this freaking room without a chaperone. To say I've been climbing the walls is an understatement.

Especially once I got my memory back and Rory filled in some of the missing details. Hunter is still in the hospital. He's stable, but they thought he wasn't going to make it at one point. Yet Rory's been here with me.

Why we couldn't all just go to the normal hospital is beyond me, but Meyer said it wasn't safe for me there with all things Trent going on. Hunter's injuries are being explained as an attack by someone they don't know.

He hasn't filled me in on exactly why, but I intend to get that information today. From either him or Meyer. Meyer who hasn't left Hunter's side the entire time.

Meyer who must be exhausted.

I get the feeling that he's going to need a hospital bed of his own if he doesn't take care of himself soon, but I'm keeping my mouth shut for now.

My lips have been sealed since I climbed in the car with Rory and Rob twenty minutes ago. The two of them have been talking quietly up front while I've stared out the window in the back. Guilt over everything that's happened with Hunter clogs my throat. Because he wouldn't be in the hospital if it wasn't for me. The guys wouldn't have nearly lost him if they hadn't taken me in.

I text Tommy again, but he hasn't responded to my message from this morning and that alone makes me feel uneasy, but no one has mentioned him since I woke up, so I'm telling myself he's busy.

That has to be it.

Except there's a gnawing in my stomach that tells me I'm sticking my head in the sand.

Too much has gone wrong.

There has to be something wrong with him too.

Why else wouldn't he answer me?

I shake my head and take a deep breath, trying to refocus my thoughts on something, anything, else.

Racking my brain, I shoot off texts to Tina and Shae, checking in with both of them. I'm fairly certain neither of them know what's going on so I keep it casual, just a friendly check in, but something to focus on as the miles pass.

I pull up my thread with Yen too. It takes a few moments of deliberation, but I said I'd try, so I send her a message too.

Me:

Hey, you doing okay? Just checking in. Been a wild few days.

Yen:

Oh thank god you're okay. I heard from Meyer. Fuck me being okay you crazy bitch. How are you? How is Hunter?

Leaning my head on the window I take another deep breath.

Me:

I'm alive, that's enough for now. Hunter… I don't know. We're heading to the hospital now.

Yen:

Okay, well if you need anything, let me know. And I mean it. Anything. Hunter is like a brother to me.

Me:

I know. And I will. Thank you.

Yen:

Anytime. Let Meyer know we're holding down the fort, he can be there for as long as he needs to be.

Me:

I will. <3

I smile softly before sliding my phone into my pocket, finally seeing the hospital just down the road. About goddamn time. We might have only been in the car for half an hour, but it felt like hours.

My foot bounces as we creep through the parking lot before pulling into a space. When the car is off, Rory glances back at me in the rearview mirror. "You ready?"

I gulp but nod. "Yes, it's already been too long. Are you ready?"

It occurs to me that Hunter is like his brother and he's been stuck with me. Another wave of guilt crashes over me because I hadn't even thought about how Rory has felt about the whole Hunter thing.

Fuck me, I'm a selfish bitch.

Rob climbs from the car without a word, and once the door closes, Rory starts to speak. "I'm fine. Seen and survived worse. You are my main concern, Quinn."

"But Hunter—"

"No, Quinn. You. Hunter has been through shit before.

Was it hairy for a minute? Undoubtedly, but he's stable. He'll be pissed that Trent did what he did, but otherwise he'll be fine. Mostly. You though…what you went through, after everything, and now Hunter. I'm worried about you."

"I'm fine," I say quietly, glancing down at my clasped hands. "I still haven't heard back from Tommy, but I'm sure he'll respond soon enough. Now, can we please go see Hunter?"

I don't look back up at him, because I don't want him to see the pain, guilt, and worry in my eyes. He always reads me too easily and I know I'm not hiding it very well right now.

"Quinn," he starts, but I shake my head.

"Please, can we just go in?" I plead, needing to see Hunter for myself.

"Okay, Jellybean. Let's go see Hunter. But we're not finished with this conversation, understand?"

Finally, I look up, catching his gaze in the mirror again. "I understand."

He holds my gaze for a moment before nodding and reaching for the door. I follow suit and climb from the car. He takes my hand the minute I'm beside him and I can't decide if I'm clinging to him, or if he's clinging to me.

Either way, the hold grounds me and the world doesn't seem quite so terrifying with him at my side.

I feel like everything with Trent has put me back so

freaking far. That him finally finding me confirmed every insecurity and fear that existed inside of me. Giving voice and power to that monster that lives within me.

Quieting it now is exhausting, like I'm almost doubting myself, because the monster was right before.

Trent did find me.

The worst did happen.

How am I supposed to be able to trust that the monster isn't right about everything else?

Rory squeezes my hand, as if he knows the monster is winning, as we walk through the entrance of the hospital, following Rob through the maze of halls until we reach the elevator. Nerves rush through me as the doors close on us and we head up toward the floor where Hunter is being held.

The ding makes me jump when we reach the seventh floor, and when the doors open, I'm surprised by how quiet and empty it is. I look over at Rory, then over to Rob, who shrugs before exiting. We follow behind him again as he leads us down another maze of halls. We pass nurses and people I assume are other visitors, but everyone is quiet as a mouse.

It's weird and kind of eerie.

It's only when I see Meyer down the hall, phone pressed to his ear, that the feeling leaves. He keeps his voice low, but when he sees us, his eyes widen. "I need to go."

Without a pause, he ends the call and strides toward us. I move straight to his open arms. He looks as exhausted as I worried he would, but that doesn't stop him from holding me so tight that I know just how worried he's been. I don't struggle or say a word, I just let him hold me like that for as long as he needs to, with my face buried in his neck.

The sound of footsteps and a door opening and closing is enough to tell me that Rob and Rory have given us some space.

"I am so sorry, Quinn." His voice is scratchy, little more than a whisper, but my heart shatters.

"You? Why on Earth are you sorry, Meyer?" I ask, pulling back, searching his face for answers I'm not sure he'll give me.

"This is all my fault. I should've kept better track of Trent. I dropped the ball. All of this, what happened to you and Hunter, is because of me. You will never know how sorry I am, and I'll understand if you don't forgive me, but know I'm going to spend as long as you'll let me trying to earn your trust and forgiveness back."

I stare at him, mouth agape, blinking. "Are you shitting me?"

He looks shocked at my response, but there's no way in Hell he's more shocked than I am. "None of this is your fault, Meyer. I brought this problem to your door. Trent was here for me. If we're not blaming Trent, then the blame sits with me."

"No—"

"It's not on you, Meyer. There's nothing to forgive," I say, cutting him off. I open my mouth to keep speaking but the door behind him opens and Rory's head pops out.

"He's awake and he's asking for you."

Hunter has been in the hospital a week and I've barely left his room since I recovered from my drug-induced coma. Knowing that he's here because of Trent, because of me…I just…

They've both told me repeatedly that it's not my fault, but the voice that lives in my head doesn't believe them.

Meyer left us an hour ago to go handle something with Rory and I've been lying here beside Hunter because every time I've tried to move, even in his sleep, his arm tightens on me. The doctor said earlier that he'd be able to come home in a few days, which is good, because when Rory first told me what happened to him, I was terrified he wouldn't make it.

I still don't know everything about the Trent situation, but I've been trying to focus on Hunter. They would've told me if there was anything else urgent I needed to know, that much I trust.

But the doctors said Hunter's healing is almost miraculous. He laughed and said he always knew he was basically a god, but also, apparently, he's always healed from stuff quickly. Though he did mention he's never been in this bad a way before either, so he didn't know if his super power would work.

I swear, that entire conversation, I'm not sure who rolled their eyes harder, me or the doctor. Meyer and Rory just laughed along with Hunter, like this is par for the course in their life.

"How is it that, even with this many drugs in my system, waking up with you pressed against me still makes me rock hard, Angel?"

His voice is thick with sleep as I tip my head back to look up at him, a wry grin on my face to match the cheeky one on his. "Hunter Myers, you are incorrigible."

"Maybe so, but I've been in this bed without tasting you for far too long."

A devilish thought takes me and I wonder if I'm not only bold enough, but stealthy enough to get away with it.

Sliding from the bed, I go and make sure the door is locked before flipping the blinds on the window so no one can see in.

"What are you up to, Angel?" he asks, curiosity and an edge of laughter in his tone.

"Well, there's no way you're going to taste me," I say

softly, glancing around the room to make sure there are no cameras. I don't see any, so I move back toward the bed. "But that doesn't mean I can't taste you."

Removing the sheets from his legs, he tears off the gown he's wearing so he's lying there, naked, save for the bandages still covering his wounds. I bite my lip for a second, wondering if this is a good idea with him still healing.

"Don't you back down now, you little minx. I'm good." His dick bobs, almost as if nodding its agreement, and I laugh softly. "Get that pretty ass of yours up here and kiss me. Better yet, get naked first."

I make quick work of my white summer dress, kicking off my sandals in a hurry to avoid giving myself too much time to backpedal. We both need this, a little lightness in this dark tunnel of scary events.

With one last quick glance at the door, I face Hunter in only my matching panties and bra before crawling into the bed with him.

His moan is long and loud, like the mere touch of my skin is enough to make him come.

Well, he's gonna have to hold off because I have plans for him and that hard, thick cock resting against his abs.

"Well, I think you said something about…a taste test?" Wiggling his eyebrows, he nods his chin to his dick just as I wrap my fingers around it and squeeze enough to make the breath woosh out through his parted lips.

"Always so impatient." I murmur, my attention too focused on how fucking gorgeous his cock is in my hand. Strong and bold, a red tint at the base of his head where I'm guessing most of his blood is pumping.

I love the power I hold over him, knowing that every move I make could be his undoing.

"Only when it comes to you, Angel." I love that and I'm sure he knows it.

Darting my tongue out, I lick up the bead of pre-cum at the slit of his cock head before wrapping my lips around it and sucking enough to earn me a deep rumble of a groan.

Emboldened, I lean in closer, taking him more and more as his cock slowly slides to the back of my throat before I pull back and lock eyes with him.

"Don't move." It's silly, really…where the fuck is he going to go?

"Wouldn't dream of it."

Shimmying out of my panties, I pop the latches on my bra off and straddle Hunter's lap, backwards. It's not exactly a sixty-nine position but he's got access to me while I feast on his cock and he doesn't waste time putting his hands on me.

"Now this is a view I could get used to, even in here." I shake my ass, teasing him with all the things we could do once he's better and we're back home, earning me a spanking on both of my ass cheeks.

As I lean down, I make sure to spread my thighs enough that he can touch me, rub me, giving me all the attention he can. Once my lips gently graze the velvety skin of his cock, the desperate moans coming from behind me only spur me to continue. To give him more.

And so I do.

When my tongue licks up the root of him, Hunter rubs me between my lips, my cum coating the inside of my thighs from all the forbidden things we're doing. When my mouth engulfs his entire length, he pushes two fingers inside my cunt and pumps them in rhythm with my sucking.

Every time I pull away, he pulls out. Every time I take him all the way to the back of my throat, he fucks me harder and harder with his fingers.

I don't know where I begin and he ends. I don't know if the thrill running through my veins is from the pleasure he's giving me or my hunger for him.

I suck him hard, just as he curls his fingers and presses his thumb into my ass with only my cum to lube me.

The touch of pain with the all-consuming pleasure only makes me suck him more, harder…longer.

I'm blinded by my need to make him come, to bring him the pleasure he deserves, but also by my need to give him my orgasm, the one he wants to give me.

So, I bury his cock so deep in my throat that tears begin

to fall over his thighs as I choke and cough and gag with every inch he gives me.

For my efforts, I'm rewarded with his entire thumb inside my ass as two of his fingers fuck me without an ounce of mercy.

I'm writhing, mewling around the thick root of him, his scent invading my nostrils with every thrust of his hips.

I thought I was in control but he's got me pinned down by just his three fingers and his hips fucking my mouth from below.

Even at his worst physical self, Hunter dominates and controls my every orgasm.

Breathing through my nose, I concentrate on allowing him to get that one last inch of him down my throat, and when I do, I feel it.

I feel myself gagging, salivating at his earthy taste, desperate to come and scream and howl.

Just when I think I can't hold off any longer, I feel it.

The first jet of his cum spearing down my throat is the only permission I need to let everything go.

My skin begins to tingle and my legs lose all muscle strength, Hunter practically holding me up by his fingers as he fucks me like making me come is the only important thing in the world.

I explode around him and he explodes inside me.

It's a powerful thing, this position, because even when

the entire goal is to make him feel good, the truth of the matter is that Hunter will never take without making sure he gives.

SEVEN

QUINN

Puttering around the kitchen, since the place seems to be a ghost town, feels as close to normal as I've felt in…well, a long freaking time. There's something peaceful and freeing in the mundanity of it all, in knowing that everything is going to be okay.

The whole thing with Trent is finally over. I can breathe again.

My life is finally mine to live.

It's like my lungs can finally inflate fully for the first time I can remember. My guys are okay, Tina and Yen are okay. Shae is coming home.

Now if only I could get a hold of Tommy, things would be perfect, but I heard someone murmuring about him and a clean up job, so I'm assuming that's why I haven't heard from him. Him being on a job was always the only reason he wouldn't get back to me, unless I sent up a flare, but I haven't needed to, so it makes sense.

The smile on my face falters for a second before my playlist switches to *Shake It Off* by Taylor Swift, and the smile is back. Cleaning and dancing, cooking and singing, this is what I always thought was normal. It feels so… boring and yet, the fact that I can do it without having to worry is enough to make me laugh out loud.

It's not like the gnawing guilt of everything is gone, especially after Rory told me what happened, but I'm trying to find peace in the small moments. My therapist reminded me in our session yesterday to try and do it, and it's advice I'm willing to try and hold on to.

God knows I desperately need a little joy right now. It's not like I don't know the fear and guilt will be back soon, it always comes back, which is exactly why I'm enjoying these moments of peace right now. The joy is fleeting, but it means so much.

The song finishes but I keep shaking my ass as I scrub the backsplash behind the stove top, hoping for something just as upbeat to pop up on the playlist.

"You look like you're having fun."

I let out a squeak as I startle, turning to find Meyer leaning up against the kitchen door frame, watching me with a smirk on his face. Pressing my hand to my chest, I let out the breath that caught and roll my eyes at him. "You move like a ninja."

"No," he says as he stands, shaking his head and moving to the panel on the wall controlling the speakers in the room that my phone is hooked up to and turning down the volume. "You were just lost in the music. It was nice to see. You smiling. It hasn't happened all that much lately."

"More since I met you guys," I tell him with a shrug, a weird kind of embarrassment curling up inside of me as heat spills across my chest and creeps into my cheeks. "I never smiled for real before then. It was all a mask."

He moves closer, capturing my cheek with his hand, stroking my reddened skin with his thumb. "I hope that all of your fake smiles are in the past."

"Me too," I admit, softly, as I give him another small smile before leaning up on tiptoe and kissing his cheek. "Busy day?"

A shadow darkens his eyes as a frown momentarily appears on his face. In a blink, it's gone, but I swallow down the unease that rises with it. What he does comes with a lot of things I have no idea about…yet.

"Not really. A few things to deal with this morning, so unless something major comes up, I'll be home all day. I'll be in the office if you need me. And don't clean too much. Carlos will curse you out if you fuck with his kitchen."

A laugh spills from my lips at his teasing and I raise my hand in a scout salute. "I solemnly swear not to fuck with his kitchen."

The smirk returns to his face, wider than before, and reaches his eyes. "You were no Girl Scout, and I don't believe your oath either, but I decided weeks ago that I wasn't getting between you two. You seem to love to antagonize each other, and who am I to stand in the way of such joy?"

"It's fun. He makes it so easy." I wink at him and he barks out a laugh.

"I'm sure he does. Have you had breakfast?"

Nodding, I turn back to the counter I was cleaning and grab my cloth. "Yeah, I made eggs. You want something?"

"Thank you, but no. I just need coffee this morning." He moves to the coffee machine and starts making his drink, so I turn my attention back to what I was doing. "I'm going to speak to the doctor today to see when Hunter can come home, and I should get a confirmed date of when Shae is back too. I'll let you know as soon as I know."

I twist so he can see my grin. There is something so… uplifting about actually being kept in the loop, in them treating me like an adult. They're equal, at least outside of the business stuff, but that will come. Meyer already said it would, and he's not the kind of guy to break his word. "Thank you."

"Anything to keep you happy and smiling." The light in his eyes falters again, but I try not to hold on to it. I have too much to look forward to with Hunter and Shae coming home. Does that make me selfish? Maybe. Or maybe, as my therapist would say, I only feel that it's selfish because I'm so used to putting everyone else's needs and feelings before mine.

Who knows?

What I do know is I feel lighter today than I have in a long time, and I'm going to protect that small piece of joy with everything I have.

Meyer moves back toward me and kisses the bare skin of my shoulder. "I'll see you soon. Come find me if you get bored."

"I will," I murmur in response. The feel of his skin on mine, even just that small contact, makes my body come alive and steals my breath.

He leaves the room, turning the volume of the music back up as he goes, and I shake my ass again to *Save My Life* by The Band CAMINO, wondering if this is what normal feels like.

The day passed in a blink. Rory took me to visit Hunter, Meyer confirmed Shae will be home next week, and it's just been…well, a normal day.

It's a little weird, but I'm sitting in the family room curled up on the sofa with a blanket, Rory at the other end, with Meyer parked in the chair beside him. The fire crackles opposite, the two of them talking about God only knows what, while I listen to a podcast about different types of therapy healing.

It's not exactly thrilling, but I'm here to do the work.

Taking a sip of my hot chocolate, I let out a contented sigh.

Who knew normal could be so…quiet?

"It's time," Rory says, snagging my attention, and I lift my gaze from the fire to the two of them. Meyer runs a hand through his hair and my stomach twists. I'm starting to learn their tells, and him doing that means he doesn't want to do something.

"Time for what?" I ask, moving so I'm sitting up, pulling my knees up against my chest, hot chocolate balanced on top of them.

"Quinn, we need to talk." Meyer leans forward, his elbows resting on his knees as his hair falls into his eyes. His tone is enough to tell me that whatever it is we need to talk about, I'm going to hate it.

Oh, God.

Hunter.

He was fine when I was there earlier…but anything could have happened.

I think I'm going to be sick.

The tension in here is so thick, my peace is long gone

and I feel like the warm air is suffocating me.

Gripping my mug to stop my hands from shaking, I look at Rory, who is a blank slate, before turning my gaze back to Meyer. Pushing all of the softer parts of myself back into their box to keep them safe, I lock up my heart as I let myself go numb to try and steel myself against whatever it is he needs to say. I feel my face lock down as the emotion drains from me. "Just tell me."

He waits a beat, assessing me, and I know he sees as I shut down. The flash of panic in his eyes, the flare of his nostrils, the way he sits back up, becoming the man I met what feels like a lifetime ago back in that warehouse when a man lay bleeding out between us.

He nods, his eyes never leaving mine. He presses his lips together and takes a deep breath before speaking, giving me one last moment to try and prepare myself for whatever it is he's going to say.

"Tommy is dead."

For a second, the words don't register, and I bark a laugh. One harsh, cold sound as my heart obliterates.

Then the words sink in and that laugh feels like it's choking me as the bottom falls out of my world.

I don't think they can see. I haven't moved, not on the outside, but inside…any protection I thought I had is laughable.

Every piece of me shatters as his words loop in my head.

Tommy is dead.

I already feared as much, but I had dared to hope.

Dared to wish that my gut was wrong.

Hoped beyond everything that he was just busy.

Foolish, childish hope because I knew that if something wasn't wrong, if he wasn't just busy, there's no way he wouldn't have fought his way to be here when I woke up.

He never would have left me alone.

"What happened?" The words are empty and hollow. I don't even sound like myself, but that's not surprising.

The version of me that they knew only existed because of Tommy.

And he's gone.

I already know it's my fault. That this is because of Trent, even before they tell me. But I need them to confirm it.

"Quinn." Rory starts, his voice softer than Meyer's. He reaches for me, but I flinch away, despite the fact that he was nowhere near touching me, and hurt flickers in his eyes as he pulls back. "I'm sorry. For all of this. You don't need to know the—"

"I *do* need to know," I say, cutting him off. My voice breaks as I speak and I close my eyes, taking a deep breath, trying to stop my devastation from taking over my body, but I feel my throat growing thick as tears well in my eyes.

Blinking back the tears as best as I can, I say, "Tell me.

Please."

My voice cracks on the please but I move my gaze back to Meyer, who has transformed from the cold businessman back to the man who has comforted me, cared for me, maybe even loved me. He moves across the room to crouch beside me and grabs my chin, turning me to face him. "This was not your fault, Quinn. What happened to Tommy…"

"What. Happened?" I ask again, tears slipping down my cheeks unchecked. Usually, I'd wipe them away, try to hide them, but there's nothing to hide right now. Trying to shut down didn't work and they can see all of my broken pieces laid out before them.

"Trent happened," Meyer says softly and I feel the sob rise from my chest and get stuck in my throat.

Of course Trent fucking happened.

"What we've been able to make out is that he went to get information from Tommy, but Tommy wouldn't give you up. He shot him. It was a quick death, but he never gave you up."

For a minute, I wonder how Trent found me, but it's no more than a flicker of a thought as the sobs in my chest win and I start to shake as I cry.

Tommy still tried to keep me safe. Even with Trent likely torturing him. They can tell me it was a quick death, but that doesn't mean what came before was quick.

Oh, Tommy, I am so sorry.

The mug of chocolate slips from my fingers, but Rory catches it as I feel like I'm breaking all over again. My world feels like the floor just disappeared and I bury my face in my arms as I grip my legs, trying to make myself as small as possible. As if holding myself together physically might mean that I can hold myself together fully.

That's never going to happen though.

Tommy…

He saved me…and I was his ruin.

"Quinn," Rory murmurs my name as I'm lifted from the sofa. Moments later, I'm cradled against his chest and I break fully. Sobs rip through me unchecked as I cling to him like a life raft against the waves of devastation that want to take me to their murky depths. "I'm so sorry, Quinn."

He strokes my hair with one hand, while his other arm locks around me, anchoring me to him.

A hand on my back tells me Meyer is sitting with us, both of them there for me in the worst moment of my life.

I cry until my tears run dry and my throat is hoarse. Rory moves me to sit in Meyer's lap and I lean against him, but even the warmth from him isn't enough to break through the ice in my veins. He rubs his hand up and down my spine, sitting with me in the silence of the room.

The sound of footsteps on the wooden floor tells me

that Rory leaves the room.

"Is there anything I can do?" Meyer asks when the door closes, and I squeeze my eyes closed.

I try to speak, but it's like my words are caught in a chokehold of grief, so instead, I shake my head. He holds me tighter, like it might make things better.

But I know better than that. Some wounds can never be healed…

And this one, I don't think I'll ever recover from.

Blinking to stop the sting of my eyes as I stare up at the ceiling of my room, I feel a pressure inside of me building up. The anger, sadness, helplessness…the guilt. I try to escape the torrent of thoughts that haven't left me all day, but it's a useless exercise.

Rory and Meyer have both checked on me today, each of them trying to make me feel better, and I know they lost him too. Deep down, I *know* that. But Tommy was…he was everything I'd never had.

He was someone I could depend on. He showed up for me. He *cared* for me in a way no one before him ever had. He taught me that some people were worth letting down my walls for. That the outcome was worth the risk.

But now he's gone.

When I woke up this morning, it was like there was a weight on my chest again and I couldn't breathe. The blood that stains my hands, whether my fault or not, is very real. Even if not physically, I know the deaths that have happened the last few weeks are because of me.

The guards.

The drivers.

My heart shatters in my chest because I can still barely bring myself to acknowledge the last one…

Tommy.

All he ever did was help me, and now he's dead.

Dead.

Because of me.

My throat tightens and I try to swallow past it, to keep the tears away. My face is still puffy from crying myself to sleep.

I'm not sure when Meyer brought me to bed last night. Or if it was Rory. I don't remember much of exactly what they told me, except the part I'll never forget. The words that will haunt me forever.

So much death…just because I wanted to escape my life.

A part of me thinks I should've just stayed in my old life with Trent. Should have just tried to survive the hand life dealt me. I'd probably be dead by now, but that's just me, rather than the long list of names currently on my soul's ledger.

The guys seem to think that by their sheer force of will alone, I'll believe this isn't my fault, but I can't see how it isn't.

Do I know that Trent is responsible for his actions and the consequences? Obviously, I'm not completely delusional. But if Trent is responsible for his actions, then I am for mine.

Which means the guys are for theirs too.

I let out a huff at the rational voice chirping up in my head, but still bite down on my lip, wincing when I taste blood. Logic and reason have no home in my mind right now. All I have is emotion and no matter how much I try not to let it overwhelm me, I fail.

Tommy tried to teach me that emotions were good, but the anger that rages inside of me like the worst kind of storm can't be good.

I don't want to be a burden to anyone while I fight the war inside of myself, which is why I've stayed up here all day. The guys have so much going on, but my guilt keeps dragging me under, like my very own monster, dragging me to the depths of my darkest shadows to cage me for bringing Trent upon them.

Rational me knows they willingly took me in. Rational me knows that Tommy made his own choices too.

But the monster doesn't belong to rational me.

The monster lives in the depths of my shame, created by my father, reinforced by my mother, and Trent fed it until it became the leviathan it is today.

I beat it once.

I ran.

But look what's happened since then.

My phone pings, and a smile ghosts my lips when I see Meyer's name.

It's like he knew…

They always know.

Meyer:

Get dressed. I'm taking you for lunch before we go and get Hunter.

Meet me in the kitchen in 20.

I want to smile at the message, but smiling feels a million miles away. Hunter is coming home and I should be happy about that.

I *am* happy about that, it's just buried beneath the rubble of devastation. Letting out a reluctant sigh, I drop my phone onto the bed beside me. Being in bed this late in the day isn't something I do, but I've also never felt loss like this. The thought of carrying on like nothing happened, the guilt of just being happy the last few days. It's hard to put everything in order inside of me.

The thing that finally gets me moving is the knowledge that Tommy would kick my ass from here to kingdom come if he saw me wallowing. Even over him.

Pick yourself up, kid. We only get one life. You might as well roll with the punches and keep living.

I smile at his voice in my head as a tear slips down my cheek. I can't count the number of times I heard him say that, usually when I was freaking out after Trent had found me in yet another town.

Part of me is angry at Trent. For not giving up. For not just letting me go. But mostly, I'm angry at myself for putting other people at risk. For caring about people.

For being human.

Shaking my head, I cling to Tommy's words and get myself ready for the day. I spend too long in the shower, letting the water hide the tears that overwhelm me again. When I finally make my way downstairs to the kitchen, I find it empty. So I grab a bottle of water from the fridge and take a seat at the table.

Meyer said twenty minutes and I went a little over.

Maybe he left without me?

"Stop it." Meyer's voice pulls me from my thoughts and back to the kitchen in his house. The house I'm still living in, despite everything.

The house I don't need to keep me "safe" anymore.

Not now that Trent is dead.

I still can't decide if I'm awful for not feeling anything but happy about his death. Especially since he is the reason Tommy is dead.

"Dammit, Quinn. Stop it."

I blink, my vision coming back to the man sitting opposite me at the table. He moves quickly, pulling my chair out and twisting it to face him before he crouches in front of me, cupping my face with a hand, stroking his thumb across my cheek.

"None of this is your fault."

I open my mouth to respond but he shakes his head, stopping the words on the tip of my tongue.

"None of this is your fault. I will say it as many times as you need me to. We all will. Tommy wouldn't blame you, Hunter doesn't blame you. This is not your fault." He stares into my eyes, as if trying to force his will upon me. Like he's single-handedly wielding a sword and trying to slay the demons in my head.

But the shadow army is legions strong, and he's wrong.

This *is* my fault.

Whether he wants to acknowledge that or not.

Rather than tell him any of that, I nod. "I'll try to do better."

He groans in frustration and runs a hand through his hair. "You don't need to do better, Quinn. There's nothing to be better at. I just hate seeing you like this. The grief

I understand, we're all going to miss Tommy, he was important to us all, but blaming yourself isn't going to help anyone. I even understand the train of thought, but I can't stand to see you beating yourself up like this."

His eyes plead with me and for a second, as I lock eyes with him, it's like the waves of emotion pull back. Like I can breathe if I just stay here, like this, with him.

He reaches over and squeezes my hand, his touch like an extra piece of armor, and when the waves crash back down, they don't hit quite as forcefully as before.

"Thank you." The words are a whisper as he grips my hand and I blink back the tears that well in my eyes.

I might not believe that this isn't my fault, but just maybe, with him, with the others, I can fight through the legions of shadows and come out of it alive.

EIGHT

HUNTER

"How is she?"

Rory looks over at me like I just asked the stupidest question on Earth, and well…fair, but still. "Look, you told her about Tommy before I was home. I was supposed to be there for that. She's going to need all of us to deal with that. She doesn't let people in, but she let him in and he was ripped away. You don't think she's going to try and do something stupid like run to protect us?"

He stays quiet, like he's thinking over what I said, as I groan, pulling up my jeans. Stupid fucking stitches. I get it, things could've been way worse for me, but a few extra scars is no big deal.

I'm healing, I'm hurting, but I'm alive.

My biggest concern is Quinn.

Losing Tommy is going to be possibly the biggest

emotional hit she's taken. She hasn't lost people before. Not anyone she gave a fuck about. I might be pissed that they told her before I was home, but I'm more concerned about exactly what I just said to Rory.

That she'll run.

She's run her entire life. Either inside herself, or the last few years, quite literally.

"She doesn't have anything to run from. I told her Trent isn't a problem anymore." Rory finally says as I shrug into my t-shirt, glad to finally be out of that fucking hospital gown.

I quirk a brow at him and shake my head. "Dude, I love you like family, but clue up. She isn't going to run from Trent. If she's blaming herself like I think she will be, then she's going to run to protect us from her. You've spent time with her, I know you've seen it. That part of her that believes she's broken. That she's the problem. She had only just started to let that go and now this."

"She still has the tracker in," he says with a shrug and I roll my eyes. "She can run, but she can't hide."

Sometimes I wonder how he can be so in tune with her *and* this dense all at the same time. But there's no point in arguing it out here. I just want to get home. Meyer and Quinn were supposed to be here too, but since Rory arrived alone, I'm guessing she's worse than Rory is willing to tell me.

I get it, I could've died, but I didn't. If they start treating me like I'm some precious piece of glass, I'm going to get real ruthless and do something stupid. There is no way in Hell I'm dealing with that.

Not when Quinn needs to be our focus.

Well, her and Trent.

"Have you checked on him?" Rory glances up at me from his seat when I ask the question. I don't need to say who *he* is.

"I swung by there this morning before coming here. He's alive. Even though he wishes he wasn't. Still got a smart fucking mouth though. Well, he did to start."

The sadistic smile on my friend's face tells me he enjoyed his visit with Trent this morning. I'm not entirely sure why the asshole is even still breathing, but talking about much of anything in this hospital has been a challenge.

Which is the other reason I'm ready to get out of here. I feel like I have ants under my skin from being stuck in bed for so long. Too much is going on and I'm severely out of the loop. We had too much going on before Trent; shit that was precarious footing at best. Meyer will have a grasp on it all, but there's only so much one person can do. If the talks with the Ghosts and Demons have gone sideways because of Trent…well, I'll be paying him a visit all of my own.

Fuck me, I need out of here.

Stat.

I chuckle to myself for the stupid pun as Rob enters the room. "Ready to go I see."

"I've been ready since I woke up from surgery and you know it."

He shakes his head as he steps into the room, the door closing behind him. "I've got your discharge papers all filled out, you can go run free, but I don't need to tell you to take it easy, right?"

Rory snorts a laugh from the sofa and I flip him the finger. "Taking it easy is relative. I'm fine."

"You nearly died, Hunter. No one thinks you should be leaving, even if you bribed the doctor to tell you that you could leave when Quinn was here. This goes against all advice, so I need you to not be a fucking idiot."

I grin at him and wink. "Me, an idiot? Never, Doc. I'm the goodest boy that ever lived."

He rolls his eyes at me and shrugs. "Just don't get yourself killed. I already saw what that looks like, I don't want a repeat any time soon."

I hold up my hand and make the Star Trek salute. "I swear."

Humor probably isn't the best route, but it's all I've got. I'm not going to promise anything because I don't know what's been happening while I've been trapped in here. I don't have any intention of landing myself back in the hospital, but if shit has hit the fan, I'm not about to ride the bench.

The door opens again and it's like a lightning bolt straight to my chest.

My girl.

"You came." The smile on my face is so wide at seeing her it almost hurts. I open my arms and she barrels right into them. My hold on her is tight enough to crush her, even with my injuries. I kiss the top of her head, breathing her in before looking up to Meyer.

He shakes his head, answering my silent question in an instant.

She's not doing well, which is to be expected. Tommy was her safe harbor in an otherwise torturous world. Maybe the only stability she knew in this world before us, and well…it's not like life hasn't been rocky since she met us. She stayed in touch with Tommy the entire time.

He was the dad she always deserved, and now the monster from her nightmares took that from her.

"Are you okay?" I murmur to her as the others leave the room, trying not to wince as she clings to me. She's worth the pain that comes with the embrace, and I'd live and die for her every day if that's what she needed.

"Me? I should be asking you that," she says as she looks up at me. Her eyes are puffy and it's obvious she's been crying recently.

"Angel, I am fine. You are the one who's hurting right now." Tucking her hair behind her ear, her eyes close at the touch, and when she looks back up at me, her eyes are glassy. "Is there anything I can do?"

"No," she whispers, before gulping and burying her face in my chest again. "Just this."

I tighten my hold on her again, resting my chin on the top of her head. "I can do that, Angel. I'm not going anywhere."

"So what do we know so far?" I ask as I lower myself onto the sofa in Meyer's office. Leaving Quinn sleeping in my bed was torturous, especially after she fell asleep crying in my arms, but I've been out of the loop for too long already.

"We know that someone working for Tommy told Trent where Quinn was. We don't know who that was yet and Trent is proving to be…elusive in being forthright." Meyer's distaste spills over his words.

Glancing over to Rory, I find him brooding as he stares at the fire. "He's not talking?"

"Nothing we don't already know," Rory says, the bite in his speech revealing his frustration. "And I can't push much harder without killing him. I don't want to do that yet. It's too soon. He hasn't suffered anywhere near enough."

I don't need to ask if Rory has been creative, he always is. The things he's done to people in the name of information is enough to make most grown men vomit while shitting themselves.

"Do you think he'll give us names?" I ask, but I have a feeling I already know the answer.

Rory shakes his head and Meyer's matching grunt of annoyance tells me they've already had this discussion.

"So, essentially, we know nothing? Just awesome." I lean back on the sofa and pinch the bridge of my nose. This isn't exactly what I was hoping to hear but I'm also not entirely surprised. Trent isn't the sort to save others, but he is the type to fuck with us by withholding. "What about everything else?"

Meyer heaves a breath and shakes his head. "It's fucking chaos out here. Word got out that we were attacked, and it's a battleground. The Demons backed out of the deal and the Ghosts are saying they won't deal alone because it isn't worth it to them. They're being giant dicks in my ass and need to be dealt with. The Demons are at least lying low for now and staying quiet, so they can drop down the priority list until we get control of this situation back. Trent fucked us, but I'm working on it. I already secured the deal with the south for the guns that are sitting with Elise, we just need to finesse the details, but I've got it handled."

I blink, a little surprised that he managed to keep that deal, all things considered. The boys on the other side of the border don't tend to like drama, especially when hospitals and cops are involved, but I guess my silver tongue is finally rubbing off on the big man. That, or he threw his weight around for a change and showed them not to fuck with him. Either way, I'm happily surprised and still itching to get to work and have something to fucking do. "Put me in, coach. What do you need me to do?"

He eyes me, like he's weighing up whether he wants me to be working.

Fuck that.

"Do not treat me like some paper doll. I can work, so put me to work. I'll go fucking stir crazy if I keep sitting around with nothing to do, so tell me what the fuck you need." We have a mini stare off, but he concedes and I do a small internal fist pump at winning. He's a stubborn fuck when he wants to be, but I also know he needs the help. There wouldn't be chaos if he didn't.

Plus, me being back out and seen will let people know the hit we took wasn't as bad as might be rumored. I'm not stupid, me being in the hospital was a weakness for our family. People see it as instability. A weakened defense system. Which is fucking ridiculous when you consider the empire Meyer has built since he took over the family business, but perception is everything.

"What do you know about Echoes Cove?" he finally asks.

"Not a lot. The Knights' home territory, isn't it?"

He nods his head and runs a hand over his face, telling me I'm not going to like what he's about to say.

"Yeah. And we've somehow managed to make it onto their radar. I don't know if they're involved with the Demons or the Ghosts, but they started sniffing around after all this shit blew up."

"We're not even close to their territory. Someone *had* to have brought them here, tattled to the big kids in the sandbox."

"Exactly my thought. Get out on the streets. Meet with the mid-level people. They're the gossips. Do the collections like you'd normally do and deal with anything that comes up and find out whatever you can. Let people know you're back. That should spread quick enough that I can get (NAME) back to the table. Get this peace treaty back in place once and for all. It's not like the threat won't always be there, but it should be lower. Check in at the clubs too, let's pretend it's business as usual for you and that should be enough to convince some people that that's real." I nod at him and he turns his attention to Rory. "That gives you the freedom to work the Trent angle with no distractions. I want to know who betrayed us. Every single name, and we will show no mercy. You do not come for our family and live to brag about it."

"Got it." Rory says with a nod, and just like that, I feel more settled.

"I'll get back to the club, as if it's business as usual, and I'll check in with Elise. She's been shouting the last week, so I'll handle her and figure out how to get her off those guns so she'll get off my ass. The drugs can wait. The clientele aren't going anywhere and I don't want you distracted, Rory. If she contacts you, let me know, and if anything else comes up, tell us for fuck sake."

Rory rolls his eyes in response, but nods in agreement again, saluting Meyer with a little, "Yes, sir."

He's obviously spent too much time with Quinn and her sassy mouth of late.

I'm only a little jealous of that.

Maybe more than a little.

"What are we doing about Quinn? And Shae?" I ask him, knowing he likely already has plans in place.

"Tonio will be with Shae when she's home, like always, and Eddie is going to come back in now that you're home to watch over Quinn. I've had him picking up for you and checking in on HellScape."

"Oh, I'm sure she'll love having her very own BFG back. Though, you know she's never going to not call him Bruno right?" I can already picture her face and it's enough to make me laugh. A somber thought steals the joy from me, but I know I need to ask the question that popped into my head. "What about Tommy?"

Just saying his name is like a twist of the knife in my heart. He meant a lot to Quinn, but he meant a lot to us too. His loss is one we're all going to feel for a long time. Especially Mama Marino. Her thing with Tommy was very much a don't ask, don't tell, worst-kept-secret kind of thing. I know Meyer hid her away after everything with Trent, but again, I'm out of the loop.

"Mama's handled it all. The service is in a few days. He'll be buried in the family plot. Mama wanted everyone to be home for it, so somehow managed to get the morgue to keep him on ice until we knew what was happening with you and Shae."

"Keep him on ice…who are you, The Godfather?" I ask with a laugh and it makes them both chuckle in response. *The clown is officially back in business, baby.* "Does Quinn know?"

Meyer shakes his head, glancing at Rory before looking back at me. "Not yet, we didn't want to overwhelm her, all things considered. But since it's only a few days away, we probably should tell her."

A sound draws my attention to the door and I jolt in surprise at seeing our girl standing in the doorway. Apparently, she's becoming a silent ninja too, because not one of us noticed her come in. She stands there with her hands on her hips, head tilted, sass out for all to see, and quirks a brow at me when I smile at her.

"Tell me what?"

NINE
QUINN

I should be excited for today. Shae is finally coming home, and God knows I've missed her so freaking much, but it's all overshadowed by tomorrow.

Tommy's funeral.

Meyer and the guys told me about it last night, and I was more disappointed in myself that I hadn't even thought about his funeral since they told me he was gone. Knowing that Meyer's mom handled all of the details… it's just another thing to add to the list of things I feel like I should've done and fumbled. But adding to my guilt meter right now isn't going to make much difference, so I'm just piling it on there with everything else about this entire fucked up situation.

Just when I think I'm doing a little better, the universe drop kicks me out of nowhere and shoves me right back down. I don't know who put Mercury in the microwave, or which planets are misbehaving, but if the universe could give me a break right now, that'd be really nice.

I hit the stop button on the treadmill and head over to the weight rack. I might have spent a little time last night trying to distract myself from everything by going down fitness rabbit holes. Being in the situation I was in with Trent isn't something I ever want to experience again. I'm going to ask Rory if we can restart my defense training, but I need to be fitter. Stronger.

So I rack up the weights on the barbell and follow the video tutorials on a few different lifts, trying to get a feel for them. I'm watching myself in the mirror to try and make sure that I'm matching the woman on the video when I notice a shadow appear beside me.

Racking the weights, I glance over and a smile takes over my face. "Bruno! You're back!" I bounce over to him and hug him. He startles at the movement, but pats the top of my head when he recovers.

"Yeah, I'm back," he says in that gruff, gravelly tone that I hadn't realized I'd missed once I release him. "Boss wants me back with you for the foreseeable future."

I put my hands on my hips, a little frustrated that Meyer just conveniently skipped telling me that my living shadow would be coming back, but I also know that he wouldn't have done it without reason. Trying to accept the reality of their world, while pushing back my reactive responses, is proving to be difficult, but I'm not a child.

Even if having a babysitter feels like I'm being treated like a child, that doesn't mean I should act like it. Making a note to ask Meyer why Bruno is back later, I nod at him with a smile. "Well, welcome back to the boring world of me."

The alarm on my phone goes off to tell me to leave the weight rack and get my ass back on the treadmill, but I pause, turning back to Bruno. "How well trained are you in self defense?"

He huffs, almost like he's offended I'd question his abilities. "Well enough to keep you safe."

"Good enough to show me some moves?" I ask. I know Rory will likely help me train again, but Rory is just one guy. I could come up against anyone, learning from different people might teach me different things.

Bruno folds his arms across his chest and observes me. "If the boss signs off on it, then yeah, I can do that. I trained forces before, I'd just need to adapt some stuff to suit you."

I grin wide and clap my hands together once. "Awesome, I'll speak to Meyer. Thank you, Bruno."

The corners of his lips twitch upward when I call him Bruno. I know it's not his name, but calling him anything else just feels weird now. And I think he actually kind of likes it. Secretly.

Deep, deep down.

"Sure thing, Little Bird."

I cackle at his nickname and head to the treadmill. Tomorrow is going to suck, but I'm going to cling to these moments of joy with both hands. Tommy didn't sacrifice for me to not embrace the best parts of life, and I refuse to muddy his memory by letting the grief overwhelm me.

Once I finish my workout, it's lunchtime and Bruno follows me to the kitchen where Carlos is cooking up a storm. Instead of interrupting him, I make my way to the fridge and pull out a ton of fruit to make myself a smoothie, along with leftovers from dinner last night. A smoothie is great, but it's not going to fill me up even a little.

"No eating! Shae will be home shortly and I'm making lunch for everyone!" Carlos says as he sees the leftovers in my hand.

"I didn't think she was home till later?" I question, glancing over at Bruno, who shrugs in response. Putting the leftovers back, I make a protein smoothie and head upstairs to shower. If Shae is home soon, then I need to not be sweaty and gross. Especially if there's some big lunch thing.

I wonder if Meyer's mom will be here too.

It would make sense for everyone to be home for the funeral. It occurs to me that I haven't seen Mateo since everything with Trent and add it to my mental list of things to ask Meyer about.

"I'll wait out here," Bruno says as I open the door to my room. I'd almost forgotten what it's like having a permanent living shadow.

"Right, yeah. Okay. I won't be long." I say a little awkwardly before closing my door and chugging back the shake before heading to the bathroom. I make quick work of the shower before drying my hair and getting dressed in a pair of jeans and a cute sweater. My phone buzzes on my dresser as I put my hair up in a ponytail.

Shae:

Bitch, you better not be hiding.

I laugh, shaking my head as I type back.

Me:

Not hiding, just showering. You home?

Shae:

You think I wouldn't have just barged in if I was home? We're just coming up the driveway. Tomorrow we get to be all in our emotions and sad. Today... Let's just enjoy the family we have with us.

Tears prick at my eyes, but I blink them back.

Me:

I will try my best. For you.

Shae:

Yeah you will. See you in a min!

I pocket my phone, take a deep breath, and wipe my eyes.

We got this.

Tommy would want this. He'd hate to know that I was moping around because he was gone. Especially since he died trying to ensure that the life I've been building was one I got to keep.

Steeling myself, telling myself that little mantra on a loop, I head downstairs with Bruno a few steps behind me. Just as I make it to the bottom step, the door swings open and Shae stands in the entrance, hands on her hips, floppy hat on her head, and a giant grin on her face.

"I'm back, bitches."

Morning comes quicker than I'd like, and despite the icy chill outside, the sun is shining and the skies are clear. It's a beautiful day to say goodbye to someone you love.

Tommy used to tell me mornings like this were

his favorite, that he could bundle up, but still enjoy the brightness of the day on his morning walks. It seems fitting that the world graces us with his favorite morning for this day.

I've cried a dozen times already, mostly in the privacy of my room or the shower. Everyone here is grieving and today is going to be hard for us all. Meyer has his mom and Shae to worry about, so I don't want to add to that burden.

Lunch yesterday was great, even if it did feel a little weird playing happy families with today hanging over us, but Shae seemed to have a good afternoon at least. I tapped out early, the smile on my face hurting my cheeks and the mental exhaustion too much to keep pretending that today wasn't happening.

No one questioned it and I spent the night tossing and turning, trying to remind myself that Tommy loved me and he wouldn't want me to torture myself.

But the guilt still ate me alive whenever I was on the cusp of sleep and stole that sanctuary from me.

Ignoring the circles under my eyes, I paint on the waterproof mascara I found in my kit, just a small piece of armor against the day, before dressing in a black pantsuit. Tommy used to make fun of my love for all things black, but I guess today it works out for me.

Once I look almost human, I stare at my reflection, trying to pep talk my way through the day. It's just one day, I can break tomorrow. In private. Likely on the floor of my shower. After that, I'll pick myself up, dust off, and do what Tommy would've wanted, but for now, I can be strong.

Just like he would've been if it had been someone else we'd have lost.

A knock at the door pulls me from my thoughts and it opens before I get a chance to speak. Rory's head appears through the gap before he steps into the room fully. His black-on-black suit almost matches mine.

"You ready?" he asks, staying back by the door, as if he knows I'll break if he tries to hug me.

I check the silver watch on my wrist. More time has passed than I realized, and I nod. "Ready as I'm going to be."

"Come on, Jelly Bean." He holds out a hand for me and I take it, squeezing it once before letting go and heading downstairs. Everyone else is already in the foyer waiting for us, all in black, no more than a quiet murmur between Tonio, Bruno, and Meyer to fill the silence.

We head out in a convoy of black limos. I'm in the second one with Bruno and Hunter. Meyer in the first with his mom and O'Connor. Shae with Rory and Tonio in the one behind us.

"Where's Mateo?" I ask Hunter quietly. I meant to ask at lunch yesterday, because I just assumed he'd be here.

"He and Tommy weren't close and he didn't want to be here, despite Meyer and Mama Marino calling him out about it. So he's out doing a clean up of Tommy's business for Meyer since most of it is delicate work. He'll be back in a few days."

Curious. I thought it was just me that Mateo didn't like. "Is that where he's been this entire time?"

"Yeah, he was out that way handling some stuff for Meyer before everything with Trent happened, so it was easy enough to reroute him rather than bring him home." Hunter watches me closely once he finishes speaking, like he's waiting for me to shatter in front of him.

"I'm going to be okay," I tell him with a flat smile. "Today is about Tommy, not me."

"Uh-huh," is all he says in response, before turning his attention to his phone buzzing in his hand. I stare out of the window while he taps away on the screen, wondering what life would have been like if Tommy had sent me here when we first met. If I'd have gone along with his plans.

Would he still be here?

Would I?

I know playing the what-if game isn't going to help anything, but that part of my mind that loves to torture me plays the game like it's playing to win.

We pull up to the cemetery and Bruno exits the car first, closing the door behind him. "Erm?"

Hunter laughs softly. "He's just checking in and making sure it's safe."

"It's a freaking funeral, surely it's safe. Who the hell is going to attack a funeral?"

He shrugs, smiling sadly. "It's exactly that reason why it'd be a good place to attack."

I close my eyes and take a deep breath. His reasoning is solid, but fucking hell. Where is the honor in that shit? "Are the threats still that bad?"

"Nothing you need to worry about," he says, and I turn to face him properly, quirking a brow.

"I have Bruno back and I'm currently waiting for permission to attend my friend's funeral, so they can't be great."

He takes my hand and squeezes it. "They could be worse," is all he says before there's a knock on the window and the door opens. Bruno appears, holding out a hand for me, which I take and climb from the car.

It takes a second, but as I look around, I realize just how many people are here.

Tommy obviously meant a lot to a lot of people, and I had no idea. Not in this capacity anyway. I catch my breath at the realization of just how much Tommy is going to be missed. It somehow makes my grief feel both bigger and smaller at the same time.

"You ready?" Hunter asks as he exits the car.

"Not even a little." I tell him honestly. He places a hand on my lower back and guides me to where Meyer, Rory, and the others are standing. Shae is standing with her mom, their hands clasped tightly, and I can't help but wonder what it would be like to have that sort of relationship with a parent. I know they have their issues, but they're still there for each other when it counts.

Like family should be.

Like Tommy was for me.

My throat clogs and it feels like an elephant is sitting on my chest. As if the realization that he's really gone is only just hitting properly. Tears prick at my eyes and Hunter pulls me into his side, tucking me under his arm. "I've got you, Angel."

I cling to him like my very own life raft until Meyer interrupts us. "It's time."

He doesn't say anything else, but I see the car arrive with the casket.

Tommy.

My guys leave and are joined by three men I don't recognize, though one looks like a young copy of Tommy. It's jolting to see.

Bruno moves next to me and offers me a tissue. "Thanks," I say quietly as the six men bring the casket from the car and walk past us with it atop their shoulders as they follow behind the priest.

The crowd moves along behind them, but I'm frozen in place.

"You can do this, Little Bird. Come on." Bruno takes my hand and I let him lead me with the crowd of people to the open grave waiting for us.

By the time we get there, the casket is in place and Meyer is standing with his mom and Shae, the other two with him. Bruno hands me off to Hunter and Rory, who place me between them before we sit as the priest steps up to the casket. He sprinkles what I assume is holy water over the casket before stepping up to the stand beside it.

"Thessalonians 4:13 reads, 'Brothers and sisters, we do not want you to be uninformed about those who sleep in death so that you do not grieve like the rest of mankind, who have no hope.'" He pauses briefly, looking around at us all before starting to speak again. "Anyone who knew our friend Tommy, knew that he wasn't one for show and pomp. That his relationship with the church was turbulent, but I know that now, when it counts, he will be with those he loved before, and will be at peace."

The words get a little fuzzy as I try to swallow back the lump in my throat, but then an older guy I've never seen before stands and moves to where the priest stands. He clears his throat, his eyes glassy as he removes the hat from his head and clutches it in his shaking hands.

"A lot of you probably don't know me, Tommy had

a tendency to keep branches of his life pretty separate, but I've known him since we were kids. Since he kicked the bully's ass during recess for trying to steal my lunch money." He pauses, laughing and wiping at his eyes. "Tommy was always that way, from the very beginning. Never a bully, unless you were a bully to someone else. Always standing up for the underdog. An angel in human form, sent to save those of us who couldn't save ourselves."

Oh god, I don't know if I can do this.

"I know there are a lot of us here who he saved in one way or another, and while T was taken from us way too soon, I like to think he's still watching us, growling at us to not be so asinine, to rise up and keep fighting, because there is always someone out there who needs our help. Just as soon as we've found the strength to save ourselves. He'd say he didn't save us, that he just helped us realize we were strong enough to do what was needed, but that was him all over. The man who deserved far more than he'd ever accept, but would give away everything to help the people he thought were deserving."

Tears stream down my face and the rest of the words turn into a buzz as I check out, dozens of heartfelt stories being showered upon the casket as I struggle to take each breath, lost in the fact that there was so much I didn't know about the man who saved my life…and now I'll never have the chance to learn it all.

TEN

QUINN

Five days.

Five days I've stared at the letter that Meyer's mom gave me after the funeral. My name in Tommy's scrawl across the envelope.

Five days I've been too afraid to see what it might say, because what if this is the last piece of him that I have?

I haven't even touched it from where I placed it in the frame of my mirror since we got home, and even when the tears haven't felt so overwhelming, like they may never stop, I've been too scared to read his words on a page.

The wake was a blur, but I know Yen and the girls were there, and Tina even dropped by briefly, but I was useless to anyone. Grief wrapped me up in its warm arms and shut me down. I thought I had a better handle on it, but I ended up back in Rory's bed, curled in his arms, hiding from the rest of the world because I just couldn't deal.

A sliver of shame wrapped around my heart while I hid and it's taken root since. Sitting deep within me, playing happily with my guilt, becoming the best of friends.

Emotions are so much freaking fun.

"We're going out." I startle as my door crashes open and Shae makes herself known. She stomps across my room and flings open the curtains, letting sunlight spill into the room. "I gave you days of moping, but no more. Life is for living, and the dead would be pissed that we're wasting it. Get your ass up out of bed and into the shower. I have a whole day planned and you are coming, even if I have to have Eddie drag you kicking and screaming."

Turning to face me, hands on her hips, her dark hair swaying loosely around her, she looks like she just stepped off a runway.

Oh yeah, the universe is really playing fair.

"Up!" she demands before ripping the duvet from me like I'm a petulant teenager.

"I was getting up, sheesh!" I grumble as I roll out of bed and she slaps my ass as I hustle into the bathroom while cackling to herself.

"Don't make me come back and get you. We leave in thirty and we have appointments to keep, so get a move on."

"Yes ma'am," I mock with a salute before closing the bathroom door.

She bangs on the door and I laugh when she yells, "Don't you sass me!"

Shaking my head, feeling a little lighter already, I turn on the shower. Stripping out of my underwear and tank, I climb beneath the hot water, taking the time to wash my hair properly, exfoliate, and just kind of pamper myself a little. She said I had thirty minutes, using half of that in the shower seemed like a great idea.

Especially since I can't remember the last time I showered.

Got to love grief.

Once I'm done, I roughly blow out my hair, slip into jeans and a t-shirt, with the black leather jacket Hunter left outside my door two days ago, and pull on my Converse. My jeans are loose and the t-shirt a little baggier than I remember.

I guess not eating and working out like I have been are having an effect.

I glance at my reflection and sigh as I turn sideways. My ass is shrinking too. That was never the plan. I guess I'll need to change up the workout stuff to help keep my bubble butt. Checking out the rest of me, I shrug to myself. I'll do, I guess. Runway ready I am not, but then, I've never tried to be.

Swiping my phone, I glance at the letter in the frame of my mirror.

Tomorrow.

Tomorrow, I'll read the letter and face my fears, but today…Shae was right. Life is for the living, so I'm going to try and have a good day.

"Are you nearly ready?" I hear Shae holler, and I laugh as I open the door.

"I'm heading down now," I yell back, before stumbling into Bruno. "Oops, sorry. I keep forgetting you're back." Wincing, I realize how bored he must have been while I moped in bed the last few days.

Oops.

I find Shae waiting in the kitchen with the guys. She's sitting on the counter, legs swinging while she sips on an iced coffee, Carlos fawning over her while the guys sit at the table, talking and eating.

"At last!" Shae exclaims as she jumps down to her feet. "See you boys later, she's mine for the day."

I glance over at my guys with a sheepish smile and give them an awkward wave before Shae grabs my hand and drags me from the room. "So, where exactly are we going?" I ask as she drags me past Bruno, outside to where Tonio is chatting with O'Connor.

"That is what you're going to find out." She winks at me and leads me to the car, where Tonio opens the door for us. "Thank you, Jailor."

"You're welcome, Brat." He responds, rolling his

eyes. I softly laugh at their back and forth. Sometimes I think they'd be perfect together, you know, if Shae liked dick, but then other times they bicker like siblings. It's an amusing rollercoaster to watch.

Tonio slides in after us as Bruno and O'connor climb into the front of the car. "We need all three of you?" I ask Tonio, who glances up front and nods. The engine rumbles on command and we make our way out of the compound.

"No, probably not, but we follow orders."

"Ignore them, we'll hardly notice they're around today anyway." Shae tags in, pulling out her phone and tapping away. Moments later, *Ready For It?* by Taylor Swift starts blasting through the speakers. "This is girls' day, and we are going to *live. It.*"

Laughing, I join her for car karaoke, a mixtape of Taylor, Demi, Selena, Kelly, and so many more powerhouses. We screech away, dancing in our seats, living life the way she reminded me earlier we should be doing while the guys all look kind of miserable.

Well, except for Bruno. I haven't missed him mouthing the words to the songs, but I'm not about to call him out on it either.

I lose track of time while we're driving, but we pull up in front of a hair salon and Shae claps her hands together. "First stop of the day! Hair!"

I blink at her, ignoring how ratty my hair has gotten

of late—I mean, I've had more important things going on.

"Come on," she groans, reaching over me to open the door, but O'Connor jumps out of the car and grabs the door as she's swinging it open.

"Thanks," I say to him with a small smile, still feeling weird about the whole escort-driver thing. Bruno appears as Shae and Tonio exit the car and heads inside first. "This will never not be weird."

"Eh," Shae grunts with a shrug. "You get used to it. Plus, Val has been my stylist for, well, forever. She's cool with the penguin parade."

"Penguin parade?" I ask, confused.

"These fools in their penguin suits."

I laugh at her response as O'Connor groans behind me. "That might be the worst thing you've called us yet."

"What can I say? I have wordy brilliance."

"Sure you do, Princess," Tonio retorts, rolling his eyes.

"All clear," Bruno announces when he returns, opening the door for us.

"Let's go!"

We walk inside to what looks more like some holistic spa that you see on reality tv than a salon.

"Shae!" An older woman calls out from across the room and walks over, embraces her, and kisses both her cheeks before turning to me. "You must be Quinn. We're excited to get to give you both your new looks!"

I paint on a smile, a little overwhelmed. New looks? What the hell has Shae got us into now?

Val steers me away from Shae into the empty salon—I guess that's why Bruno was so quick to call all clear—to a room at the back. "We're going to start you with a massage and facial, then get on with your hair. Have a think about what you want us to do, but you're going to need a trim at the very least."

Blinking at her, trying to process it all, I nod. "Erm, yeah okay. I will."

"This is Yvonne. She'll be looking after you first. Would you like anything to drink?"

"No, thank you," I respond, still a little overwhelmed but trying to get to grips with it all.

She pats my shoulder before opening the door and ushering me inside. A short, black-haired woman is in the room, setting up a tray. She smiles warmly at me and waves me in. Closing the door, I step inside, the scents and music all curated to be relaxing, I'm sure, but this is just… foreign.

"You must be Quinn. Please, come in. Shae booked you for a full body and facial, so I'll leave you to get ready. Just undress, then pop up on the table, lay face down, and cover yourself with this towel."

My overwhelm must be showing because she walks over to me, squeezes my bicep, and smiles again. "Deep breaths. This is supposed to be relaxing. I'll give you a few minutes and knock before I come back in." She winks at me before leaving the room and I take a deep breath.

Right. Relaxing.

A stranger rubbing over my body, feeling my scars. So freaking relaxing.

I know Shae means well, but damn, this is not my idea of a chill out. Regardless, I strip down and hop up onto the table.

Life is for living.

I repeat the words like a mantra and take a few deep breaths.

Life is for living, and that's what I'm going to do. Push myself outside my comfort zone. Experience new things.

And apparently, that starts right now.

After a day of pampering and shopping, with my newly trimmed, styled, and re-highlighted hair, I asked Shae if we could swing by and check in on Tina. She stopped by the wake, but I wasn't coherent enough to speak to her. It's been a hot minute since I checked in with her properly and I know she starts at HellScape tonight.

Which is how I find myself in the elevator of my old building with Shae, Tonio, and Bruno, heading up to see my friend. The ding announces our arrival on the floor and the guys pile out in front of us.

"I know it's their job, but seriously? Meyer owns this building. Surely, we're safe."

Shae snorts a laugh beside me as we leave the elevator. "Nothing is safe for precious cargo."

Rolling my eyes, I head to my old apartment and knock on the door, ignoring Bruno and Tonio's sounds of disapproval.

"We called up for goodness sake, chill out. Sam or Eric would have said if anyone else was up here."

The sound of locks turning alerts us to Tina, and moments later, the door is open. I find my slightly-frazzled friend chewing on her thumb. "Hi."

"You okay?" I ask as I give her a quick hug and step into the apartment. There are clothes thrown everywhere.

Bruno pushes past and looks around the apartment before nodding to Tonio. "We'll wait outside."

"Yes, yes you will," Shae says, her new sleek bob, now styled sharp enough to cut, swinging around her face. She ushers them out of the apartment and shuts the door before turning back to face us. "What in the name of wardrobe tornadoes happened in here?"

"Tina, this is Shae. Shae, Tina. She's Meyer's sister."

Tina nods, obviously freaking out a little.

Shae rolls her eyes and folds her arms across her chest.

"Yeah, yeah, I'm my own person, now back to the tornado."

"I can't decide what to wear for work." Tina's words are mumbled, but I squeeze her with a hug anyway. Focusing on her seems like a much better distraction than shopping.

"I was the same my first shift," I tell her as I release her. "But honestly, you'll be fine in almost anything. Harper's bark is worse than her bite."

Shae barks out a laugh. "Yeah, she's a pussy cat, really. Just with really sharp claws. Now, let's go through this mess and figure it out. Go shower, wash your hair, and we'll prep you. It's kind of my thing, just ask Quinny baby here."

I roll my eyes at Shae, but turn to reassure Tina. "She's kind of a pro at this stuff," I say, gesturing to my hair, waxed brows, and curled and tinted lashes with a flourish. "Go shower, we'll sort this stuff out."

"Thank you," Tina whispers, squeezing my hand and smiling at Shae before escaping to the bathroom.

"You're sending her to Harper? I thought you liked her…" Shae jokes once the shower turns on.

"I do like her, and you know the club will be a safe, steady income for her. Her ex…well, he's a giant fucking flaming dumpster who beat the crap out of her. He can't get to her here or there."

Her face softens and she nods. "Now it makes sense. Okay, we can totally prep her for HellScape. I assume she's taken your old spot at the bar?"

"Yeah," I tell her as I start rounding up the discarded clothing strewn around the room and putting it in a clothes basket that's lying in the corner. "She's more nervous than I thought she would be though. Feel like going to the club with her for a bit?"

I look over at her, hopeful, and the wicked grin on her face is a dead giveaway of her agreement. "Hell yes. But we should probably tell Tonio so they can have their little conniption now and let Meyer know."

She drops the clothes in her hands into the basket at my feet before heading to the door and wrenching it open. "We're going to HellScape. Do not throw a fit, Princess. Do what you need to, but it's happening."

She slams the door closed and I'm too busy laughing at the look of shock on Tonio's face as she just laid out her demands to even wince at the loud noise.

"Well, that's one way to do it."

She shrugs as she walks back over to the main of the room. "Needs must, and I'm bored of asking for permission. I've done that enough for one day. I'm all out of spoons for their bullshit."

"Understood. Now, what do we put Tina in for tonight?" I ask, picking up the last of the clothing that's been thrown around.

The wicked grin appears again and she winks at me.

"Quinny, baby, we went shopping. If I can't find something here, you think I don't have something downstairs? Plus, if we're going too, we need to change." She claps her hands together as her eyes sparkle in delight. "We're about to have a total nineties's *Clueless* moment. Just call me Cher."

"Are you sure this is right for tonight?" Tina asks, tugging on the micro skirt that Shae persuaded her into after having Tonio and Eddie haul our entire shopping spree up to the apartment earlier.

We're sitting in the back of the car outside of HellScape, the line already wrapping around the block, and I feel for Tina. I've been her.

"It's perfect," I try to reassure her. "It's going to be hot, and in the words of Lil from *Coyote Ugly*, you need to make the kiddies drool."

She looks at me a little confused while Shae cackles next to me. "Showing your age there Quinn."

"Fuck you," I retort, flipping her the bird as she continues to cackle.

"Yeah, I have no idea what that is, but I get what you mean. I can totally do this. It's just bar work, right?"

"If that's all you want it to be, absolutely. And Yen is great, she'll keep an eye on you. Harper…like we said earlier, her bark is worse than her bite. But Matthew isn't going to be able to get to you in here, the guys did a deep dive, so none of his associates can either. You're safe here." She grips my hand and I squeeze it back. "You've got this, and we'll be there if you need anything tonight too. But I don't think you will."

She lets out a shaky breath and nods. "Okay, let's do this."

"Hell yeah, baby!" Shae bounces in her seat, and before we get a second to move, Tonio and Bruno are out of the car and opening the doors for us. The people in the line turn to stare and I shudder. Having all eyes on me is something I've run from for forever and I don't think I'll ever be comfortable with it, but tonight isn't about me, so I straighten my shoulders, put on a smile, and pretend they're not looking so I can support my friend.

Tina climbs from the car and I follow behind. She exits on her side and walks around to us with Tonio on her tail. Before we can take a step forward, Hunter appears in the doorway, that lethal swagger out for all to see as he walks toward us. He looks every part the dangerous business man; black slacks, white shirt, sleeves rolled up, blonde hair mussed. He's freaking delicious and he is all mine.

"Ladies, you made it." He takes my hand and kisses it, winking at Shae as he does before turning to Tina. "Tina, it's nice to finally meet you. I'm Hunter. Welcome to HellScape. Harper is waiting for you inside, so let's not keep her waiting any longer, shall we?"

Tina's eyes go wide as he talks to her, that weaponized smile on his face. I can practically see her heart beating in her chest. I press my lips together to not smile. When I was a kid, I thought I'd be jealous if I had a man that other people found outrageously attractive, but the upside of knowing what he's done for me, is that I feel so secure that Tina's reaction to him is just, well, kind of amusing. I remember the first time I saw him, I had a pretty similar response.

Shae links arms with Tina and leads her inside, Tonio and Bruno behind them, while Hunter places his hands on my hips and leans in close. "You look good enough to eat."

"Oh, this old thing?" I tease, rubbing my palms up his chest. "Just threw it on."

His head tilts back as he laughs. The bobbing of his Adams apple does things to me that shouldn't be possible from something so…simple. Yet I still clench my thighs together because goddamn.

"Just threw on a leather skirt, fishnets, and corset with a lace choker. Oh, Angel, I'm pretty sure I'd have seen these before now. Did you have fun with Shae?"

I nod, grinning at him as he presses his forehead against mine. "I did, it's been a good day."

"I like this smile on you," he murmurs as he pulls back

and tugs on a strand of my hair. "I like this lighter color on you too."

Heat creeps across my chest and up my cheeks. "Yeah, I've never been quite this blonde before."

"It suits you. Now come on, let's get you inside so I can drool over you appropriately without wanting to take the heads of every guy out here staring at you."

Rolling my eyes, I take his offered hand. "No one is staring, and even if they were, I'm pretty sure you just laid alpha claim on me for all of them to see."

His eyes sparkle as he winks at me. "Oh, Angel, that was nothing."

I let him lead me inside and to where Tina and Shae are already talking to Harper. Music plays lowly as people finish setting up, getting ready for open, and I realize I kind of miss this place. Before we reach them, Yen pops up beside me and squeals as she tackles me from Hunter. "You're here!"

"I'm here," I respond, laughing. "I told you earlier I would be."

Hunter motions to me that he's heading upstairs and I nod, knowing I'll find him later, before turning my attention back to Yen.

"Yeah, but I didn't know if you'd be up to it." She shrugs, smiling sadly. "I tried to catch you last week, but—"

"Yeah I was kind of out of it. Thank you for being there though."

She hugs me tightly again. "Always. Now come on, introduce me to the new girl."

We make our way over to the others and somehow, Harper is smiling.

Weird.

"Harper, what is that thing on your face?" Yen questions, obviously as creeped out as I am.

"Do you want to keep your job, Yen?" Harper snaps at her, smile dropped.

Yen rolls her eyes before turning to Tina and they start talking like old friends. It warms my heart how instantly they click. Tina is younger than us both, but she just seems to fit here.

"Play nice," Shae says to Harper, who huffs before walking away toward the basement. "That went better than I thought it would. Now, let's get this party started, shall we? I didn't dress like this to not dance."

Almost as if on cue, the lights lower, the music volume increases, and people start flooding into the club. Following Shae to the bar, Emma pours us a round of tequila shots, which we make easy work of before heading out to the dance floor.

The tequila warms my insides and helps me loosen up as Shae and I start to dance. My hips sway to the beat of the music and I let myself get lost in it. Tonio and Bruno stay by the bar, a watchful eye on us, but it's like they all fade away. She keeps the shots coming and the music is just as intoxicating as the liquor in my system.

Hours pass as I let myself just live, enjoying the time with my friend and just…being. Shae makes out with a dozen different beautiful women who dance with her throughout the night and I find myself glancing up at the windows to the office above. Knowing that Hunter is up there, likely watching, even though no one can see him.

I wonder if the others are up there too.

Tapping Shae's shoulder, I point to the office and she winks. "Go have fun!"

I return her grin, feeling bold, and make my way to the stairs. Slinking up to the office, heat pools between my legs. Could be the tequila, could be the dancing, or it could just be the way Hunter held me earlier.

The only thing I can't decide on is if I want him to be alone in there or not.

You'll find out soon enough.

Strutting down the hall to their office like I own the place, I lift my hand and knock once before opening the door, finding Hunter leaning against the edge of the desk, watching me, like he was expecting me.

"I guess you were watching." The words are almost a purr as I step into the room and let the door close behind me.

"Oh, Angel, I am *always* watching."

His eyes rake over me and my heart races. If I hadn't already come up here with an agenda, I'd have one now, regardless.

He watches me like he's a wolf and I'm his prey… but he doesn't realize that, right now, it's the other way around. Biting my lip, I run my fingers through my hair, then down my neck to the top of my corset. "Want to do more than watch?"

I step up in front of him and place my hands on his shoulders as he cups my ass and lifts me so my knees rest on the desk as I straddle him.

"I thought you'd never ask," he murmurs before his lips meet mine. I keep the kiss slow, teasing, as I grind down on him.

His hands squeeze my ass cheeks as his tongue delves deeper. And just like that, I'm already frantic with need.

Burying my hands into his perfectly styled hair, I take sick pleasure in ruffling his public persona and uncovering the man that only exists for me.

He knows what I'm doing, and judging by the way his fingers hook around my fishnets and pull the material apart, I'd say he loves it just as much as I do.

"You're daring the wolf to come out and play, Angel. Careful what you wish for." I don't answer, I just pull him in tighter, his head cradled in my arms as I rub my aching pussy up and down his covered cock—hard and ready—and moan straight into his mouth. "I'll take that as a yes."

In a fraction of a second, I'm no longer straddling him but sitting on his desk as he pushes my skirt up and over my hips and rips into my fishnets like they're a personal threat to his safety.

This is the side of him that I love most. Crazed eyes focused only on me, bared teeth ready to bite into me, and nostrils working overtime as his heart beat tries to catch up with his libido. He's barely in control and I'm loving every second of it.

"Whatcha gonna do now?" I spread my legs as wide as possible, putting my heels on the desk and leaning back on my elbows. I've got a surprise for him and I'm not sure if he's going to spank me for it or fuck his gratitude right into me.

"Oh, Angel. You lied to me." Two fingers push into me without any preamble, his thumb pressed against my clit and his eyes watching me like a hawk.

"Not a lie, an omission." I moan, my mouth speaking while my brain tries not to check out from the pleasure.

"Lying by omission is the same thing when it comes to us. You know this." Three fingers and I'm about to start rutting on his hand like a fucking cat in heat.

"Doesn't count if it's for your pleasure, right?" My head falls back between my shoulders as he lowers his head to my pussy and sucks, without a hint of mercy, on my clit. I can't open my eyes, can't speak, as the suction draws me closer and closer to him.

Just as my first orgasm begins to take flight at the base of my spine, he stops everything and places his palms on either side of my thighs, his lazer sharp gaze fixed on me.

"Any number of those men down there could have seen your cunt while you were dancing. Twirling around without a care in the world. Do you know the danger you're putting those guys in, right now?" My head snaps up so I can fully look at him and there it is…the craze, the jealousy, the possessiveness.

Fuck, it's hot.

"I'm sorry." I say what he expects me to say because, goddamn it, I want to come.

"I don't think you are." Leaning down closer to my mouth, he places a tender kiss on the swell of my breast before sinking his teeth and sucking deep. It's the exact same thing he did with my clit and it makes my entire body jolt, a cry erupting from between my lips.

"There, now I've shown my alpha—as you like to describe it." Looking down, I see the purplish mark right above the line of my corset and sigh. To be clear, I'm not sure if that sigh is in exasperation or because I'm completely turned on by his show of possession.

I'll say the former but I'm almost convinced it's the

latter.

"You're impossible!" I huff out, but secretly, I'm enjoying this little alpha show.

With my ripped fishnets barely hanging on for dear life and my skirt covering half my corset, I look like I've been in a fight with a feral animal. Hunter must see the same thing I see when he decides to rip whatever was left of my nets and pull my skirt off completely.

"Nothing is impossible when it comes to you." His lips slam back against mine, one hand at the back of my head with his fingers curled tight around my strands. The sound of his belt being unfastened and the zipper pulled down invade my senses. My hands roam his neck, his chest, his abs as I pull up his crisp shirt.

Before I can even dig my nails into his toned muscles, Hunter wraps his long, nimble fingers around my wrists and pulls me up to a standing position.

"What if the entire club could see you come for me?" His whispered words make my knees buckle but he's right there catching my potential fall. "What if every single asshole down there could see your face pressed against the glass—mouth drooling as I push two fingers between your teeth?"

We move—well, he practically carries me—to the wall of windows that overlook the bar. Just as he promised, he pushes me against the glass and presses his hard, thick cock between my ass cheeks as he continues whispering in my ear.

"What would they think of you?" Turning my face to the side so only one cheek is pressed and the other is at his mercy, he licks the side of my neck. "Would they say you're a whore? A slut?" Using the fingers he just had in my pussy, he pries my lips open and gags me. "Would the women be jealous knowing you're about to come harder than they could ever imagine?"

Hunter's not expecting an answer. This is him narrating his fantasy and living it out for me. Only for me. Every shocking word out of his mouth only gets me wetter and wetter, my knees weaker and weaker. So much so, he needs his weight against me to keep me upright.

"Do you know what those men would be thinking?" I try to shake my head but it's impossible with the hold he has on me.

Suddenly, I'm turned around and on my knees as he shoves his impossibly hard dick in my mouth and slams right to the back of my throat, making me choke and cough.

"Breathe, Angel. Breathe through your nose for me." I follow his instructions while he just waits for me to catch up to this little plot twist. Once I've regained my senses, he continues his little sex-time story.

"That's my good little angel, sucking on my cock like it's candy." He's hunched over me, one hand on the glass, the other at the back of my head as he fucks my face for his imaginary public. "All those men, they'd be wishing they could have their cocks in your mouth." His thrusts increase, his rhythm a tiny bit more erratic as he talks himself into a frenzy.

"But they can't. They'll never have you. Never taste you. Never know how fucking…fuck!" My mouth is suddenly empty as he pulls away and brings me back to my standing position. I'm pretty sure his imagination was working a little too well but he didn't want to come in my mouth.

Pity, really.

"What's wrong, baby? Is my mouth not good enough for your cum?" Oh, I'm getting sassy tonight.

With a growl that makes my pussy throb with how much I need him, he closes his mouth over mine, tasting himself and me at the same time. He's fucking my mouth again, except this time it's with his tongue. It's not enough for him, I know it's not.

Slamming my chest back against the windows, he bends at the knees just enough to thrust up into my pussy as he snakes his hand up to my throat and turns my head to the side. "Watch me as they watch you." His words are a feral growl and I'm almost coming all over him from his animalistic need of me.

"Then fuck me like you mean it."

Oh shit.

Turning his hand to the perfect angle, he pushes one thumb between my lips and presses it against the row of my bottom teeth as his cock ravages me. In and out he slams so hard I'm afraid I might get a fucking concussion.

I don't fucking care because this orgasm is going to kill me first.

"My little angel. Every. Time. I. Fuck. You." He pauses, his teeth sinking into my collar bone. "I. Fucking. Mean. It."

Just as he utters his last words, two of his fingers push down my throat. His cock finds that perfect little oasis inside my body that ignites every fucking fire in my veins. When his free hand reaches around to my clit and pinches that hard little nub just the way I love it, I scream out around his fingers, come on his cock like a fucking waterfall, and almost fall to the floor from the sheer power of it all.

Except he won't let me. I'm completely pressed up against the windows as spurt after thick spurt, he coats the inside of my cunt with his seed.

His moans are in my ear, his promises that this is the map to the rest of my life ring like a favorite song in my brain.

"Yes! Yes! Yes!" I cry out, begging for more or less or now and forever. I don't fucking know what I'm saying except that I can't imagine my life any other way.

ELEVEN

RORY

I've always known that I'm a monster, that my lust for inflicting pain was not something most people had, but watching Trent dangle from that chain like a limp doll brings me more joy than I've felt before, and I've barely even started.

The dried blood staining the concrete at his feet is from my last session with him, as is the dried blood that mars his skin. But seeing him so fucking helpless after what he did to Quinn brings a perverse sense of pride.

Especially when his humiliation from soiling himself is clear for all to see.

"Just get on with it," he grinds out. "I know that look, I wear that look, but you won't win."

A sadistic grin spreads across my lips. "We'll see. I do love a good challenge."

I turn to the table at my back, poring over the array

of toys I have there, trying to decide where to start. I've kept things reasonably typical for extraction thus far, but it hasn't worked.

So maybe I need a new tactic.

I glance at the sedative at the edge of the tray. That will definitely help to move him, but I want to hear him scream first.

Picking up the crow bar, I turn back to him. He doesn't need his knees. And I can break things before I cut them off.

Way more fun.

"All you need to do is tell me who gave you Quinn's location."

He spits at me, hatred shining in his eyes. "I won't tell you a fucking thing other than, if you think you only have one person in your operation that's willing to betray you, you're a fucking fool. I see why you're drawn to her, you're just as fucking stupid as she is."

I bring the crowbar down on the side of his knee at full force, his cries of agony like a symphony to my soul. "You don't speak about her, think about her, or utter her fucking name." I swing again at his knee, reveling in the sounds that I pull from him.

"Now, I can do this all day, but can you?"

He sucks in a few breaths, trying to compose himself, and I laugh loudly, the sound echoing around the cavernous space. He just glares at me, which makes me laugh all the more.

Sauntering back to the tray, I grab the syringe with the sedative before turning back to him, keeping the smile that he seems to hate oh so much plastered on my face. "Oh, Trent, you might think you're a monster, but you have no idea what I'm capable of. And that was before you came for the woman I love. You have no idea."

I push the needle into his throat, about where he did it to Quinn—a poetic kind of justice in my eyes—and slowly administer a small amount of the sedative, enjoying the clench of his jaw as the poison stings in his veins. "Now, go to sleep and dream of me while I prep you for the ride of your life."

"Fuck. You." The words are quiet, slightly slurred through the mixture of drool and blood, as the sedative takes hold. I let the smile drop from my face as he goes limp. He won't be out for long, just long enough for me to do what I need to.

I'm not stupid enough to let him down yet, so I grab the clear metal table from the corner of the room and drag it to where I've set up my work space. It seems almost out of place being so clean and shiny, but it won't stay that way for long.

Untying the leather restraints on the table, I think through the optimal punishment for someone like Trent while still getting him to speak.

Once the table is prepped and I've cleaned my blades, enough time has passed that I know the sedative has taken hold. I release the chains holding Trent up, taking a small sliver of pleasure as he crumples to the ground.

Heaving him onto my shoulder should be harder, but he's lost weight since he's been here. The worst part is the stench coming from him. Dumping him on the table, I buckle the restraints around his head, neck, wrists and ankles before cutting the clothing from his body.

Nothing quite like being naked to make a guy feel nice and vulnerable.

Once he's strapped in, I make sure the grate is open to drain fluid from the table, then grab a bucket and fill it with icy cold water. Splashing it over his blood, dirt, and shit-covered body, he startles awake with a yell, making me laugh once more.

"What the fuck?" he shouts as I lift one of the smaller blades from my spread.

"I told you, Trent. I'll get the names I need, and I won't let you die beforehand. You can make this stop at any time. Just give me names."

I start at his feet, running the scalpel around his cuticles then along the flesh of his nail beds, launching his toenails across the room with a careless flick of my wrist. I ask him the same question repeatedly, and when he's too busy screaming to answer, I begin on the pads of his toes, cutting away small segments of the skin and peeling it from the meaty flesh beneath the dermis.

Once he's finally stopped screaming and his breaths hiss through clenched teeth, spewing spittle into the air to land back on his face, I take a more direct approach. The blade slices through the tender skin in the arch of his foot with ease, blood finally flowing freely from the incisions.

This draws fresh screams from him, nourishing the darkest, most twisted parts of my soul.

I cauterize each cut to make sure he doesn't bleed out, the stench of burning flesh making him gag through his cries of agony.

When I move to his hands, having discarded the finesse of the scalpel for the brute force of pliers, fear finally glistens in his eyes as he tries to thrash around on the table. I grab each of his nails, prying them from his fingertips, before crushing each of his knuckles in their grip.

I've gotta hand it to him, nobody's ever been dumb enough to withhold information for me for this long.

I sigh, growing weary of his screaming, and reclaim my blade before grabbing his balls and stretching them taut, the tip of the blade poised and the first droplet of blood dripping onto the table.

"Harper Williams! That's who told me where she was!"

I pause at the name, keeping my shock tucked away,

because I don't quite believe it. But he also said there was more than one person, so I'm not going to stop yet. I use the soldering gun to seal the wound I just made, his screams now filling me with deadly, brutal annoyance.

"YOU WANTED A NAME!" he screams.

"I did. But you got cocky and told me there was more than one person. I want them all."

A tear slips down his cheek, like a balm to the scars on my soul from what happened to Quinn, but it's not enough.

Protecting her at all costs is what I vowed, and that means enjoying this a little more than I should.

Putting down the soldering gun, I grab another blade and move toward his right eye. "You don't need to see to speak," I say with a smile as I tower above him, his pathetic whimpers hanging in the air between us. "Now give me the other names."

After a day with Trent, I'm both invigorated and exhausted, but my work isn't done yet. Meyer might have told me to focus on Trent, but I had a pre-arranged meeting with Dario for tonight about this fuck up with the Ghosts.

Hunter might be better with most people, but Dario is more like me than the others.

We speak the same language.

Well, sort of.

I push open the wooden door to the bar the Ghosts own, the stench of beer, piss, and sweat filling my nostrils as my feet stick to the floorboards.

Fuck, I hate this place.

Trying to make a deal with the devil is never fun, but getting the devil to agree to not traffic people while also trying to stop a flood of low-grade drugs choking our streets is kind of a priority. There's money in vices, that's how we survive, but when people start dropping…it's not good for anyone.

The problem is the Ghosts are known to try and cut corners to make a bigger profit. Which is exactly why I'm here.

We have their guns still, Meyer's doing a deal for them with the boys across the border, but the drugs? They're still in my warehouse and, after testing, they're basically rat fucking poison. So I get to find out who supplied them, deal with that, and try to put a better option on the table while bringing them in on the gun operation we've been running to make it profitable for them, but more so for us.

All while delivering apt punishment for breaking our original deal. The truck of girls we intercepted…I clench my fists just thinking about it. I might be a monster, but I'll never be *that* kind of monster.

Fuck, I hate this part.

Politics isn't my strong suit, I don't exactly play well with others.

Give me wet work any day.

I spot Dario across the room and lift my chin in greeting before heading to the bar.

The blonde behind the pine gives me a wide smile, her low-cut top barely containing her tits, which are as real as the blonde of her hair. I give her a tight smile as I lean against the worn bar top, scanning over the booze available. This is going to require whiskey. "Rory, not often we see you here. Slumming it with the riff raff."

"Hi Tor. Just a whiskey," is all I respond. I'm not here to flirt with Dario's niece. That's a dangerous game, and since Quinn…well, women who aren't her just don't appeal to me.

Tor frowns at me but slams a glass in front of me and pours the amber liquid. I slide some cash across the bar, throwing back the booze before motioning for her to pour again. It's cheap-ass whiskey and tastes like shit, but whiskey is whiskey. She pours another, all while looking like she'd rather smash the bottle over my head, and I lift the glass in thanks and head over to Dario.

If I believed in a god, I'd be praying for the will to get through this without shedding blood. Fortunately, I have a stronger motivation to keep it on track: the knowledge that this will benefit Quinn and keep her safe.

That is what matters to me.

"Dario." He looks up as I say his name and slide into the booth on the bench opposite him. The dainty redhead draped over him looks put out by my arrival but I don't give a fuck. Dario was expecting me, she can get fucked if she had other plans.

"Rory, good to see you." He pushes the girl away and points across the room. She lets out a huff of frustration and slides out before stomping away. "Fucking women, man."

He takes a swig of his beer before refocusing on me. "So, what's the sitch?"

I take a sip of the cheap whiskey, my nostrils flaring at the shitty taste as I lean back, glancing out at the bar as I do. Usually, I'd want privacy for this, but I also know that, bare minimum, Dario would cut out the tongue of anyone who spoke about his business to an outsider.

Fuck it.

As I lay out Meyer's plan to work and split the drugs, guns, and money, he keeps quiet. The details are what Meyer planned, and he looks pissed when I talk numbers, but I remind him that the girls he tried to traffic were found by us, and of the fact he threatened Quinn.

He's lucky to be alive.

His jaw clenches as I remind him that pissing Meyer off is a bad idea, and that everyone here is still alive because

Meyer decided to give them another opportunity rather than clear the board of players.

It's something we've done before, it's exactly how Dario moved in, but apparently he got overzealous.

"I'll let you know by the end of the weekend."

I stand and shoot back the rest of the shitty whiskey before slamming the glass back down. "Let me know by the end of tomorrow."

Without another word, I leave the bar, the Ghosts, each in their cuts, eying me as I go. Fucking bikers.

Once I'm outside in the fresh air, the temptation to just set their bikes alight is real, but I keep my shit in check and head back to my truck. It's almost midnight and I want to see my girl. Wasting time on these fuckheads isn't worth it.

At least that's what I tell myself as a group of them appear outside the bar, watching me as I start up my truck. One of them has a crowbar in his hand, others guns, a few with knives, and I grin at each and every one of them. A silent challenge.

But they remain by the door and I pull out of my spot, heading home.

They might think I'm the asshole here, and I probably am, but I dare them to test me.

My monster could use an unrestricted outlet, but for now, I tuck it away.

I can play with biker entrails another day.

I get back to my room after the longest fucking day, wanting nothing more than a shower and bed, to find Quinn sitting on the end of my bed in tiny little fucking shorts, a see-through tank top, and those ridiculous fuzzy socks Hunter has been getting her…and all thoughts of sleep disappear while my dick twitches at the sight of her.

"Well, I could get used to coming home to this," I say with a grin as I pull off my t-shirt and undo my belt, my dick twitching again as her eyes drop to it.

She looks back up at me and I can see the hunger there, but I have a feeling that isn't why she was waiting for me. "What's up?"

She clasps her hands together in front of her and her smile widens. "You mean, other than your cock?"

"Yes, Quinn." I groan as I harden even more. Her talking about my dick is never a bad thing. Ever. "Other than my dick."

"I was coming to try and win you to my side with convincing Meyer to let me have the girls over." She pauses, biting her lip, her eyes wandering back down to my now-undone jeans. "But I can think of more fun ways to spend our night."

"Maybe we can kill two birds with one stone," I tell her

with a wink. "I can think of a few ways you could persuade me to your team."

Her eyes widen before she blinks at me, biting down on her lip again before she bounces over to me, her pert tits bouncing right along with her, and drops to her knees in front of me, rubbing her hands up my thighs to the opening of my zipper. "I can think of a few too."

My mouth waters as her fingers wrap around the base of my cock and squeeze hard enough to make my teeth clench and my blood pressure rise with how much I want to pound into her tight little cunt.

Quinn knows my trigger button, the one that pushes me to do unthinkable things to her body and still make her scream my name loud enough to damage her vocal cords.

"Who's in charge, here, Quinn?" My words are deadly, spoken through a clenched jaw. Lightly, she scrapes her teeth across the head of my dick while the tip of her tongue flicks at the slit already leaking precum. I'm fascinated by the scene below, the way she keeps her stare only on me. The way one corner of her mouth twitches with a smirk as my breathing becomes more and more erratic. My body tightens with a need so deep it takes every ounce of self-control to keep still, yet she keeps on pushing me.

"Who the fuck is in charge, here, Quinn?" I repeat when she doesn't answer, my entire body trembling with the need to rip her clothes off and slam her down to the floor as she chokes on my dick.

My control falters as my favorite thought enters my mind…why would I deprive myself of that pleasure. More importantly, why would I deprive *her* of that pleasure?

Just as Quinn slides her plump lips over my shaft until the head hits the back of her throat, I groan and enjoy the brief moment of bliss.

One second…fuck, her mouth is hot and wet and everything I love.

Two seconds…my fingers latch onto her hair as I pull her those last inches closer until she's unable to breathe with her nose flattened against my groin.

Three seconds…my hips rear back as I slam my dick right back into her mouth as I hold her head in place.

Four seconds…I'm fucking her face like she's a porcelain doll and I'm the motherfucking elephant in the room.

The most beautiful thing about it all is that she moans with every thrust of my hips and that just motivates me to give her more.

My girl is going to earn her night in with her friends. Because if they're here, I can't fuck her like the depraved asshole I am. She'll have to pay in full beforehand.

With a steady line of drool falling from the corner of her lip where my dick meets her mouth, I decide to change tactics. It would be a shame to waste all of that natural lubrication.

Pulling out, I hook my fingers in her mouth, just behind her bottom teeth, and while I stroke my dick my other hand, I pull her close and command, "Suck my balls" before releasing her and bracing myself for her next move.

And fuck me, she does it so well. Her saliva is coating my balls as she rolls one, then the other, in her mouth, her tongue flicking and caressing until I'm pretty sure I'm going to lose my fucking mind.

But I'm not ready to come. Not yet. Not until she's screaming my name with pleasure and…a little pain.

"Enough." I stop stroking my cock, bringing my hand to her hair again and pulling her away when she doesn't follow my instructions. I should punish her for that.

Fuck it, I will punish her for that. Right the fuck now.

Stepping back, I smirk at the sound of frustration that leaves her throat, her gorgeous eyes now staring daggers at me as if that has ever fucking worked with me. If anything, it just makes me want to do worse.

And by worse, I mean make her work for her orgasm. Make her cry for it. After all, she's so fucking beautiful with her tears streaming down her cheeks for me.

Bending at the waist, I pull up her tank and watch as her tits bounce from the roughness of my action. Her nipples are so fucking tight and hard I could cut my tongue on them.

The image of blood in my mouth as I suck on her flesh makes my dick so fucking hard, it physically hurts.

"Don't move." Quinn growls and just as my back is to her, I smile. She'll pay for that, too.

Walking to the closet dresser, I open the drawer and pull out my favorite knife. It's the size of a dagger making it practical and easy to use for exactly what I have in mind.

Quinn's eyes widen as I bring the blade into view, making my way back to her.

"This will sting a little." The flash of fear in her irises makes the monster inside me chuckle, restless with anticipation. "Buy you'll be a good girl and take it, won't you, Quinn?" This side of me belongs to her. I may sound like a fucking psychopath but she sees my nurturing side, placing all of her trust in the palm of my hand.

The hand holding the butt of the knife.

The knife I'm currently bringing to her nipple.

The nipple I've just lightly sliced open.

Her sharp intake of breath makes my cock leak even more, my hard dick a painful reminder that fucking her is the goal, not playing around.

And yet…

As soon as the first drop of blood slides around her otherwise flawless nipple, my mouth immediately waters.

"You're so beautiful when you bleed for me." Her moan turns to a gasp as I drop to my knees and bring my mouth to her tit, sucking on her nipple and filling my mouth with crimson essence.

In a fantasy world, I'd be a vampire and she'd be my only source of nourishment.

"Rory, oh my God." Quinn's moan only makes me suck harder and when she brings her hands to my head and pulls me even closer, I decide that my dick has been patient long enough.

That thought is obliterated when I pull away, ready to turn her on her stomach and ram my cock inside her tight little pussy, and see her other nipple just begging for my blade.

Who am I to say no?

Quinn's eyes follow my slow movements as I bring my knife to her other nipple and slice in the exact same spot as the first, my nostrils flaring as her blood overflows from the small incision and begins to slide down her flesh.

Fuck, I'm a goner.

My mouth is on her again, sucking and licking at her nipple as I drink every drop she has to offer.

When I pull back, Quinn is staring at my mouth as I stare at her eyes.

"You wanna taste, don't you?"

Our stares collide and I don't waste time crashing my mouth to hers and letting her savor herself.

We're not kissing, we're devouring each other. Our

lips firm and our tongues searching, we're fighting for dominance with every nip of our lips and collision of our teeth. It's feral, animalistic sounds coming from deep down inside our chests, and our bodies are acting on pure adrenaline and instinct.

Seconds before I lose my entire fucking mind, I pull away, picking her up by a handful of her thick, lush hair and throwing her on the bed like a rag doll about to get the fucking of a lifetime.

Quinn scrambles to avoid falling off the other end of the bed. I may have used a little too much force but I'm too distracted by her bouncing tits to feel bad about it.

As soon as she's settled in the middle of my bed, I use my knife to cut off her tiny, taunting little shorts, ignoring her cries of protest.

"Dammit, I loved those shorts!"

"Too fucking bad, they're in my way." Once her pussy is on display, her plump lips coated in her cum and her clit so full and hard I can see it throbbing for me, I throw the tattered remains over my shoulder and kneel at the apex of her thighs.

Thighs that are too fucking perfect for a monster like me.

Before I set out to mar her skin into a beautiful, bleeding mess, I bring my mouth to her cunt and suck on her lips, one then the other, before wrapping my lips around her clit and bringing her a little pain with her pleasure.

When my teeth scrape her bundle of nerves, I know how she feels. I hear the pain in her gasp, feel it in her quickening breaths, crave it as her hips buck, seeking out more.

Lapping up her cum, my tongue buried inside her pussy, I groan as her thighs squeeze my face, holding me in place as she tries to take control of the situation, fucking my face from below.

Now, that won't do, will it?

Placing the knife on the bed beside her, I bring both of my palms down on her knees and dig the pads of my fingers into her skin, prying them apart and pulling myself away.

"Tsk, tsk, tsk. Topping from the bottom, Quinn? Really? Is this any way to act?" I don't actually give a fuck, to be honest, but any excuse to bring her pain with our pleasure is good enough for me.

Sitting back on my haunches, I wink. What I'm pretty sure is a demented smile forms over my lips as I watch her staring back at me.

The widening of her eyes, her pupils dilated, her mouth slack are all signs that she's both afraid and intrigued by my next move.

"I suggest you don't move an inch."

Quinn's body goes completely still, only her heavy

breathing echo around my room as I spread her legs impossibly wider and angle her hips so her pussy is wide open for me.

"Do you know how enticing your cunt is? All pink and red, smooth skin and luscious flesh?" As I speak, I make myself comfortable, my eyes roaming, deciding on my next move.

To be honest, I already know what I want to do but I give myself an out in case I'm pushing her too far. Then I remember that Quinn is mine to do with as I wish and that singular thought makes my chest fill with satisfaction only she can give me.

Just as my knife gets close to my target, I raise my gaze to hers, popping a brow to make sure she remembers my previous order.

If she moves, there's a good chance I'll fuck up.

And I do not fuck up, ever.

Concentrating, I reproduce the exact same movement to her clit as I did to her nipple. A nip of the blade at the base of her nub has her crying out in pain, but when I latch my mouth onto it, sucking away all the hurt, I revel in the music of her moans.

Pain with pleasure is an aphrodisiac most don't know how to indulge in. Luckily for my Quinn, I excel at everything I undertake.

"Oh fuck, Rory. Fuck, fuck, fuck." The more she cries

out, the harder I suck. My arms are now wrapped around her thighs as I taste the blood from her innermost private nerve endings, taking, taking, taking until all I can taste is her.

Once I've had my fill, my tongue coated in her blood, I slide down to her pussy and bury it in her opening, lapping up her cum. Like a five starred chef, I create the most delicious elixir known to man and I'm the only motherfucker allowed to drink it.

Rising, I bring her hips with me as I stand on the side of the bed with her pussy still glued to my mouth. I'm drinking her in, devouring every inch of her cunt until my dick is so fucking hard I'm afraid I'll never be able to satisfy its hunger.

Quinn's shoulders are the only part of her body still touching the bed besides her hands as they white knuckle the sheets.

Thrashing and screaming my name as she comes all over my face, I refuse to back away. I'm not fucking moving my mouth until I have every drop of her inside me.

As her body goes slack, I flip her over onto her stomach and tuck her knees under her belly, keeping her thighs nice and wide for my dick.

There's no waiting, no probing, no warning. I slam my cock inside her cunt and wrap my fingers around the long strands of her hair as I fuck the remaining life right out of her.

Deep, rhythmic thrusts in and out, in and out, bumping that precious button only we three know about every time I'm buried inside. She's arched back, her face staring at the ceiling as I ride her like a fucking thoroughbred about to win the goddamn race of a lifetime.

There's nothing more fucking erotic than watching my dick sliding in and out of her pussy as her tight little asshole is in plain view, just begging to be touched.

As I've said before, I'm not one to deprive myself of pleasure and even less when it comes to giving pleasure to Quinn.

"Mmmmm, looks like your ass wants to play."

I pull all the way out of her cunt only to replace my dick with the handle of my knife, pumping it in and out a few times so it gets nice and wet with her cum.

Good thing it's a small dagger or else I'd have to get more creative.

Once I've got it nice and wet, I slide the wooden handle up from her pussy to her tight little hole and just as I slide my cock back between her lips, I push the knife into her other entrance. The muffled noises coming from her mouth make my entire body twitch with need for her.

One hand still holding tightly to her hair, the other fucking her ass with my knife, I begin to thrust my hips slowly, methodically, so she can feel the entirety of my length as I destroy her from both holes.

It's all a tight fit. It doesn't matter how small the handle is, her pussy is just that narrow.

"Do you feel me destroying your cunt, one hard thrust at a time?" I grit my teeth at the feel of her muscles clamping down on me every time I bottom out. "Maybe next time you'll think twice about asking for a favor?" I fucking hope not.

"Never." Her one word answer comes out like a mix between a mumble and a gargle as she gasps at my more fervent thrust.

The sounds of skin slapping skin and the smell of our depravity lingering in the air only make me want to rip her apart just so I can put her back together again.

"Good girl. Now come for me."

I can barely hold on to my need to fill her up with my cum. I want to see it spilling out from inside her.

Like a detonator, she freezes then bucks wildly as her orgasm trembles throughout her body. The goosebumps on her skin are like a map to her pleasure as she cries, literally, with pleasure, and screams my name while I continue to slam my cock and my knife inside her holes.

Lost and so close to losing my ever loving mind, I still as her pussy lips squeeze the cum from my cock and I unleash all of me into her.

Strains and strains of my semen fill her pussy to the rim, making me grin as a white, thick liquid seeps out between her lips and my shaft.

"Fucking beautiful." Sliding out, I replace my cock with the handle of my knife and roll it around her opening until I'm satisfied it's nice and soaked before pushing it back into her ass.

"There. Your friends can hang out but my cum will stay inside both of your holes the whole fucking time they're here."

TWELVE
QUINN

Thanks to having Rory on my team, Meyer caved and I get to have my friends over. Tina, Yen, and the girls are coming over for dinner and I'm not sure who's more excited, me or Shae. She's been clucking around the dining room for the last hour making sure everything is just right.

Needless to say, the karaoke machine is set up in the corner, the sound system is prepped, the bar is stocked, and everything looks like something out of a magazine.

"Is this too much?" Shae asks hesitantly as I look around the room, taking in the twinkle lights laid out between the leafy vines in the center of the small table that she's put in here rather than the usual giant one, the flower crowns for each person coming sitting atop the place settings, and the little goodie bags on each chair. "I've never really had friends, and I've definitely never done a girls night like this. I thought the smaller table would be better and give us more room to dance later, but maybe the bigger one would've been better. Made the room look bigger or something."

"It looks great, Shae," I reassure her, loving the effort she's gone to for me. Because I know that she'd have done any of this if it wasn't my idea. "Maybe a little extra, but well, it's you. I'd expect nothing less."

She pokes her tongue out at my teasing and I laugh.

Today was a hard day. I swear, every single thing has made me think of Tommy, even down to Shae caring for me in her own way and taking over the prep for tonight. I am loved, I am cared for, and that's all because of him.

I still haven't had the courage to read the letter from him. I might be actively avoiding my room just so I don't have to acknowledge its existence.

"I am extra, it's why I sparkle so much. Just call me Twilight, bitch."

I pull my phone from my pocket, pull up her number, and change her name in my phone, adding the sparkle emoji to the end of Twilight, then show her.

"You're such a bitch," she says, laughing. "Should I change?"

Her quick switch up from joking to self-conscious throws me. Shae doesn't do self-conscious.

"Shae, firstly you look amazing, secondly, you know these people probably better than I do, so stop stressing it.

It's just a chill night." I motion to my cozy band tee and jeans with accompanying fluffy socks. "Do I look like I'm out to impress?"

"You always look good enough to eat," she jests, winking at me. "But for real, I don't know why I'm so nervous. Maybe it's because I've been away for so long. Maybe it's because of what happened last time we had a big gathering here. But I feel on edge."

I frown, remembering what happened last time. Maybe this wasn't such a great idea. "We can call it off if you're not good."

"Are you kidding me?" she squawks. "Carlos would have a conniption after how much he's planned food wise for this. He's had a freaking ball of a time. Plus, I need to move past it. This is a good way to start."

"As long as you're sure."

She nods once, firmly. "I am." Her phone pings and she grins widely at me. "Good thing too, because the girls are here."

We head out to the front door, opening it and waiting for everyone to arrive. One of Meyer's concessions was that the girls get picked up by O'Connor in one of our cars so that he could make sure nobody was followed.

What he failed to mention is that a five-car freaking convoy was with O'Connor. I swear, there's more protection in this motorcade than the president has. Shaking my head, I smile as the cars pull up to the entryway. At least this explains where Tonio went. I did wonder, but Shae's shadow is less prevalent than mine.

Speaking of Bruno, he moves past us out of nowhere to open the car doors. "Freaking silent ninja."

Shae chuckles beside me just before the squealing starts as Yen, Belle, Tina, Sofie, and Amelia climb from the car and rush to us. There are hugs all round, and I deal because that's who these girls are at their core. They're sparkle-sunshine-twenty-something woo girls. Tina looks like she fits right in with them, and she already looks happier and healthier after being around them for almost no time at all.

"Y'all better have munch, because I am starving," Belle croons as we usher them inside and the five of them pause in the foyer.

Sofie lets out a whistle as she takes in the space. "This place looked like a palace from the outside, but this is something else."

I chew on the inside of my cheek, nervous all of a sudden about letting people inside our lives like this. What Shae said about last time is gnawing on my nerves, and while these guys work for Meyer, and I know them…well, betrayal is the downfall of many.

It's never your enemies who betray you.

Tommy's voice in my head soothes me for a second, but then the nerves come back with full force. He was right.

Maybe this was a mistake.

Shae leads the girls to the dining room, Tonio wandering behind them, glancing back at me with a look like he'd rather chew on glass than partake in tonight's festivities. I start to follow when Yen grabs my arm and holds me back. "Don't stress, I know these girls. I wouldn't have let you bring them here if I thought there would be problems."

"You psychic or something? Holding out on me, Yen?" I joke to hide my worry.

"Nah, it's just written all over your face. They were too busy paying attention to the shiny things in here, but I know you better than they do too."

I let out a deep breath and Bruno closes the front door. "Ready?" he asks with a comforting smile.

Yen releases my arm and I shake myself out. This night is going to be fun, I wanted to be normal and that's what tonight is.

Normal.

Shoving down the insecurities, worries, and all the other swirling bullshit emotions inside of me, I cling to the joy and paste a smile on my face.

I open my mouth to tell him I am when Carlos's shouts beat me to it. "Starters incoming!"

"I guess I better be," I chuckle and take Yen into the dining room where the others are already seated. I take my seat next to Shae and Yen sits beside me, bubbles are already flowing and the laughter in the room is infectious.

Feeling lighter almost immediately, I sit back and enjoy listening to the gossip of HellScape as Carlos brings in the charcuterie-style starters he's prepared. The whipped feta and homemade hummus with the selection of veggie sticks, meats, and cheese makes my mouth water.

The night passes almost too quickly, and by the time dessert is over, everyone is already more than a little tipsy. So when Shae stands and shouts, "Karaoke!" everyone is very much on board.

I start piling up the dishes on the table and startle when I feel hands on my hips. "You not partying and singing too?" Glancing back, I spy Meyer, a smirk on his face as he watches me.

"I will, just in a minute. I wanted to help with cleanup. Carlos has done enough."

He gently tugs on me, so I step back from the table and lean my back up against his chest. He rests his chin on my shoulder as his arms tighten around me. "Carlos will be offended if you try to help him. He loves this shit. Makes him feel needed."

I let out a sigh and tip my head back to lean on his shoulder. "Carlos needs to be offended by less stuff. You doing okay?"

"I'm good, are you having a good time?"

"I am," I reply honestly. It's not like my sadness has

vanished, but it's more like shadows on the edges of my vision rather than clouding it entirely. "I needed tonight, thank you."

"You're welcome. I fully intend on claiming my thanks in full later," he teases, biting softly on my neck, pulling a low groan from me. I feel his hardness pressing into me and the thought of partying disappears.

"You could always whisk me away and claim it now," I utter.

He kisses the spot he bit before whispering in my ear, "Not a chance. Go have fun with your friends. Drink, dance, sing your heart out. It's safe here. Enjoy yourself. I will find you later. Maybe I'll even sing for you."

He pulls back and slaps my ass and I turn to argue but he's already walking away from me. Letting out a frustrated sigh as my insides flip flop at the teasing, I turn back to the girls just as *Girls Just Wanna Have Fun* starts on the karaoke machine.

A grin spreads across my face and I bounce over to them, lifting my hands in the air and dancing as the music starts.

Yes. This is exactly what I need. And the other thing I need? Well, that I'm going to claim later.

Ready or not, this living life thing is going to happen. Just so long as life keeps cooperating. Things can only look up from here…right?

After the hilarity of girls' night last night, I'm thankful the guys let my sleep in today. I know Meyer had plans last night, but a few too many glasses of bubbles followed by shots because the girls are terrible influences meant that I was poured into bed by Meyer rather than ravaged by him.

Which is why, when I woke in his bed this morning with a bottle of water and Tylenol on the bedside table, I called his name like my own personal savior.

Mostly, I'm glad that I'm not the type that cries when they're past tipsy. Because that could have been horrific.

Instead, it turns out I'm the sing-Taylor-Swift-at-the-top-of-my-lungs-and-dance-like-I'm-twenty-one type.

The latter I'm reminded of as I make my way downstairs after my shower. My body *aches*. I hobble into the kitchen, desperate to find caffeine, and find Meyer humming to himself while he's cooking.

"No Carlos?" I ask as I shuffle up beside him and pinch his pert and peachy hiney. He laughs softly, leaning over and kissing my forehead before seasoning the sauce he's putting together.

"Gave him the day off after last night." I grab a bottle of water from the fridge, wistfully looking at the coffee machine while I ponder if the caffeine is worth the noise and hassle that machine causes.

These guys don't keep soda in the house, which usually doesn't bother me so much, but Coke is a great coffee substitute when I feel like this.

"What are you making?" I ask as I decide the coffee is worth the risk and start tapping away on the machine, wincing when the bean grinder whirrs to life.

"Tuscan chicken," he responds casually. "Some people call it marry me chicken, but I prefer the original name."

My heart races in my chest as my eyes go wide.

He.

Did.

Not.

I turn to look at him and he's down on one knee. My breath stutters in my chest as my mouth opens and closes like a stupid mute freaking fish until he cracks up laughing. "Oh, your face, pretty girl. Do not fear, no planned proposals here. Good to know where you're at."

Blinking at him, I try to regulate my breathing back to normal. "You're such an ass."

He climbs to his feet, still chuckling. "Yeah, but you adore my ass."

"Yeah, I do. It's peachy."

He turns and struts back to the stove, sashaying that peachy behind of his while I shake my head. This version of Meyer is one of my favorites. The playful, not so serious version. He doesn't come out often, and that might be why I treasure these moments the way I do.

As I keep being reminded lately, life is way too fucking short not to.

"So, we were thinking, since you're likely feeling a little delicate, the four of us could do an old-school, classic cheesy date night of movies, good food, snacks, obviously, and just relaxation. What do you say?"

Grinning, I nod. "Sounds like perfection, as long as there are no horror films."

"How about we give you first pick?" He teases and I poke my tongue out at him. "Do that again, and I'll put it to better use."

"Promises, promises," I toy with him. "You said something similar last night."

"That I did, but I'm not one to take advantage of a lady. Tonight, however, depending how much of my chicken you eat…well, it's not called marry me chicken for nothing."

Laughter bubbles from my lips when he winks at me over his shoulder again.

Once my coffee is made, I hop up on the counter since Carlos isn't here to bitch me out and just enjoy watching him cook.

Everything he does is done with such ease, yet it appears to be flawless. It smells amazing anyway.

The silence between us is comfortable in a way I'd

never known before finding these three.

"Food's nearly done, want to head to the cinema room? The other two should be there already. I'll bring down the food once it's plated up."

I jump down from the counter and move toward him, feeling a little awkward about just leaving him. "You don't want help bringing it down?"

He shakes his head as he turns the stove off. "No, I've got this. Go get comfy. Thank you for keeping me company while I finished."

I push up on my tiptoes and chastely kiss his cheek. "I'll always keep you company, and if you're sure then I'll go pick a movie."

"Just no cheesy romcoms." He pleads and I grin widely.

"I make no promises. Musical romances are a weakness of mine."

He groans again and I cackle as I skip from the room, feeling much better than I did when I came down earlier.

"You will be the death of me, Quinn Summers."

"Maybe," I call back over my shoulder. "But at least you'll die with a smile."

THIRTEEN

MEYER

This fucking world is getting more and more twisted and complicated with each day. Long gone are the days when Pops ran this city with ease. No, now we have unruly fucking bikers thinking they can stomp on whatever ground they want to and break deals when I've allowed them to work *with* us rather than *for* us...

And now the Knights have come calling.

I knew they would eventually. As soon as I heard about them, I knew the days were numbered before Echoes Cove wasn't big enough for them anymore. Businesses like ours don't grow like ours has and stay off their radar. Hell, they probably knew about us before I took over, but Pops kept the ship tight and small. I've been about expansion and growth.

Apparently, I was too ambitious. I don't want to work for someone, and I have zero intention of doing so.

You don't work as hard as I have, as *we* have, to bow to someone else.

Knights or not.

There might not be a ton of information out there, but I've done enough research to know the sort of people I'm coming into contact with.

The rich kids whose veins run blue; that want a piece of every pie because they feel entitled to it. Their organization runs far and wide, deeply rooted across the world, with members at all levels of life from what I can see.

But I don't want to be a part of it…

I'm not sure what sort of weight they're going to throw around though. Once upon a time, our world kept family out of dealings. These days, family is weakness, which means I have a fuck ton of it.

O'Connor pulls up to the pretentious-as-fuck restaurant at which my presence was demanded, and I hear his snort as he shuts the engine off at the valet stop. "This place is… something," he sniggers.

"You're not wrong," I retort, eyeing the place up. "I bet the food is shit too."

"Usually is at places like this. All about aesthetics rather than good food."

Letting out a frustrated sigh, I reach for the handle and climb from the car. O'Connor climbs out moments later and tosses the keys to the kid at valet, whose eyes go wide when he takes in the Bentley. "Look after it," O'Connor says, glaring at the kid, who nods a little too fast.

Can't be the only decent car he's seen here, so maybe he's just got a hard on for Bentleys. Can't blame the kid, it's a work of beauty.

We head inside, O'Connor never more than a step behind me. I wanted Hunter here too, but with Rory out today dealing with Dario again, as well as accompanying the drug truck we took from them down south, we figured it best if Hunter stayed home with our girl. I grab my phone and shoot Rory a text to remind him to only play a little nice, before sliding it back in my pocket.

Dario blew past Rory's deadline for an answer, which means they either get a worse deal, or they get cut out entirely. Even if that means clearing them from the map. Again. But before I decide to do that, I need to work out what the Demons are up to and figure this shit out with the Knights today. O'Connor is the person I trust most, after Mateo, but Mateo has been a brat lately, so I've left him out East dealing with Tommy's stuff. O'Connor might just seem like my driver, and that's exactly how I want the world to see it, but he's so much more than that. Everyone underestimates the staff.

I step up to the maître d' desk and smile tightly at the guy standing behind it. His eyes go wide when he sees me and I hold back a smile. I guess he knows who I am.

It's always nice when my reputation precedes me. Makes my life easier sometimes. "Meyer Marino. I'm here to see Edward Riley."

The guy's brows dart up but he nods without even checking the tablet in front of him. "Of course, sir. Your party is already seated. Please, follow me."

Of course they are, I'm twenty minutes early and he's still here early. Though, by the sounds of it, he's not alone.

I glance at O'Connor, who rolls his eyes, mirroring my sentiments, then follows the maître d' through the busy restaurant. It's like something out of a country club advertisement; all dark wood paneling, marble floors, plush chairs, and just money thrown around recklessly on decor.

Our visitors are easy to spot on the far side of the restaurant at the corner table, backs to the wall so they can watch the entire room. Usually, I'd be pissed they took the advantageous spot, but it makes me smile.

They have something to fear here, otherwise they wouldn't have positioned themselves like that, and that's an advantage for me. They haven't dabbled in our city before, and now I have an inkling that there's more to that than us potentially just being a small fish in their world.

I recognize Edward. He summoned me here, so I did my research. Marc Garcetti, our city's mayor, is a shock though. As is Stone Royal. I thought he was a musician, not someone I expected to see, even though I discovered his family was interlinked. What I saw was more to do with his father than him, but I guess that's the way of an organization like theirs.

"Meyer Marino, it's good to finally meet you," Edward says, standing as we reach the table. The other two stand with him and it's a power play, dick measuring handshakes all round.

"Nice to meet you. This is Mikey O'Connor." O'Connor plays his part well and takes a seat beside me when Edward motions to the chairs.

The maître d' takes our drink orders before practically sprinting away from the table. We make small talk until our drinks are bought over to us before placing our order. I get the filet steak with lobster tail, because obviously, ordering is a dick measuring contest too. Just like ordering the top-shelf whiskey. I'm also assuming I'm picking up the tab today, not that it bothers me, but fuck I hate this political bullshit. There's a reason I'm not in politics. I might be good at it, but I despise it.

Once our server leaves, the smile drops from Edward's face as he leans back in his chair and takes a sip of his whiskey. "Let's talk business, shall we?"

"I didn't realize we had business," I retort, and O'Connor knocks my foot with his under the table. I get it, play nice, he's the one who's going to have to get us out of here if shit really hits the fan since I could only carry light. He, however, is armed to the eyeballs beneath that somewhat-baggy getup of his. "What is it, exactly, that you'd like to discuss?"

Edward smirks, but it's Marc who leans forward. "As I'm sure you're aware, Marino, your family is known to the law enforcement in our city. You've been garnering attention that I'm sure you're not fond of as of late, especially since a cop seems to have mysteriously gone missing, who is linked to your new…acquaintance. Miss Summers?"

I keep my face blank, even at the sound of her name in his filthy mouth.

"No idea about any officer going missing, mister mayor. Sounds like police business to me." I take another sip of my drink, leaning back casually, popping my ankle up on my knee. "But if you need some help searching for him, I'm sure we could ask some of our more street-level friends. I'm sure your friends look in higher places than mine."

"I'm sure," he responds tartly. "As I was saying, recent activity has drawn attention and we can help with that."

Letting his words hang in the air, like I'm contemplating his offer, I take another sip. It's good whiskey at least, this visit won't be a total waste of my time. I glance over at Edward, who is smiling like a cat with the canary in his teeth, while Stone looks bored out of his mind. "In return for what, exactly? What is it you want from my family and me?"

"Well, Meyer. May I call you Meyer?" Edward says, pulling a cigar from the inside pocket of his jacket. I wrinkle my nose as he lights it. The stench is vile, but I keep my mouth shut. "What we want, is to help you. For a piece of the pie, as it were."

I quirk a brow as I lean forward, keeping eye contact with him. "And why is it you think we'd want your help, Edward? The Knights have stayed out of my city until now and we've been doing more than just okay without you. I understand how this deal benefits you, but I'm yet to see how it is that this would benefit us. You say we're garnering attention, but if you think I don't already have that covered, you've sorely underestimated me. There's a reason we've grown to what we have, and it's not because I'm a stupid businessman."

Edward's jaw ticks and it's enough to cause the corners of my lips to tilt upward. This fuck wants something for nothing and I'll be fucked if I'm going to bend to him just because of the potential power behind him. The Knights definitely pose a threat, and I'm not opposed to an agreement with them, but not over something so pathetic and flimsy as help with the local police force.

"What is it that you'd want in return then, Meyer?"

Edward asks. Marc opens his mouth to chip in, but is silenced by a look from Edward. It's very obvious that our Mayor isn't used to being put in his place, but he's not the big fish at this table, even if he does supposedly run this city.

If only he knew how little power he truly had. I could have him removed from his seat with ease, but until now, he's never been an issue for me. The police commissioner is an old friend of Mama's, he'd be perfect for mayor if I really wanted, but that's an ace in the hole for later.

"I'm not sure what you have to offer us," I finally reply. "Like I say, we've been doing just fine on our own. Is there a reason that you're only now looking at my city?"

Stone snorts a laugh. "He's not stupid. Got to give him that."

Edward glares at the rockstar, who gulps back his second glass of vodka before picking up the third that was bought to him. "We previously had an agreement with someone who was dabbling here. He's no longer a problem."

My stomach drops at the realization. "I assume you're talking about my godfather, Tommy DeLuca?"

"Your godfather?" Edward asks, his shock apparent. Oh, good. "I didn't realize. My sympathies."

"Appreciated. But yes, my godfather. Technically, he worked for me, his contacts were and still are mine. His connections were and are mine, so whatever agreement you had with him still stands."

Edward grips his glass, his rage apparent.

"Any agreement he had in place would've been on either mine or my father's behalf, so I'm afraid I'm going to need to look into that before we discuss anything further." I finish my glass and stand, O'Connor following suit. "I'm going to get right on that, so apologies for cutting this short, but I want to get this cleared up. If you'll excuse us."

I tip my head to him, re-button my jacket, and stride away from the table. Tommy had way too much shit in place that he apparently didn't fill me in on. I loved the old man, but fuck me, I could've used a heads up on this one. We make it outside and the kid at the valet runs to grab the car. It takes less than thirty seconds before the car is in front of us. O'Connor checks it over before getting in while I slide a hundred to the kid.

"Where to?" O'Connor asks once the door is closed, and I pinch the bridge of my nose.

"Home, I need to call Mateo home or head out east. I don't want to do either, but I need to look over Tommy's stuff, like, yesterday."

After an exhausting day, I find myself on a private jet,

Quinn opposite me, wide-eyed about the plane, even though she's fidgeting enough for me to know that she's on edge about going to Tommy's place.

Hunter strides toward us from the pilot's cabin, smiling at the air host who hands him a glass of what I'm assuming is whiskey, not apple juice.

"Should you be drinking while you're still healing?" Quinn asks him as he sits opposite her.

He leans forward and rests a hand on her knee to stop her leg bouncing before busting out that megawatt smile of his. I smirk as I glance back down at my phone and the petulant response I just got from Mateo, which steals some of the joy of watching their exchange.

"Whiskey is good for the mind, body, and soul. Rob would never tell me not to drink it."

"He isn't the doctor I'd be asking for advice," she grumbles. "He caves to you guys too easily."

Oh, if only she knew.

I wonder if Rory told her about the tracker yet. Actually, there's no way; we'd have had Hurricane Quinn if she knew. Should probably do something about that, but it's kept her safe thus far, and too many things are still uncertain.

Especially with the Knights now sniffing around. I get the feeling that kidnapping isn't something that they have issues with if it serves their needs.

They continue their light-hearted bickering, which I know is more to keep her distracted, and I'm thankful. By the time Rory, O'Connor, Eddie, and Rob finally board, Quinn and Hunter are in full war mode with their back and forth, while I try to not clench my jaw so hard that my teeth crack over how to deal with Mateo without beating him to death.

He's my brother, and I love him dearly, but sometimes I want to choke the life from him with my bare hands. Glancing back down at my phone doesn't make it any easier.

Mateo:

I don't need a fucking babysitter, I can just send you whatever. But if you need to swing your dick for the princess, I guess I'll see you in a few hours.

I have no idea what his issue with Quinn is, they've hardly interacted that I'm aware of. I pocket my phone, finish my drink, and start a game of chess with Rory, while Rob reads behind us next to Eddie, and Hunter and Quinn play a game of snap.

Some things never cease to amaze me, but she's smiling and that's what matters.

The flight passes with ease, almost too much, and the host appears to let me know we're only about an hour out.

At that point, Rory heads to the bathroom, and Quinn jumps seats to sit next to me, leaving Hunter pouting. I smile, shaking my head at how he can be entirely himself with her. We all can. She makes it easy.

She snuggles under my arm, curling her legs up on the seat and getting comfy. "You doing okay?"

Looking up at me, it's impossible to miss the sadness still in her eyes, but she gives me a soft smile anyway. "Better than I expected to be."

I squeeze her against me, wishing there was something I could do. "Anything I can do to help?"

"You can distract me for the next hour?"

"And how would you like me to do that?" I ask, my mind going to places it definitely shouldn't be while we're on this plane.

But then…there *is* a bed in the back.

Focus, Meyer.

She doesn't look back up at me, but I feel her stiffen. "You could tell me more about the business. What you guys actually do. Why we're having to go to Tommy's place, because I know it's not just a simple visit. And maybe why I still require a silent ninja shadow everywhere we go?"

Well shit. Not exactly what I expected, but I did tell her I'd tell her what she wanted to know about our lives, as long as it was safe for her to know. But where the fuck to start?

I don't really want her to know about the Knights, but I also can't decide if it's safer that she knows about all the threats or none of them. That said, she's a grown-ass woman, and despite my caveman ways, I know that she's capable of making her own decisions.

Doesn't mean I'm not going to agree with them, or find ways to keep her safe regardless, but…I suppose I can divulge some of it.

Running a hand down my face, I let out a breath. "Okay," I start, and she pulls back, sitting up straight as Rory returns. He looks at me, and I don't know what he sees on my face, but he sits down opposite Hunter, giving us space.

"Let's start with this trip. A new player on the board, an old-school power player that's never bothered us before, made themselves known, but it turns out they had an agreement with Tommy and Pops from back in the day. I need to go through all his shit to see if he has any details anywhere about it. Unlikely, because it was probably a gents agreement, but Tommy made meticulous notes. I want to know what he knew."

"Okay," she says, nodding. "Do we need to worry?"

"Not yet," I answer honestly, scanning her face as she digests my words.

"Okay, so what about the rest?" she prompts, and I can't help the smile on my face. Our kitten definitely has claws;

they're put away, but she's impatient today, apparently.

"You wanted to know about the business?"

She nods eagerly, crossing her legs and leaning toward me, her elbow resting on the table.

"Well you already know some, the clubs for example." I pause, and she nods again. "Okay, so you might know some of this already, but basics, we work in drugs and guns and launder money for that through the clubs. We also help victims of human trafficking while working with some other…organizations to ensure the trafficking is kept to a minimum. I wish it were zero, but I'm not foolish enough to think we can get there yet."

I scan her face again, her wrinkled nose and forehead telling me she's processing what little I told her, likely making her own assumptions, but that's fine.

"Is that it?" she asks and I can't help but laugh.

"There's a bit more to it, it's not like you don't know that. Look at how you, quite literally, fell into our laps."

Her cheeks redden, her hands squeezing together like she's remembering watching me shoot that dickhead in the warehouse. "Yeah, I know that stuff too."

"There's more to it, but that's the basics."

"So there's nothing I can do to…help?"

Shaking my head, I place a hand on her knee and squeeze gently. "No, you don't need to worry about helping with the business. If you want a job, we can talk about it, but it's not necessary. You could do what Mama and Shae do—enjoy life, work with a few charities—but you do not need to work. You will never. We will look after you."

Her lips twist before she chews the bottom one. "Not sure how I feel about that entirely." She untwists her hands and shrugs. "So if everything's so simple, why do I still have Bruno as my shadow?"

"Bruno?" I ask quickly, then remember. "Ah, yes. Eddie. Your safety is important to me. To all of us. There are some things not quite ironed out right now, which might pose threats. We let our guards down once. We won't do it again. You're too important to us. So even if there's no immediate threat, Eddie or someone else will always be with you. I'm not willing to risk you."

"Oh," she says softly, deflating like I just took the wind out of her sails.

"Any more questions?" I ask, having expected way more from her, but she shakes her head. I have no doubt she'll ask more in the future, especially since I'm not that certain she got *that* much new information. I open my mouth to speak again when the pilot's voice comes over the speaker, letting us know we're prepping for landing.

Quinn stiffens again, her entire body tense as she turns to sit properly and puts on her seatbelt. I guess she's less prepared for this trip than I'd hoped…

Here's hoping for no more surprises.

FOURTEEN

QUINN

The time at Tommy's was…painful. Healing. Heartbreaking. Uplifting.

Turbulent.

That's probably the best word for it.

Not that Mateo made it easy. I really don't get what his problem is. At least he was civil before, but during this trip he was just a brat…and that's me being nice.

Really, he was a giant raging dickhead. A stale ham sandwich of a human. A toddler stuck in the body of a twenty-something.

Any of those are fitting and still not quite hitting the mark.

It was annoying as shit for me, but mostly, I feel for Meyer. He's trying so hard to hold everything together for everyone else, that I don't think he's taken time to grieve.

Or even noticed that he hasn't.

I don't know if any of them have, which makes me feel shitty and selfish for being so wrapped up in my own grief, but I also know that my grief is acceptable and not something I have to feel guilty about. Lord knows I'm carrying enough guilt as it is. My poor therapist might not be getting paid enough.

We've been back home a week, tons of boxes that Hunter and Rory drove back are scattered around Meyer's office, and he's been holed away in there for basically the entire time we've been back.

I get it. He said he needed some important details about a deal, and if he hasn't gotten them…well, I'm not surprised he's still holed away. There were a lot of boxes that got brought back.

Sliding my phone into the pocket of my leggings, I glance at my letter from Tommy.

Yes, I'm still a chicken shit.

No, I still haven't read it.

Tomorrow. Maybe.

Hauling ass out of my room, I almost run straight into Bruno. "Sorry, forgot you were out here."

"It's fine, I'm used to it," he says, chuckling. "To the gym?"

"Well you did say you'd teach me some stuff. Want to do that today after my workout?"

He shrugs and glances at his watch. "Can do, probably

better tomorrow though. I've got a thing tonight."

"No worries," I say with a smile. "I can work out plenty on my own."

I don't mention that I haven't talked to Meyer or the others about my plans to learn how to defend myself. I know I could ask Rory again, but they all seem to have a lot going on at the moment. Being an additional burden to them isn't something I want.

Boredom spurs me down the stairs and to the gym. I know I asked Meyer if I could help with his business and he said not to worry, but that wasn't a no.

Maybe Bruno will have an idea of what I could do to help them.

Lord knows I can't just keep working out and lounging around. I'm going to lose my ever-loving mind. How Shae and her mom manage it baffles me, because if I stop for too long I'll end up in my head, and that's not a fun place for anyone to stick around too long.

Am I totally avoiding dealing with my grief? Avoiding asking too many questions about Trent? Avoiding…well, all of the freaking emotions? Absolutely I am. Emotions don't seem to get me anywhere, contagious little bastards.

Would I rather lose myself in getting sweaty? In all ways imaginable? Yes, please, sign me up. But I need something to occupy my mind for the in-between.

At least until I'm ready to deal with this shit I'm

avoiding.

Is it healthy? Of course not. My therapist is probably the most frustrated human on the planet right now. But this is how I deal. I need processing time before I sit in it anymore. I did the initial wallowing, guilt-ridden thing, but I can't anymore.

Everyone deals with shit differently, this is how I'm doing it.

My way.

Might not be the "right" way, but fuck it.

Who says there is a right way?

Once we reach the gym, I hook my phone up to the speakers and play *Middle Fingers* by Aston while I warm up on the treadmill. I run like my demons are chasing me, the music keeping me focused as it switches to *Shake* by The Haunt and my mind finally quiets.

"You think the boys will let me help out with the business?" I ask Bruno, who quirks his brow at me.

"You want to help with the business?" he asks, basically parroting my question.

"That's what I said."

He laughs, just once, but shakes his head. "I doubt it, Quinn. They want to keep you safe, which means as far away from the business as possible. Why do you think you're not even at the club anymore? Too many variables. Outside of this compound, the risk…well, it's higher. Even here isn't entirely safe, as you discovered, but it's easier. Until they find out who was helping Trent—"

"What do you mean, helping Trent?" I hit the stop button on the treadmill and turn my full attention to him.

"Shit," he mutters, shaking his head. "Nothing. I meant nothing. But no, I don't think they'll let you help with the business."

Folding my arms across my chest, I stare him down, fairly certain he's laughing on the inside at just how terrifying I'm not, but I want to know what he meant. "Bullshit to nothing. What did you mean?"

"Fuck," he grumbles, staring back at me. "Trent had help, we just don't know who. If they find out I told you, I am fucking fish food."

"So dramatic," I respond, rolling my eyes before jumping off the treadmill. "But thank you. A few things make more sense now."

I'm a little frustrated that Meyer didn't tell me, but he did say there were threats I guess. He just wasn't specific.

"Secret's safe with me." He visibly relaxes at my words and I smile. "Trust goes both ways, right? I'm not going to tell on you, not when I wanted to know. Now, I feel like sushi. You hungry?"

"I don't think Carlos—"

"I don't mean Carlos," I tell him with a smile. "Let's go grab lunch!"

After the bust of trying to help with the "family business", since I got back from my lunch with Bruno, I've been scrolling online looking at part time jobs and volunteer work that I might be able to do, just to pass some time. I've never really sat well in the housewife role, and since Carlos does the cooking and grocery shopping and the guys have a freaking team of cleaners, there's nothing in that role for me to do anyway.

The only things I have to pass my time are TV and working out, and I'm getting restless. I want to do something. Find some purpose. Too many sacrifices were made for me to get to this point. The whole point was so that I would be free to live my life, and while I am free—admittedly with constraints, which are mildly understandable after what Meyer told me last week—I don't feel like I'm free.

Even knowing there are threats, I can't just do nothing. I'm still tucked away like a little lost bird in a cage, like I have a broken wing. And I'm not saying I'm not broken, lord knows the multiple weekly sessions with my therapist are testament enough to that, but I don't need to be squirreled away.

A broken wing never mends if it isn't given the chance to stretch and fly.

Which is exactly how I find myself in Meyer's office with Rory and Hunter, trying to plead my case.

Again.

I tug on the cuffs of my sweater, giving them the best puppy dog eyes I can muster, before saying, "Pleaseeeeee."

It feels gross having to almost beg, but all things considered, between Trent, Tommy, and the other stuff they have going on, I realized going full-scale wild child and just doing it without speaking to them would be childish.

Even if I feel like a child right now, this is definitely the better path.

At least that's what I keep telling myself.

"You know if you guys are on my side, Meyer will cave." I flutter my lashes at them and Hunter starts laughing.

"You definitely make a compelling case, Angel, but I don't know if now is the right time. I know you hate being cooped up, God knows I would too, but we'd have to send Eddie with you wherever you went, and that might raise more questions. We have to think about potential collateral as well."

"Well, I'm on board," Rory says with a shrug. "I know the benefits of being team Quinn." He winks at me and I grin wide, thinking about the night I cornered him in his room and had him join team me for my last battle with Meyer.

"Benefits?" Hunter asks, wagging his brow. "No one

said anything about benefits."

"Oh, the benefits are fucking great," Rory tags on and I start to laugh. "Might be even better if we got to share those benefits."

He stares at me and I feel my cheeks heat. "You'd want that?"

He nods in answer and I glance over at Hunter, who is already on his feet and moving toward me. "You have no idea how much we'd want that."

He kisses me with so much want that my toes curl as I clasp his t-shirt. When his lips leave mine, he moves so he's standing behind me, his hands on my hips, and Rory stands.

"You sure you want to play this game, Angel?" Hunter whispers to me, and I suck in a raspy breath. It's not something we've done, but I can't say it's not something I've thought about happening.

"Yes." The word falls from my lips like a whisper then Rory is in front of me, his lips on mine as Hunter kisses down my neck.

Holy fucking shit that feels so good.

I have a tingly sensation with every touch of their fingers and lips. Every whisper they breathe across my skin.

"Turn around." Rory murmurs over my lips just as the warmth of Hunter's body leaves me bereft.

Still, I do what Rory tells me to do and turn so his front is now flush against my back.

Hunter has taken a seat on one of the sofa chairs, his demeanor calm and collected, almost bored. Until, that is, I look into his eyes and see it all like a high-definition screen. With eyes fixed on me, his irises dilated and his nostrils flaring with every touch of Rory's fingers down my sides, his hunger is plain to see. Legs apart, elbows pressed on the arm of the chair as he fists his fingers under his chin, he licks his lips as though he can already taste me.

"Aren't you going to join us?" I'm suddenly feeling shy, like maybe he's not interested, which is crazy, right?

"I will. But first, I want to see what these benefits are." The glint in his eyes is filled with both humor and dark promises to come and goddamn, I'm here for it all.

Without taking his eyes off me, Hunter brings one hand to the buttons of his jeans and pops them open, one by one.

Behind me, Rory is licking a path from my collar bone to the base of my ear before pinching the flesh between his teeth.

"Look at his dick, Quinn." My eyes drop to where Hunter is spreading the lapels of his jeans and pulls out his cock. Commando, of course. That's just how he rolls.

I barely have time to lick my lips before Rory's palm connects with my neck and his fingers instantly press on my pressure points. This position gives him complete access to my neck but his only interest at this moment is to get me nice and wet without even needing to touch me in all the places I want him to destroy me.

"I bet you can already taste him in your mouth, can't you? Do you want to gag on it, Quinn? Maybe see your life pass before your eyes as you wonder if he's going to choke you out of your last breath?" Rory's words would be concerning if I didn't know him…this is foreplay.

And how fucked up is that?

I don't bother answering him. All of his questions are rhetorical, a means to get me worked up for them.

Rory slides one hand down my front, tweaking a nipple as he goes. Curling his fingers around the hem of my sweater, he pulls it up and over my head but doesn't take it all the way off. Instead, he stops the fabric mid-way down my arms, trapping them as he twists the sweater in his fist and tightens his hold on me.

My chest is heaving, my nipples poking through my bra as he slides the hand on my neck down my sternum until he reaches the thin, lace material. With rough jerks, he pulls the cups down and exposes my tits to Hunter, who darts his tongue out to lick his bottom lip as though he can taste me.

My gaze drops to his hand again as it squeezes his dick, stroking himself long and slow.

"I think he likes what he sees, baby. But I think he

needs the whole picture, don't you?" That same hand glides down my stomach right to the button on my jeans, which he pops open without a hint of resistance. The zipper is next, cool air lowering my body temperature enough to give me time to breathe.

It's so fucking hot in here, that can't be normal.

Rory twists my sweater tighter as he pulls down, forcing my chest out more and my head back, bringing my ear to his mouth.

"If I put my fingers in your cunt, how wet will they be?"

This time I do answer.

"Very."

"Good girl."

Using my sweater as bindings, Rory does quick work of tying the sleeves around my wrists like he's been doing this his entire life. Maybe he has. Once I'm tied up to his satisfaction, he slams his palms against my hips and hooks his thumbs in my jeans, pulling them off right along with my undies.

That's all it takes for me to be completely naked for them. Oddly enough, he doesn't take my bra off, just leaves my tits out on display, but I don't question any of it because my mind is too focused on Hunter and the way he's pulling out his balls as he pushes his jeans further down his thighs. My God, he's fucking delicious. Intense. Mine.

I'm ripped out of my musings when Rory pushes me to the office floor, keeping one hand on the top of my head before tunneling his fingers into my hair and pulling my head back.

Standing to my side, he smiles down at me and whispers, "Open." It's then I realize he's got his own dick out and I'm about to get the Rory face fucking I love so much.

My mouth drops open, my eyes never veering from the intensity of his state as he pushes his dick between my lips and grins. It's not a loving grin, it's everything primal and depraved, like he knows a secret and will only tell me once I can't refuse.

"Remember, baby, this is you giving us the benefits of being on your side. Time to earn your alliances." I don't have time to register his words before his cock is pushed into my mouth all the way down until my nose bumps his groin and the head nudges, then invades, the back of my throat.

I gag, earning a long, sinful, groan from Rory. My eyes instantly water and saliva starts dripping at the corners of my mouth.

The Rory face fuck is almost cruel in its intensity but I can't get enough of it.

"Look at those tears, Hunter. She's crying for us." Then he pulls out just an inch, allowing me to breathe easier, but not long enough to get a good gasp in before he's gagging me again.

*Tsk*ing, Rory, tightens his grip on my hair to the point of delicious pain. "Breathing is for the weak, baby. You gag and you fight for your life. I decide when you get to breathe." My eyes widen as I try to keep my lungs filled with air, letting out as little as possible through my nose but getting more and more desperate. Stars are flashing at the corners of my eyes as he pulls me back an inch more and palms my neck, no doubt feeling his cock down my throat.

"You look so pretty with my dick choking the life out of you." I blink, my tears running into my ears and my saliva only making his deep, slow thrusts easier for him.

My vision starts to blur and his face, cruel and loving all at the same time, disappears with every slow blink I take.

Just when I feel my entire being on the brink of giving out, he pulls out and orders, "Breathe."

I gasp, gulping in mouthfuls of air and coughing at the sudden freedom from his grasp.

"Now crawl to Hunter and show him how much you appreciate his generosity."

It's not exactly easy crawling with my arms tied behind my back and my chest burning from the earlier lack of oxygen, but I do what I promised I would.

I earn my freedom.

Once I reach Hunter, the scene shifts from depraved to loving in an instant. As I crawled, Hunter made space for me by taking his jeans completely off and spreading his thighs for me. Leaning up, he palms my cheeks with both hands and brings his hot, possessive mouth to mine, searing me with a kiss I feel all the way down to my swollen clit.

Rory wouldn't be disappointed by how wet I am. I'm fucking soaked because I, apparently, love fearing for my life.

Again, how fucked up is that?

But Hunter is my flip side. He soothes the rough edges, makes Rory's corners a little more rounded and gives me the balm after the burn.

Pulling away, Hunter looks right into my eyes and murmurs, "Watching you like that was fucking beautiful, Angel." I smile at his words then do what I was told.

Fisting his cock at the base, Hunter uses his other hand to push my head down. I swallow him up in one smooth move, the musky scent of him invading my nostrils and warming my chest with the familiarity of him.

I'm well aware that my ass is on full display for Rory, so it's no surprise when I feel the heat of him at my back, pressing against my bound arms.

"That's it, baby. Suck his dick like it's your last meal." Two fingers push into my pussy and I moan around

Hunter's dick, earning me a long, satisfying groan.

I love making my men lose even the tiniest bit of control because it means that I hold it. They're only pretending to be in charge.

Rory adds another finger, hooking it deep inside me and causing a gasp to fight its way out of my mouth as I try to release Hunter's dick.

I can't though.

One hand is pushing me down and it doesn't take a genius to know it's Rory's handiwork.

Meanwhile, Hunter is rubbing soothing circles with his thumb over my pulse point.

It's a whole new taste of pleasure and pain.

"You're so fucking wet. We could both slide into your cunt at the same time." At his words, my pussy clenches like it's actually yearning for that exact scenario, and judging from the dark chuckle beside my ear, Rory knows it too.

Oh fuck.

No. He can't actually be serious.

"Is that what you want, baby? Two dicks fucking this greedy little pussy?" Again, my walls squeeze his fingers and again, he chuckles, all the while pushing my head down until I'm choking on Hunter's impossibly hard dick.

"Oh, Hunter. I think our benefits just doubled."

"Is that what you want, Angel?" My eyes fly up to

Hunter's concerned gaze and whatever it is he sees in them only makes his irises dilate and his nostrils flare like a predator.

He may be the more docile of the three but I'm not crazy or naïve enough to think he's not just as hungry as Rory and Meyer.

In a matter of seconds, I'm torn off Hunter's dick and Rory's fingers are no longer inside me.

I blink up, a little disoriented, to see them both gazing down at me.

When did Hunter stand up?

It doesn't matter, I've got bigger problems right about now. Very, very big, and hard, and ready to pummel me, problems.

Still on my knees, I wonder why they're just standing there, staring at me.

"The desk is too high." Hunter muses.

"From behind won't do, anyway." Are they discussing how they're going to fuck me?

"The loveseat won't do." Rory shakes his head at Hunter's words, and although they're both looking at me, their minds' eyes are all over this office.

"The carpet it is, then." They both say at the same time.

This whole situation is surreal, being discussed like they're trying to move furniture around a small space and not sure if it'll fit.

"I'm right here, you know?" I say, the corner of my lip rising in a small growl.

"Get the lube." Hunter calls out just as he squats to my level and buries his fingers in my hair.

"This might sting a little."

My logical brain tells me I should recoil, yet that's not what happens. In fact, I lean into Hunter, almost purring at the thought of him and Rory using my body to the brink of sanity just to bring me right back to reality.

"What's the use of an orgasm if you don't work for it?" I sass back but my gaze catches on Rory rummaging through the desk, who stops and raises a brow at me like my comment just gave him permission for all kinds of kinky shit.

Palming the side of my face, Hunter brings me in for a deep, soulful kiss. The kind that starts at my lips but travels like lightning down my spine and around to my clit.

I want to reach out and touch him, wrap my arms around his neck and devour every inch of his mouth, but that's not what they have in mind. My arms are still securely tied behind my back and even though I could probably manage to free myself, I don't want to disobey.

At least not yet.

As Hunter explores my mouth so thoroughly that I lose myself in the taste of him, his scent is all around me, intoxicating, like an age-old bourbon. My body is leaning in his direction, my balance teetering as I search for more of him. Almost more, always closer.

"Such an eager little slut, aren't you, baby?" I startle at the sound of Rory's voice right behind me, my mind too consumed by Hunter's mouth.

Both men lead me to the carpet and my first thought is that it's going to burn. If they fuck me on this rug, I'll have the marks to prove it.

I can't fucking wait to wear them proudly.

"Can you untie me?" I'm already anticipating them giving me the green light as I lean to the side and try to untangle myself from the sweater when the sharp sting of a large palm slams against the entrance of my pussy.

My yelp is both surprise and red-hot pain that spears through me.

"What the fu—" Rory is suddenly straddling my chest, one huge, rough palm pressing against my mouth and nose as he stares down at me with savage intensity.

"Who gave you permission to free yourself, Quinn?" Even if I could answer, I wouldn't. In fact, there is no acceptable answer and trying to justify my actions would only delay my orgasms and no one has time for that.

Shaking my head, my eyes pleading with him, I kick out my legs as the oxygen begins to run low in my lungs.

Hunter stands, getting the full view of me struggling against Rory as he plays his favorite game. The one where he's in control of my breath, of my very right to live.

I suppose there's a primal power in knowing his decision could end me. Or give me the gift of life. He's Satan and he's God all wrapped up into one beautiful, kinky package.

Once the fight leaves me and my legs go limp, I lose sight of Hunter as he kneels behind Rory and between my legs.

It doesn't take him long to push not one or two but I'm guessing three fingers inside my cunt as I fight for air, my lips crushed against Rory's palm as I try to heave in even a small increment of oxygen, but all I get for my effort is nothing.

No, not nothing. Hunter is fucking my pussy with his fingers, causing my heart to fight for every beat of its chambers, every pulse in my veins and arteries.

It's when my eyes roll to the back of my head that Rory takes his hand away and crashes his mouth to mine.

He doesn't just allow me to breathe, he's the giver of life, kissing me back to consciousness.

I'm drunk on his tongue ravaging my mouth and Hunter's fingers crooking just right until I'm bucking for a whole different reason.

"That's it, Angel, fuck my hand like a wild mare." My hands behind my back are getting the brunt of my hips pumping up and down as I search out the orgasm Hunter is offering me on a fucking silver platter, all the while distracted by Rory's vicious mouth.

Then he's gone and I'm dazed from the loss of him and delirious from the Hunter's fingers fucking me like it's the last time he'll ever touch me.

"Next time, you assume nothing." Rory whispers in my ear. "In fact, there won't be a next time." As my eyes finally focus on the intensity of his stare, I do the only thing I can do: I nod.

"Good girl. Now, come all over Hunter's hand." Those fingers curl once more and I'm lost. Completely and utterly disintegrated as he hits my trigger and my hips bolt upright and my breath is caught once more in my lungs. The moan that escapes from between my lips is swallowed up by Rory's mouth again and I just when I think I can't take it anymore, Hunter presses his lips to my pussy and drinks every fucking drop of my cum like water after a marathon.

My brain checks out for a minute, my eyes darting from side to side behind my lids as our tongues continue to battle in this scorching-hot kiss.

The sound of the bottle of lube has Rory moving back, our mouths separating and leaving me cold without the heat of him on me.

Still straddling me, he takes out his dick and rests it in the deep groove of my cleavage, eyes returning to mine with a glint that sends shivers down my back.

"It's go time." Squeezing the globes of my tits together and rubbing himself between them for just a beat, Rory stands with all the ease and grace of a lion before he joins Hunter, who's now kneeling at the altar of my cunt.

"Hmmm, look at all that lube, baby. Just think…it's still going to hurt." He could have been talking about the weather, his voice is so even and matter of fact.

"Maybe we shouldn—" This time, I cut myself off with just a warning look from Rory. If they think it'll fit then I just need to trust them to have my best interests in mind.

Fingers crossed I don't fucking bleed out.

Hunter's hands are all over me, spreading the lube down my slit and over my clit. Coating my lips and covering my inner walls. He's thorough and meticulous, but he's also hard as a fucking rock and I want to suck his dick again. Feel him swell in my mouth before ropes of his cum make their way down my throat.

Moaning and mewling like a cat waiting for her male to impale her, I plant my feet on the carpet and search my men out, my hips fucking the air as Hunter slides his fingers down to my ass and, without any preamble, breaches my rosebud entrance before pumping a dollop of lube inside.

The slickness is everywhere, my pussy, my thighs, my ass. Even my knees are coated in lube from where Hunter held me down as I grew wild with lust.

"Fucking beautiful." Hunter's voice is reverent and it

gives life to a burst of heat in my chest.

"I can't wait to destroy her." Although less romantic by societal standards, Rory's words are reverent all the same, making my entire body bloom with lust and need for these men.

By this time, I can barely feel my arms anymore, not when the only thing I can feel is the heat of Rory's cock teasing the entrance of my pussy, sliding between the lips and pressing against my still-swollen and greedy clit.

Then, in one hard press of his hips, he's buried to the hilt, his head thrown back and his mouth parted with a curse escaping through his lips.

He's never looked more powerful, more commanding. More all-consuming. My eyes dart to Hunter and he's watching me watch Rory, smirking when my cheeks flare with heat. Given all the depraved shit we've done, I can't believe getting caught staring at Rory is what makes me blush.

"Do you see what you do to him? To me? To Meyer? It's the closest we come to perfection." With those words, Hunter spreads my legs wider and lifts my ass up off the floor—my arms rejoicing—and turns me to the side.

"Fuck, the way she just clenched down on my cock? I almost came from that alone." I don't have any control over myself anymore, Rory and Hunter are the only ones directing my movements, my position, my leeway.

Once I'm lying on my side, Rory hooks my leg over his arm as he slowly fucks my cunt like he's cooly rowing on a placid lake. Hunter covers my entire back and his dick lines up next to Rory, and just as one pulls out, the other pushes in.

My scream is instant as they try to fit not one huge cock inside me, but two.

The sensation that I'm being ripped apart is almost too much. Almost enough to make me scream a safe word, yell *no* at the top of my lungs. Run for the fucking hills.

The feeling of muscles and ripping skin is too much to bear until suddenly, I don't know where the pleasure begins and the pain ends. Until the rhythm is so lulling that I decide to concentrate on the pulsing of the in and out, the squirting of lube every so often. I focus on every little groan that escapes the guys, the long, drawn out groans as my cunt clamps down every time they're pushing in together and causing my entire sex to burn, burn, burn.

Funny thing about a woman's body. It adapts to survive and right now, my cunt is opening up and willingly swallowing them up like last night's dinner.

"That's it, Angel. Fuck, you feel so goddamn good." Hunter grunts in my ear, one finger on my clit while his mouth drops kisses up and down the column of my neck.

Rory's gaze finds mine and, with every added second that he fucks me, his intensity grows tenfold. And as his intensity grows, so do his thrusts. Soon, I'm gasping for air, but this time, no one's clamping down on my mouth. No one is forcing me to hold my breath.

No, this time it's the sheer force of his thrusts that is causing my lungs to empty out without permission.

"You're fucking perfect, baby." Rory's words have him losing some of that tightly-reined-in control, and as his hips begin to speed up with erratic thrusts, Hunter pulls out of my pussy and moves his body just a little higher, the head of his dick suddenly at my puckered entrance.

Oh, God.

Oh fuck.

God, yes.

As though he's waiting for the perfect moment, Hunter doesn't breach my entrance right away, he just presses lightly, giving me time to accept the inevitable.

Gripping one ass cheek, Hunter doesn't hold back just as Rory pulls out of my pussy before slamming back in again. It's like they've done this a thousand times.

"Fuck, fuck, fuck. " It hurts, it really fucking hurts until Hunter and Rory both reach up and pinch my nipples. It's a distraction method; give new pain so I can ignore the older one.

By this time, I'm too far gone to care where they're fucking me, I just want to come again and I want to do it now.

Hunter's hand returns to my clit, a thumb rubbing uneven circles as he fucks my ass nice and slow.

It's Rory that destroys me first.

Just as I'm about to feel the cresting power of another orgasm, Rory bends his head down, so close to Hunter he can probably feel his breath on his lips, before sinking his teeth into my flesh.

I lose my fucking mind.

In fact, my mind shuts down completely as an electric current runs down my spine and a tingling feeling at my clit makes me think I want to pee.

"Fuck yeah, she's losing it."

I gush all over Rory, squirting for the first time in my life and not understanding what the actual fuck is happening to me.

"Holy fuck." Hunter's voice is awe-stricken, his movement losing some of it's fluidity as he continues to fuck my ass.

Then it's Rory's turn, almost howling up at the ceiling as he releases string after string of cum inside my cunt, refusing to pull out until Hunter's dick releases his own orgasm into my ass.

Three mouths moaning and gasping as we each ride the wave of unfiltered pleasure with a big dose of pain. It's beautiful, it's vicious, it's pure.

It's all us.

Getting a job was a no go, though trying to persuade Hunter and Rory to my way of thinking was definitely a fun distraction. Except that was days ago and all I have left to deal with is my grief.

I want to know more about what's going on with who helped Trent, but I promised Bruno I wouldn't tell and I have zero intention of breaking that promise. So that leaves me with my freaking emotions.

Sitting cross legged on my bed, I stare down at the letter from Tommy.

Still unopened.

Slightly battered and bent at this point.

His almost illegible scrawl across the front.

It even smells like him, that spicy dad smell that he always had. No idea what it is, other than comforting. Except right now, the scent is enough to carve my heart from my chest.

I'm not ready to deal with this letter, but I have a feeling I'm never going to be ready to deal with it.

Taking a deep breath, I turn the envelope over and peel it open. Tears well in my eyes before I even take the folded pages from their resting place. My hand shakes as I reach for the letter and unsheathe it.

I wipe at my eyes before unfolding the paper. Tears on paper doesn't seem like a great idea.

Staring down at the pages, my heart picks up pace, beating against my ribs like it's trying to escape whatever is to come.

I take another deep breath, blinking back the tears that threaten to breach again, and read his scrawl.

Quinn,

My precious little pain in the ass, if you're reading this, well, I'm sorry, because it means I left you, and way before I ever intended to.
I know letters aren't really what the kids do, and you can tease me all you like for my old-timer ways, but I swear, you keep calling me old man and I'll haunt you from whatever grave I'm put in.

A laugh spills from my lips as his voice sounds in my head. I wouldn't put it past him either, haunting me just for shits and giggles. Shaking my head, I wipe away my tears again and keep reading.

I know this isn't exactly our way. Feelings aren't something we talk about, not really, but I need you to know that letting me help you that day...it saved me in a way I didn't even realize I needed. Not until we were already in the thick of it and you were being a giant pain in my ass.

You were the daughter I got to save, you gave me new purpose in a world that was becoming monotonous and breathed life back into me just as I was getting too set in my ways and turning hard. You helped me live again. Feel again. Reconnect with life again.

Because of you, I dared to try and experience what life had to offer. You inspired me with your strength. Even when you thought you were weak, you were my inspiration to keep going. Especially when I got to kick your ass for doubting yourself.

Kid, you were the light of my life and there isn't anything I can ever say or do to tell you just how much you did for me. Especially with this spider scrawl of mine. How am I two pages in already? See, you infected all of my life, even the way I talk to myself.

But you infected it in the best ways. I had no family left until I met you. I'd cut pretty much everyone out, and then you blasted the ice away from my dark, unbeating heart and showed me that happiness can be found in even the smallest of things.

I failed you. Because if you're reading this, it

*means someone got to me and I didn't hold up my
end of our deal.*

A sob chokes me as I remember the stupid deal we
made that one night he found me with a bottle of vodka
and a bottle of pills. The night when Trent had found me
yet again, and I didn't see the point in going on. The deal
that we'd both grow old and decrepit and only go out when
we'd done everything on the list we wrote together.

*That list we wrote is in here for you, cause it's on
you now, kid. You need to complete it for the both
of us. I'm sorry that I won't be there to watch you
grow, to watch you thrive, because I know you will.
You're too special not to. There is a light in you
that I don't think you even realize is there, but it's
what woke me up from the longest darkness I've
ever known, and I know the boys see it too.
Enjoy your life, kid. Live it for the both of us.
Know that even if I'm gone, I never regretted
helping you. Not once. Even if it's what led to my
end. You were worth all of it. Every single grumble,
every headache, every paperwork trail that I hated.
Worth that and so much more.
I've sorted my will so you'll be looked after, Meyer
should get it not long after I'm gone.*

Be good to yourself, kid. Dream big and chase every single one.
I love you. Always have. Always will.
Keep smiling, and don't waste those tears on me you hear?
Live big, live loud, love wild and relentlessly.
Regret only the things you did and not the things you don't.
I'll never regret you. Not in this life or the next.
Now take that list and run free.

Miss you already,
This old man.

Tears fall freely down my face as I finish the third page of his letter and find the bucket list we made together tucked behind it. A smile graces my lips when I see some of it crossed out, but there's still so much we were meant to do.

Oh, God.

He's really gone.

I'm never going to see him again, hear his grouchy voice again, witness him bitch me out for something small, or see the joy on his face when he puts a scoop of vanilla ice cream on top of his coffee in the evening.

Fuck.

He's really gone and he's not coming back.

I don't know how to do this without you, Tommy.

I push the paper away and fall back onto my pillows, curling up into a ball as the sobs wrack my body. He might have told me not to waste tears on him, but they're not a waste at all.

Nothing about him was.

He was the only dad I ever got to have and he was ripped away from me too soon.

By the monster he was protecting me from.

One day, I'll want revenge, but today, all I have is utter devastation at the fact that I'll never have the chance to finish the list with him.

FIFTEEN

QUINN

After crying so much that not even splashing my face with cold water half a dozen times is enough to hide how red and puffy I am, I head downstairs in my hoodie, shorts, and a pair of fluffy socks I found tucked away in the depths of my stuff, finding all three of my guys in the sitting room.

It startles me for a second because they're all sitting around, chill, watching a football game, with beers. I didn't even realize they liked football…

I really need to start paying attention and being present, because that's a little shameful.

Rory is the first to notice me standing in the doorway—which, in reality, is way less of a shock, all things considered—and the ease slips from him instantly as he stands. "What's wrong?"

The other two turn, looking ready to launch into action,

and guilt trickles through me. "Nothing's wrong," I start, trying to wave them off. "Calm down, you were enjoying your night. I'll find you guys tomorrow."

"You don't want to come relax with us?" Hunter asks, sounding a little hurt, but the smile in his eyes lets me know he's only teasing.

"Football has never really been my thing."

"You mean you've never tried it," he teases again.

"You've been crying," Rory interjects, raising his brows at me, still not having sat back down.

I nod, shrugging before wrapping my arms around my middle. "I read Tommy's letter."

"Oh, Kitten," Meyer says softly. "Are you okay?"

"I'll be fine. I have questions—"

"Shocker." Hunter snorts before picking up his beer again and turning back to the game. I flip him the finger and he laughs again, obviously catching the movement.

Rory sits back down in his chair and Meyer pats the cushion next to him on the sofa. "Come sit. We'll teach you how the game works, and when you're ready, you can ask questions."

"After the game," Hunter adds on and I roll my eyes before heading over and settling onto the sofa next to Meyer. It's always funny to me that there's always like, a dozen chairs and sofas in all of their lounging areas. Other than the guards, there are rarely people here, but they have enough seating for a literal football team.

Rory watches me instead of the game so I blow him a kiss, trying to reassure him that I really am okay, even if I feel a little dramatic after that entrance. He eventually relaxes his shoulders and sinks back into his seat, picking up his drink before turning his attention back to the game.

I try to watch along with them, but clueless is an understatement. Figuring out what the different lines on the field mean, why grown men run at each other to battle over a ball before running like their ass is on fire toward a giant H is…well, I just don't really understand it. And they have breaks. A *lot*. Aren't they supposed to run around for like, hours? Or is that a different game?

Officially clueless.

Even with Meyer trying to explain why they shout or cheer at the screen like armchair coaches.

Eventually, O'Connor, Tonio, and Bruno join us and even Shae swings by at some point and offers to rescue me, but I decline the offer. Despite not knowing what's going on, this feels…dare I say, normal. It's entirely different from how I've seen them before.

It occurs to me that I've been here for a year.

Well, not living here, but in this city. I didn't do the whole Halloween, Thanksgiving, Christmas thing last year…or for the last however many years since I ran from Trent, honestly. I don't remember what was even happening with me during that insanity last year.

Was I at the house? Did they just not celebrate?

Do they not celebrate?

I realize I missed my last birthday too…and I haven't heard them talk about theirs either. Did I just completely miss it all being *that* wrapped up in my own bullshit, or did they just not make a fuss?

Chewing on my lip, picking at my nails, I try to scour my memory for this time last year, but it's like it's fuzzy. Which doesn't make any sense to me, but it's like the details, other than the giant steaming moments of fuck up, are just…foggy.

A round of cheers goes up, startling me from my thoughts. They're all on their feet, high fiving, having a total "bro moment", and I realize their team won. Which team that is is beyond me, the guys on the screen were in red, others in black looking like pirates, beyond that, I'm lost.

Bruno, Tonio, O'Connor, and Hunter leave the room still talking about the game—I think. They're talking about downs; I can only assume that's something to do with the game—leaving me with Rory and Meyer.

Rory's phone rings and he glares at it as he pulls it from his pocket. "Fucking Elise," he grumbles before standing and leaving the room.

Who the fuck is Elise?

"She runs one of the clubs," Meyer explains, obviously seeing the confusion on my face. "So, did you want to ask questions now? Or talk about the letter? Or did you want to sleep on it?"

I pull my feet from under my ass where I've been sitting on them and pull my knees up in front of my chest, resting my chin on them. "The letter…did you get one too?"

"I did," he replies softly, nodding. The light in his eyes dims a little. "He said you'd likely have questions. He knew you well."

"He really did." The words come out croaky as I play over the letter in my head. I reread it enough times that I've practically memorized it. "He called me an infection."

Meyer bursts out laughing at the admission and I smile too, because Tommy really did have a way with words. "Jeez, old man. So eloquent."

"Wasn't he?" I say with a smile. "But he said something about a will, that you'd explain, but I thought your mom was handling that."

His laughter ends and he smiles at me. "She was, but only because she wanted to. It was supposed to be me, he left me as his power of attorney and estate manager, or whatever bullshit you want to call it."

I shrug, a little confused. "I don't know what most of that means, but okay."

"It's just a fancy way of saying he wanted me to deal

with all the legal stuff. He left some stuff to my mom… they've been friends a long time; a few things to me and the guys; but mostly, he left everything to you."

I blink at Meyer, trying to process what he just said. "He did what?"

"Tommy was a clever man. Frugal is an understatement, but he was very smart with his finances. He had more than even I realized. And he left it all to you. I can go get all of the paperwork if you want the specifics right now, but he left you money, stocks, shares, and a whole portfolio of property. Including a few businesses, totally legit, that I had no clue about either. They run themselves, have a full staff and management structure in place, Tommy was just the guy behind the scenes, but now they're yours."

"I don't understand…" I trail off, shock flitting through me.

Why would he leave it all to me? I didn't even know he had stuff to leave.

"He loved you," Meyer says simply, like that makes sense of it all. "He didn't have much family left anymore. Not after what happened. You, me, the guys, Mama, we were his family, but you? You meant a lot to him and he wanted to make sure you'd be okay, even once he was gone."

Tears prick at my eyes as my throat constricts and my chest feels like someones hit me with a sledgehammer.

"But he's only gone because of me."

"No," Meyer says sternly, shaking his head. "He's gone because of Trent. Because of me if we want to get technical about it. My people let us down and Trent got to Tommy, but it's not because of you."

"It doesn't matter how we frame it. Trent wouldn't have been around if it wasn't for me." I try to clear my throat so I can speak up. "But if the blame isn't on me, then it's not on you either. And what do you mean *your* people?"

He lets out a sigh and runs a hand through his hair. "We had a leak, someone Trent got to. I don't know all the details yet but we're working on it. Regardless of fault, Tommy was a big boy, he made his own decisions, he'd say that his death was his own fault for being too old, too slow, whatever shit he'd come out with, but he'd also say that he never regretted a decision when it came to you, so he'd own that shit too."

I swipe away a tear that slips down my face with the cuff of my hoodie. He's right and I know it, but I keep bouncing between acceptance and guilt.

"Grief is such a bitch," I say, half laughing.

He smiles and reaches over to squeeze my hand. "It really is, and no one is saying that you have to hurry through it. Grief is different for everyone, and sometimes it will hit you out of nowhere."

His eyes go distant and it occurs to me that all of this

with Tommy must have brought some stuff up about his dad.

"Are you okay?" I ask, linking my fingers with his. "I realized earlier how selfish I've been since I came here, how little I've actually asked or learned about you guys. Like, I have no idea when your birthdays are, what happened with your dad, what you did for Christmas last year, if you guys even do Christmas or Thanksgiving. I didn't even know you guys followed football. I don't remember it from last year, or even if I should. I don't even remember Christmas last year..."

He laughs softly, shaking his head. "I'm okay. Losing Tommy is hard, sure. He kinda stepped up when we lost dad. But death is a part of life, I learned that young. As for everything else, this last year has been a little different than usual. Mama and Shae did Christmas away, so with just us, we didn't really do much. Our birthdays…we never really make much fuss for those either. Don't stress about not remembering or not knowing, we aren't always the most forthcoming. Mostly because we've all known each other our entire lives, so we forget that people don't just know that stuff. But if you want to do all of the celebrations this year, we can, just let me know. I'm sure Mama will be delighted to do a big family Christmas."

"I've never really done a big Christmas…or any holidays, to be fair. When I was a kid, it wasn't really a thing, then with Trent we did what we needed to for appearances, but he worked most holidays, and since I left, I've been too busy looking over my shoulder to do much celebrating. Tommy always got me a gift, but we just had an awkward exchange and left it at that."

He blinks at me, his jaw clenching momentarily before he relaxes again. "Well, then this year, we celebrate everything."

"We don't have to—"

He cuts me off with a finger against my lips. "Nope. I said it, it's happening. If I tell Hunter—"

"Tell me what?" The man in questions asks as he walks back into the room with Rory.

"That Quinn has never celebrated Thanksgiving or Christmas properly."

Hunter turns to me, horrified. "I'm sorry, what now?"

I shrug in response because there isn't really another way to say it.

"Absolutely not." Hunter utters, still sounding like Meyer swore at him.

"I didn't do holidays till I met you guys," Rory interjects, smiling at me as he takes his seat again. "Not everyone has the childhood of wonder." He turns back to face me as Hunter paces the room. "Hunter, however, is a big kid. He *loves* the holidays. When we didn't do much last year he had a tantrum for a whole week."

I press my lips together, trying not to laugh, but I can't say I'm that surprised. Hunter seems like the type to go way over the top for holidays.

Hunter pauses, turning to face me, hands on his hips. "Did you do Halloween? Like, trick-or-treating, dressing up, all the good shit?"

Shaking my head, I tell him no and his brow furrows further.

"This is obscene," he mutters. "Okay, we're throwing a Halloween party at HellScape. I'll get on Yen. We'll make it a birthday bash for Quinn since we missed your birthday last year too."

"We missed everyone's birthdays last year," I tell him and he grins.

"Then we have a joint belated birthday Halloween bash, then go straight into Thanksgiving, then Christmas, *then* a New Year's party."

"Look what you've created," Meyer teases. "He's a holiday monster."

Two weeks later, I find myself dressed up like a slutty Snow White, the guys are three of my sexy dwarves, and I don't know that I've laughed so much in my entire life. We're sitting in one of the booths in HellScape, the entire place looks like Halloween threw up on it, Hunter is proud as punch of how the place looks, and everyone is having a great time.

How he pulled it off in two weeks is beyond me, especially when Harper has been away—something to do with her mom Yen told me—but it's great. It's not actually the thirty-first, because that's Tuesday, but Saturday night at HellScape is our Halloween party, open to all, though the basement is closed to non-members. There are games set up in various booths and you can bob for apples at the bar to win free drinks. He's even done a best-dressed competition thing.

Meyer was right, he's a holiday monster, but it's the happiest I've seen him since I met him, so I'm almost glad I've never celebrated the holidays properly before so he gets to have this moment.

Though this is definitely not how I expected to celebrate the last year of my twenties, but then, I didn't even acknowledge my birthday last year, let alone celebrate it, so who am I to know what I expected? In reality, I probably would have just let it glide by again if it wasn't for these three.

"Come dance!" Shae whines, fluttering her giant lash extensions at me. She's a butterfly, so that required giant lashes to match her rainbow wings. Unsurprisingly, she looks incredible.

She grabs my hands and tugs at me until I slide out of the booth. "Fine, fine. I'm coming." I wave back at the guys, who all grin at me because I've already danced most of the night away and spent the last twenty minutes complaining about how much my feet hurt in these bright red skyscraper heels.

Shae stops one of the girls passing with a tray of shots, takes two and hands them to me before taking two more. "To your birthday and this insane mash-up party."

"I guess I can drink to that," I say with a laugh and drink down the bright-green sour apple liquid. "Wow, that's gross."

Shae giggles when I pull a face. "Yeah, but Hunter went all out with the Halloween theme and you're Snow White, so of course he did the apple thing. The house is going to look like Christmas threw up on it this year, I can feel it. Now, let's dance."

She takes my hand and pulls me through the writhing crowd. I lose track of time and dance with her until my feet can't take it any more. Checking my watch, I see it's almost two in the morning and it's like seeing the reality of it swipes what little is left of my energy.

"I'm out," I shout to her and she pouts, but I shake my head. "I'm old, officially, and I need my bed. This princess needs her beauty sleep."

"Wrong princess." She sticks her tongue out at me.

"But fine, let's turn back into pumpkins."

"Still the wrong princess," I joke and she rolls her eyes. Once we get back to the table, I find Hunter waiting for us. "Ready to go?"

"Oh, I'm just waiting on you, Angel."

"Where are the others?" I ask, glancing around the room.

"They had to head back already, but we didn't want to spoil your fun, so I offered to stay behind till you were ready to leave."

"Well, I am more than ready to leave," I tell him, clasping my stomach when it growls at me. "But nuggets on the way home?"

He chuckles at me but laughs as he grabs his phone and taps away on the screen. "We can get nuggets. Come on, let's go. Eddie is outside."

Hunter leads us through the bar and I wave goodbye to Yen and Tina as we pass them. They had to work tonight, but that doesn't mean I didn't get to see them a little. I invited them out for lunch in a few days, quiet girl birthday celebrations because, according to Yen, that's what friends do.

Who would've thought?

The drive home is quiet, especially once I have my nuggies. Bruno and Hunter quietly talk up front and Shae has been stuck to her phone since we got in here.

"Everything okay?" I ask her, and she glances at me, smiles, and turns back to her phone.

"Just worried about Teo. He's been off lately. His girlfriend left him for someone he thought was a friend just after everything with Tommy and I just…he's a little lost, I think. Everyone worries about me so much that I worry he gets a little lost in the chaos."

"The chaos isn't your fault," I tell her softly. "But if Teo is struggling, maybe he should come home?"

She sighs and drops her phone into her lap. "That's what I said, but he's being a bullheaded dick. I guess it's kind of a family trait."

I snort a laugh, nearly choking on a nugget and drawing Hunter's attention while Shae giggles at me. "It's okay, death by nugget seems fitting. But yes, definitely a family trait."

We get home and Hunter drags me to his room, not that I'm complaining. He jumps in the shower while I get undressed and climb into his bed, curling into a ball wrapped in the smell of him.

A kiss on my shoulder startles me. "Didn't mean to wake you, Angel. Sleep."

Hunter pulls me into him, my back against his chest, and wraps an arm around me, pulling the duvet over us before settling his hand on my boob, making me smile. "Thank you for tonight. For everything."

My murmur is ended with a yawn as I snuggle against him.

"This is just the beginning, Angel."

Waking up on my birthday in a puppy pile of Rory and Hunter was a great way to start my day. The last few days since the party have been a little chaotic, so I haven't seen much of the guys, and I've only been losing my mind a little with almost nothing to do around the house.

Maybe I'll talk to Shae about volunteering or something, because there are only so many lunches with friends and shopping trips I can do to keep myself busy.

Not that lunch and shopping with Shae and the girls yesterday wasn't a great time, I just…I am *so* not that girl.

At least, I don't think so. I've spent so long being what everyone else wanted and needed me to be, or running, that I've never really focused on who it is I am, but I'm pretty sure that the lady of leisure isn't a hat I can wear.

Not when sitting still makes my hands itch.

Obviously, that doesn't include scrolling through videos on my phone while binging TV, but a girl can only do that for so long.

Extracting myself from the tangle of limbs I find myself in, I throw on Hunter's sweatpants and Rory's t-shirt before tiptoeing from the room and heading to the kitchen.

"Good morning, Miss Quinn," Carlos says with a smile. We've come a long way from being the demon woman he thought I was. I'll still never accept cucumber in my pico though. "Happy Birthday!"

"Thank you, Carlos." Grinning at him, I make my way to the coffee machine, but he tuts at me and flicks the towel in his hand at me before waving at me to sit.

"It is your birthday, you do nothing."

I roll my eyes as I sit. "I'm older, not incapable."

"Hush, child. It is not about being incapable, but letting people do things for you because they want to." He shakes his head after the minor chastising and I think on his words. My therapist said something about my hyper-independence likely being an issue because I've always had to do everything for everyone, be it out of fear, or a desperate attempt to feel like enough. That I should work on trusting other people to come through for me, but surely, getting my own coffee isn't that?

Is it?

Fuck knows, but I thank Carlos when he places the steaming mug before me.

"Is Meyer around?" I ask him and he nods.

"Si. He went down to the gym a while ago, he will likely be here soon. What can I get you for breakfast?"

I press my lips together, pondering my options before

grinning. "Breakfast burrito?"

He rolls his eyes at me but nods. "If that is what you wish. No pico?"

"No pico," I confirm, grinning.

It doesn't take long before he has the breakfast wonder before me and the guys all appear together, arms laden with gifts as I'm taking my first bite.

Blinking at them as they place the gifts on the table around me, I put down the food and lean back.

"Happy birthday!" They cheer together, grinning wide.

"Thank you…but, erm…that's a lot of—"

Meyer interrupts me as he sits beside me and places a finger on my lips. "Do not start. We missed your birthday last year. And Christmas. Let us spoil you."

"You spoil me every day," I tell him and he rolls his eyes at me.

"Hardly. Now, eat, so we can do gifts."

Hunter kisses the top of my head before sitting opposite me and Rory kisses my cheek as he sits on my other side. Carlos makes them food while I eat my burrito, listening to them talk about birthday memories of them growing up.

It's nice, just listening to them reminisce. Hearing about them just being kids, pulling stupid shit for birthday pranks, it makes them more human. Not that I don't see them that way, but I know I don't know them as well as I'd like to. Meyer can say that's on them, but it's on me as well, so I enjoy the opportunity to learn these little parts of them.

"Don't forget the surprise party you entirely ruined for your fifteenth birthday," Hunter jokes, as Meyer sits back down with another mug of coffee for him and one for me.

"How did you manage that?" I ask as Meyer groans.

Rory laughs and answers for him. "We went out, totally forgetting what Mama had planned, got him trashed because that's what stupid teenagers do. We got in a fight, ended up in the ER, and Mama had to send everyone home before coming to get us."

"I'm still sure I sustained more damage in the punishment from her than I did in that fight, even with the broken arm," Meyer says, chuckling.

"Yeah, I felt that dressing down she gave us for weeks. I felt about two inches tall," Hunter adds. "Never missed a gathering since."

"Oh, God no," Rory says before gathering the empty plates and putting them in the dishwasher before sitting back beside me. "Anyway, gift time."

"I really don't need gifts. We had the party, I live here, you won't let me work so every time Yen and Shae drag me out, I'm getting gifts really."

"Those aren't gifts," Meyer tuts. "That's just life. And if it makes you feel better, I'll sort out the money from Tommy so you don't feel like you're spending our money, though, what's ours is yours freely."

I press my lips together and nod. "Yes, please. I know you don't even think about me spending the money, but having my own money would make me feel a little more independent."

"Consider it done," he says, before kissing my hand. "Now let's focus on the main attraction here. Presents!"

I open each gift carefully, thanking each of them as I go. There's so much stuff. Hoodies, fluffy socks, jewelry, bags, art.

Once I'm done, my arms almost ache from it all. "Thank you, I feel officially spoiled. You're all amazing." I kiss each of them thoroughly, working myself up in a wondrous way, and when I pull back from the last with Meyer, he pulls me down onto his lap.

"You are welcome, but I have one more surprise for you, and this one…well, it's a little different."

SIXTEEN

HUNTER

"Are you sure?"

I've asked the same question like, four times, but the thought of Harper betraying us, betraying Meyer, is outlandish to me. I get that she isn't exactly Quinn's biggest fan, but to help Trent? It doesn't seem like her style.

"That's the name he gave me, and in the two weeks we've been questioning her, she hasn't confirmed or denied, but I'm being nice." Rory explains again, obviously frustrated at my disbelief. He turns to Meyer, who has been staring out the window for the last fifteen minutes since Rory started his update. "I think it'd be best if you spoke to her, Meyer."

"You think she'll tell me anything different?"

"Honestly? I don't know, but she's been in love with you for forever and a day. If she's going to admit shit to anyone, it's likely going to be you. And since we're playing nice with her, my methods are kind of useless here." He leans against the wall by the fireplace while I sit here, leaning forward, head cradled in my hands, trying to work out why the fuck Harper would betray us.

"Was her name the only one he gave you?" I ask Rory.

"So far. I know there are others, he said as much, but apparently he has a high pain tolerance. That, or he thinks dragging it out will hurt Quinn. Which it could. We don't know who it is, so we don't know if there's something else going on."

Meyer punches the drywall with a frustrated growl. "This is bullshit. How did we get to a place this fucking chaotic and out of order? Do we need to scale back and start over?"

His question is to Rory, which I'm glad for because I don't have answers. Rory is the guy that looks after our guys, which is probably why he's so pissed off about Trent, because it means people he hired are the people fucking with us. Not that it's his fault, but he'll be bearing the blame internally.

"I don't think we need to start over, but I do need to get back to normal. This last year, shit has been sideways. Everything has been blowing up all at once and it's possible I've missed shit going on." He stuffs his hands in his pockets and I blow out a breath as I rack my brains as to what I can do to help.

He isn't wrong, this last year has been insane. Even since before Quinn came into our lives, shit was already blowing up. Then I got distracted with Quinn, so my routine greasing of the wheels probably wasn't as good as usual, then *everyone* got distracted with Quinn... and well, we need to get shit back in line.

"What can I do?" I ask them both. It's no secret that Meyer is the brains, Rory is the brawn, and I'm the charm, but that means I need to be pointed in the right direction to get shit done. I'm not really the ideas guy.

"Start working your friends in the P.D. I want new checks done on everyone," Meyer starts, running a hand through his hair. "I want new burners for everyone. Tapped and tracked. We're going to need a tech team to stay on top of that, so we need people we trust. And if you can do the run down south this weekend so I can be here to try and deal with this shit with Harper?"

"I can do that," I say, nodding. "I'll check in with Mattie and Denton, get the checks started. Denton can probably figure out the burners and tech shit too, we both know he's good for that. I might see if he knows someone who can help with keeping an eye on the tech shit too. Frees me up for the weekend, then I can be more hands-on with it when I'm back. Do you want me to speak to Yen about staying in Harper's place indefinitely?"

"Yeah, do it." Meyer agrees before turning to Rory. "I want you talking to the guys, see if we can't figure out that way who the fuck was working with Trent. Give him a few days of the silent treatment, let him heal a bit before we go back at him. I need us focused for this run over the weekend."

"You want me to go with Hunter?" Rory asks, and while some would feel offended, I know he just wants to have my back. We don't do that petty bullshit here.

"You think you'll need him?" Meyer asks.

I think about it for a second, but shake my head. "Can't ever go wrong with more hands that we trust, but if he's needed here, I can handle it."

"Okay, Rory, go with, just in case. With us not knowing what's happening in our fucking house right now, it's better that we're there just in case. And while you're dealing with that bullshit, I'll deal with Harper." He drops into the chair opposite me and pinches the bridge of his nose. I swear I can practically feel the heartburn of his stress from all the way over here. Which is exactly why I try not to smile when he grabs the Pepto from the little cabinet on the table beside him and chugs it.

"Once this weekend is over, we need to wrap up this shit with Trent and get everything back in line. The Knights are sniffing around and with their power, it won't take much to swallow us whole if we're in disarray."

For a moment, I wonder if that would be the worst thing. We have money, we have property, we have each other. Sometimes I think we keep doing this because it's the only thing we've ever known... and for Meyer, because of his dad.

I shove the thought down because such blasphemy would likely see me in a noose. Doesn't stop the niggle from being there now that I've thought it though.

Maybe I'll talk to Meyer about it later. When it doesn't feel like we're on such a crumbling foundation. But the thought of a stress-free life with our girl, where all we need to focus on is her?

Yeah, that doesn't sound so bad at all.

SEVENTEEN

QUINN

It's been weeks since Tommy's funeral and I still wake up every day missing him. But the sun shining through my window this morning makes it seem a little less intense. The guys and Shae have been amazing, giving me space to grieve, but also being there for me whenever I need them.

I'm starting to really realize that Tommy wasn't the only person in my life that truly cared for me, and he gave me a whole new family of people that he loved. Reminding myself of that each morning is helping relieve the pressure on my chest.

A yawn takes over me as I stretch out in Meyer's bed, enjoying the cozy feeling of being snuggled beneath the duvet. The sun might be shining but it's cold enough that jeans and sweaters make up all that I wear currently.

That and fuzzy socks.

Hunter has taken to gifting me a new pair each morning

and it's almost the highlight of my day seeing what weird and wacky wonders he's found. I have no idea when he's finding the time to hunt for them, but so far we've had typical patterned and different colors, then moved on to Grinch knee highs, Nightmare Before Christmas ones, Oogie Boogie ones that glow in the dark, and so many more. How he knew about my weakness for those movies is beyond me—I don't think Tommy even knew about them—but I'm not about to talk him out of it.

They're just socks, but to me, right now, they're everything.

I take in a deep breath and hold it for four seconds before pushing it out slowly, repeating the motion a few times before throwing the duvet off and climbing from bed. Padding over the plush carpet to the bathroom, I quickly shower to wake myself up before throwing on some workout gear and heading to the kitchen.

Carlos is dancing around the kitchen, singing in Spanish, and I can't help the small smile that graces my lips as I watch him.

Tommy really did give me so much. And while guilt still gnaws at my insides that I took all this from him... that Trent took this from him... I am so grateful that Tommy found me, that he loved me, and that he gave me these people.

I clear my throat to make myself known and Carlos

spins, but when he sees me, he doesn't stop his morning dance show. Instead, he cha chas over to me, takes my hand, and pulls me along with him, dancing with me around the kitchen while he croons.

Laughter spills from me as he spins me around, because I have no idea what I'm doing, but this is fun and I'm so tired of being so sad.

The song ends and Carlos pulls me to a stop before taking a step back and kissing the top of my hand. "Thank you, *belleza*, for dancing with me this morning. Would you like an omelet?"

"Be still my beating heart. A dance *and* breakfast? You spoil me, kind sir." The warmth in his eyes at my teasing response warms my heart.

"A beautiful woman should not be so sad... or so small. You have not been eating. I am not a man if I cannot make you smile or feed you."

I press my lips together as tears prick my eyes. "Thank you, Carlos."

"No need to thank me, Belleza. Now, would you like an omelet?"

Shaking my head, I refuse the offer. "Thank you, but I was going to grab a protein smoothie and work out for a bit. Maybe after?"

He quirks a brow at me. "Work out? I'm going to have words with Meyer. Pfft. Work out. I will make you the smoothie, but at lunch, you are going to eat."

"Yes sir," I mock, teasingly saluting him. He rolls his eyes and grumbles in Spanish, and just like that, normality is back. I could have made the smoothie myself, but somehow I feel like that would've offended him even more.

Instead, I pull my phone from my pocket while I wait and throw together a playlist. I haven't made a new one in forever, but thanks to Shae, Yen, and Tina, I've found a ton of new music the last few weeks and some of it just slaps. Plus, the new function I discovered on the app where it gives me a new playlist of music it thinks I'll like every week is freaking genius. Whoever thought that up deserves a raise.

"Smoothie. All the calories." Carlos hands me the *Hocus Pocus* tumbler and a bark of laughter falls from my lips.

"Where on Earth did this come from?" I ask, already having an idea.

"Hunter, of course. You think I would buy this monstrosity?"

"Never in a million years, Carlos. Never in a million years. Thank you for my smoothie. And all the calories," I say with a wink, taking a sip while he watches me with his eagle eye.

No banana.

Gods, Carlos is awesome when he wants to be.

"Tastes like Heaven," I tell him as I move to leave and he laughs.

"Of course it does. All of the calories, Belleza."

Laughing again as I leave, I feel lighter than I have in weeks. I sip away on the smoothie as I head down to the gym. Unsurprisingly, it's empty. The guys all get up at the ass crack of dawn, to do what? I have no idea, but after talking to Shae, I get the feeling that ignorance might just be bliss with their business.

It's not that I don't want to know, quite the opposite, but I'm starting to realize from the letter left to me, that he kept some things from me for my own good.

Turning on the lights, I hook my new phone up to the speakers and blast *Do or Die* by Natalie Jane as I start up the treadmill.

I spend the next hour losing myself to doing intermittent sprints and lifting weights. The joys of down time is the rabbit hole I went down trying to make my body healthier. The distractions I've dreamt up while trying not to lose myself to grief have been wild and wonderful, but also, useful.

Finishing a set of hip thrusts and pushing the barbell off the mats, I lie back on them, chest heaving. Whoever said that cardio was the best way to work up a sweat was lying. Lifting makes my heart and lungs work just as hard as running.

"You look exhausted." I push up onto my elbows and find Meyer in a pair of sweats and no top. Just a smirk on his face. "I guess my idea of coming down here to get a workout in with you are squandered."

The look in his eyes as he drinks in the sight of me in shorts and a sports bra, even when I'm sweaty, is intoxicating.

"Oh, I don't know if I'd say I'm exhausted. What sort of workout did you have in mind?" It's been a hot minute since he came to me like this, all hot and teasing, and well... I'm only human. Just thinking about him working me out is enough to make my mouth water.

Other things too.

"I don't know. I had a pretty vigorous workout in mind." His eyes sparkle as he stalks over to me, dropping to his knees before climbing on top of me, caging me beneath him. "But I'm sure I can encourage you to expend the energy."

He ducks down, kissing my neck, working down my collarbone to tease the skin along the top of where my bra sits. A gasp slips from my lips as I grip his forearms when he bites down on my nipple beneath the material.

Fuck yes, I need this.

Need him.

His fingers grip the top of my bra and pull it down

enough to pop my tits out right over the top, trapping me in the most erotic of ways.

The intensity in his gaze roaming all over me, from my tits to my exposed stomach right back up to my hardened nipples, is making me instantly wet. There's no denying he knows exactly what he's doing.

"Hip thrusts, huh? Seems fitting." Meyer takes out a knife from the back pocket of his sweatpants and raises his gaze to mine. A challenging glint in his eye that's this side of evil dares me to deny him his fun.

I'm pretty sure I know what he's going to do, but any hope that he'll be gentle with my belongings dies a silent death as he brings the knife to my shorts and places the sharp blade at the waist, cutting all the way down until there's nothing between him and what he wants.

And what he wants is now on full view for his eating pleasure.

Spreading my legs wider and pushing my chest higher as I arch my back, I taunt him. I like him on the edge of his control when he's at the border between faintly aware of his humanity and completely overtaken by his obsessions. One of which is me.

"*Tsk, tsk, tsk,* teasing me with your cunt wide open is a dangerous, dangerous game." His words are at complete odds with the spark in his eyes, the one that says playing with me is the only thing that truly makes him happy.

"I can handle your kind of danger." I'm so close to the fire that I wouldn't be surprised if he said fuck it and devoured every inch of me until there's nothing left.

The worst part is that I'm okay with that.

Flipping his knife around, he pushes the handle inside my pussy and fucks me with it like he's fucking me with a dildo. The move is quick and surprising, not giving me the time to anticipate.

I did ask for it so I'm not complaining. Not in the least.

When he pushes the knife as far as it'll go without actually inserting the blade, he stops, watching me as my pants become more and more pronounced, my chest heaving uncontrollably.

"Do you trust me?" Fuck, that's a double-edged sword, right there.

On the one hand, I trust him with my life in any circumstance, but on the other, he's fucking crazy in all the best of ways and when he gets an idea in his head, it's not always something predictable or... sane.

"Yes." Fuck it. In for a penny, I guess.

Meyer leans in, his eyes solely on me, and pinches my clit between his teeth, making sure to give me that ounce of pain that always drives me to the brink of orgasm faster than I can say, "fuck me."

"I fucking love that and I'll make sure to reward you for it." By the time his words register, he's got my legs falling over his shoulders with only my shoulder blades touching the mat, the rest of my body in mid-air as he pulls out his knife and fucks my cunt with his hungry mouth.

I'm almost there again, panting and seeking out my orgasm like a fucking wanton bitch.

I'm so lost to the wave of pleasure that's coursing through my blood—my lids tightly shut and my fingers gripping the edge of the mat—that I instantly jerk at the sting on the inside of my thigh.

My eyes pop open, my jaw dropping at the realization that he's just cut me.

"What the fuck, Meyer?" He doesn't answer right away, mirth dancing in his eye as he leans in and makes a show of his tongue licking up the wound, sending a new, tiny sting up my core.

"You said you trusted me." My eyes dart from his stare to where he's holding the blade to my thigh then back again. I'm hesitant but I don't deny him this moment, especially when he goes back to eating my pussy and distracting me with his pure talent.

I jerk again, this time half expecting it and more curious than anything as I watch him lick my thigh again before burying his tongue into my pussy again.

Why does that make me so fucking hot for him?

"What are you doing?" I was hoping my voice would

be steady but my words come out in a panting mess of hormones.

"I'll show you when I'm done."

That's when I decide that I do, in fact, trust him and let myself enjoy the dance between pleasure and pain as he repeats his action twice more. The last time, he's fucking my pussy so hard and fast that my orgasm takes complete control of me and has me screaming to the ceiling in irreverent pleads for him to never stop.

"God, yes! Oh my God, Meyer!"

In an instant, Meyer drops all pretense and as soon as my orgasm subsides, I look up to see he's ditched the sweats and has his dick in his hand—thick and hard and ready—right before he pushes my thighs against my chest and rams into me. My gasp is guttural, a force of nature pushing from my lungs as he thrusts to the hilt before stilling and taking a breath.

When our eyes meet again, he grins that psychotic-yet-fucking-gorgeous smile of his and it's so fucking contagious that I can't help mirroring it right back.

"Nothing tastes better than your cum and your blood mixed together."

My nose screws up, letting him know that sounds disgusting. Instead of trying to convince me, he brings his firm lips to mine and kisses me like I'm the whipped cream on a chocolate sundae.

Our tongues fight for dominance, which is a joke considering the only one here capable of dominating anyone is Meyer, but I like to at least try. As he devours my mouth, his hips begin to move, his thrusts starting slow then rising in a crescendo, as though he's fucking me to a beat only he can hear.

Through all of this, I realize he's right. I taste fucking fantastic. But only because it's mixed with his scent and his mouth and everything he's doing to me. Over and over again, he fucks my pussy the way he fucks my mouth: hard and passionate.

A second orgasm is calling to me as I wrap my thighs around his waist and meet him thrust for thrust, only getting hornier and hornier at the sound of skin slapping skin and my wet pussy swallowing his entire length every time he bottoms out.

It's crude and it's a primal but it's everything I need from him. He always knows what I want—no, what I need—and I'm grateful for his particular brand of psycho because every time he gives me a glimpse it only makes me better.

Meyer releases my mouth, his lips constantly touching mine as he reaches over for the knife and brings it to my neck.

"When you bleed, you bleed for me." There's a tiny prick at the base of my ear but the pain is quickly overridden as Meyer fucks me harder and harder, chasing his own orgasm, no doubt. "Your essence is my sanity."

He then licks beneath my ear and slams his mouth right back over mine and I'm a fucking goner.

I come so hard I think I pass out. There's total darkness for what feels like a second but when I come back to awareness, Meyer has his back arched, one hand on the mat the other around my neck as he releases rope after rope of his cum into my pussy, the warmth coating my insides like a soothing, erotic blanket.

When he roars out his final spurt inside me, his gaze comes right back to me and his grin spreads across his entire mouth.

Fuck, he's gorgeous. Wild yet vulnerable like this. All fucking mine, too.

"Look."

Meyer takes my knee in his palm and, without pulling out of my pussy, spreads my thighs as far as he can as I prop myself up on my elbows to see what he's showing me. I don't know where I get the strength but curiosity is a powerful motivator.

Right there, at the crease between my pussy and my inner thigh are four straight lines that make up the letter M.

"M for Meyer. M for mine."

After showering together, and getting messy all over again, I'm feeling much more relaxed than I did when I woke up. My days are a weird mishmash of emotions lately, and the guilt over having a good day only makes it worse.

Maybe one day I won't be such a colossal freaking mess.

Maybe.

Who knows what the future holds?

"You got any plans for the rest of the day?" Meyer asks, tearing me from my thoughts as I finish drying my hair. I smirk at him in the mirror and his smile stretches wide. "Not what I meant."

Poking my tongue out at him, I shake my head. "No, no plans. Why? Is this the not-quite-normal present you mentioned the other day?"

His smile drops for a second but is back so quick I almost believe I imagined it. "No, not that. It's not quite ready. I promise as soon as it is, it's all yours."

"So ominous," I tease. "But okay, so what did you have in mind for this afternoon?"

He moves to stand behind me, gripping the top of the chair, and the veins in his forearms make an appearance.

Focus on his words, Quinn, not those mouthwatering

arms. Goddamn, Adonis of a man.

He notices what I'm looking at and leans down with a smirk before kissing the top of my head. "I have to talk to someone, about Trent, about what happened to you, and I think it might be useful if you're with me."

I take a deep breath and clench my hands, digging my nails into my palms. Doing business stuff, I'm fine with, but helping him talk to someone about Trent? Someone that could be partially responsible for what happened that night? For what happened to Tommy?

Am I strong enough for that?

I must have spoken the thought aloud because he moves to my side, crouches, and turns the chair so I'm facing him. Gripping my chin, he looks me in the eyes, and the love and conviction on his face is enough to make me squirm. "You don't have to come, but I wouldn't ask if I didn't think you could handle it. You're stronger than you give yourself credit for."

Resisting the urge to kiss this man as I look down at him takes the willpower of an olympian, so if I can do that, survive what I have this far, I can go with him to talk to someone. I probably won't even have to open my mouth.

"Okay," I agree. The word sounds soft and shaky, but his smile in return is reward enough.

"That's my girl," he responds, and I swear, butterflies the size of eagles take flight in my stomach. Apparently, that like for praise from him counts outside of fuckery too. "But you could have said no and that would've been fine too. I want you to know you can say no and push back without there being consequences. I know that's not something you're used to, and that we can all be a little…"

"Bull headed?" I interject, teasing.

"I was going to go with strong willed," he says, laughing as he stands. Pulling me to my feet, he wraps his arms around my waist. "But what I meant was, you don't need to be afraid to speak up for yourself here. I know you've been doing a ton better, but I see it in your eyes sometimes. That wariness."

I open my mouth to speak, but he lifts a hand and presses a finger against my lips to stop me interrupting.

"I'm also aware that it has nothing to do with us, so you don't need to apologize. Yes, I saw the sorry coming. I just want you to know that you are always safe here. You don't need to ever worry about your past repeating itself here."

My heart swells because I hadn't even really noticed I was doing that, but he did. Maybe this setup of ours really will work. Because they all seem to really see me, even when I don't.

"Thank you," I say breathily, reaching up on tiptoe to kiss him. "Now, who do we have to go and talk to?"

That blank shutter that he gets when he's working

drops over his features before he shakes his head and rests his forehead on mine, closing his eyes.

"Someone I never expected to be mixed up in this." He pauses, and I don't push him, I give him space to work through whatever is going through his head. "We're going to speak to Harper."

Wait, what?

My mind has been reeling since Meyer told me that we were going to speak to Harper. Of all the names that could have fallen from his lips, I never would have expected hers. She basically worships him, and from what I've heard, she's done so since the day they met.

Why the hell would she have helped Trent?

I mean, I understand getting me out of the picture if she thinks she loves Meyer, but surely, if she knew him anywhere close to as well as she thinks she does, she'd have known that betraying him was the one thing he'd never get over.

Especially like this.

Maybe she thought she wouldn't get caught. Trent has a way of convincing you that what he's saying is entirely truth and that there's no way in all of the worlds that anything he has planned could go wrong.

That charm and manipulation of his…

I fell for it. Hell, the entire population of Reddale fell for it, he's practically worshiped as some kind of hero there.

The good guy.

Never in a million years would they believe who he truly is. What he's capable of.

So I can see it.

But for her to betray Meyer... that's the bit that leaves me reeling. I can't even imagine how Meyer feels, but he's been silent since we got in the car. His hand has stayed on mine, which he placed on his thigh, but his focus is razor sharp as he maneuvers the car, likely far faster than he should be, down the back roads toward wherever it is he's taking me.

Where it is they have Harper.

The journey doesn't take too long, likely because of the speed we were going, but the warehouse in the middle of butt fuck nowhere isn't where I expected us to be.

Meyer shuts off the engine but remains sitting, so I wait for him to move or say something, but minutes pass and he doesn't do either.

"Can't one of the others do this?" I ask him, the conflict he's battling internally is obviously intense. Surely the others can help. Rory has no love for Harper, at least not that I've noticed. Hunter might have, but he's more team

Yen of their merry band of helpers.

I snort inside my own head. I'm sure that Yen would love that title. But between Harper, Yen, and Elise—despite having never met her—they definitely have their own merry band of women obviously happy to help them.

At least, happy until recently in Harper's case.

Meyer finally shakes his head and lets out a deep breath. "Rory tried. He's the one who thought that me speaking to her would be a good idea. Don't get me wrong, I have zero issues doing the dirty work, and betrayal isn't something new to me, but—"

"But you thought she was your friend." I smile at him tightly. "That's the worst part about being stabbed in the back. It's not the knife. It's turning and seeing who brandished it."

He nods, the agreement in his eyes shining back at me. "I brought Harper in after... well, what happened to her, I just didn't imagine she'd betray us. I guess that will teach me for being so—"

"Absolutely not. Her decisions are no reflection on you. We're human, we crave connection on a literal biological level. You trusted her, you guys were friends, but what she did is on her, not on you. If you can tell me that Trent is responsible for his actions, and that I'm not to blame for them, then the same applies here buddy."

He cracks a smile as he turns to look at me. "You took

that little standing-up-for-yourself speech of mine to heart I see."

His teasing gives me hope, so I stick my tongue out at him. "Technically, this is standing up for you, and I've always been good at standing up for the people I love."

"You love me, huh?"

My cheeks heat as he squeezes my hand.

"I love you too, Quinn." Leaning over, he softly kisses me, leaving me craving more. "Now come on, let's get this over with so I can go home and show you just how much I love you."

EIGHTEEN

QUINN

It's been four days since I went with Meyer to speak to Harper and I can still see the tears streaming down her face as we left.

"You mean nothing to me," Meyer hisses and she writhes in her bindings. "You nearly cost me the woman I love, and Hunter nearly DIED!"

"I didn't mean for Hunter—"

"I don't give a fuck what you meant to happen," Meyer roars as I stand in the doorway, watching the scene play out before me. Her hatred shines bright when she looks at me. I didn't see it before; none of us did, I guess.

"This is your fault. If you'd have just stayed gone—"

Meyer grips her face, his entire body shaking with anger from her confessions. "You don't get to speak to her, look at her, or even fucking think of her."

Harper's whimpers would affect me more if she hadn't explained just how much information she gave Trent. Or even if she'd explained who else was working with Trent. She swore she didn't know, but the look she gave me after left me doubting. Meyer obviously didn't believe her either.

I cross the room and place my hand on his back, feeling his anger radiating from him. "Meyer."

Like his name on my lips is a release, some of the tension leaves him.

"Let's go," I say softly. "She doesn't have anything else to say to us."

He shudders as I run my hand down his spine before releasing her and turning to face me. "You're right. This is a waste of our time. Let's go."

"No," Harper cries, sobs racking her body. "Meyer, please. Don't leave me here."

I look back once, seeing the terror shining from her glassy eyes, her cheeks stained with tears, red from his hold on her. Meyer doesn't give her even that. He escorts me from the building, opens the car door for me, and drives us home without another word.

It's not like I have any sympathy for her, not after everything, but still, her face haunts me if I think on it too much. She truly did love him and it twisted her into what she became.

I wonder if that's what happened to Trent. Was he always a monster? Or was he made to be that way?

Shaking my head, I push the thought away. I didn't ask what happened to Harper. Just like I never asked what happened to Trent. Sometimes I wonder if I even want to know. Mostly, I know that I have enough things that live in my nightmares, and I could probably use the blissful ignorance.

I finish my bowl of ramen in the little restaurant I found on my outing today. Meyer dealt with my inheritance stuff, so I asked Bruno if we could come into the city. I want to get ahead on my Christmas shopping. I got the guys small trinkets for their birthdays because, well, one: I had no idea what to get, and two: buying them gifts with their money felt gross.

So freaking gross.

He didn't want Ramen, so I told him I'd be fine for ten minutes while he grabbed a sandwich from the deli across the street.

Lo and behold, I've been absolutely fine. I haven't seen him reappear yet, but I basically annihilated my ramen when it appeared. Apparently, shopping for the holidays makes me hungry.

My phone rings as I pay the bill and I smile when I see Tina's name on the screen. We had to reschedule our girls lunch because Yen is covering for Harper, so I haven't seen much of her lately.

"Hey Tina!" My grin is wide as I answer, but her crying freezes me in my tracks. "What's wrong?"

"He... he got... he got in the building, Quinn." Her words are stuttered and broken, but I make out what she's saying. "I don't know what to do. Oh, God. He's going to kill me."

"Did you call for Sam or Eric?" I ask as my heart rate picks up. I'm already out of the restaurant looking around for Bruno but I can't see him.

Fuck.

"They didn't answer. I think he hurt them. He's going to get in here. He's banging down my door."

Without thinking, I start running toward the apartment building.

Thank God I wore leggings and sneakers today.

It's not far from here. I can tell the others where I'm going, but I can't just leave her.

Fuck.

"Tina, I need you to hide. I have to call the guys, but I need you to get somewhere safe."

She sobs, but I swear I can practically see her nodding. "Okay."

She's still crying and I can hear the fear in her voice. It makes me push harder. Thank fuck Bruno put the shopping in the car before lunch.

"I'm in the bedroom closet."

Cliché, but it works.

"Okay, I need to end the call for a minute. Put your phone on silent, I'll call as soon as I can, okay?" I need to call Bruno. He'll get to us first. He's going to be so pissed I left without him but there just isn't time to worry about that right now.

I hear a loud bang through the line, my eyes going wide as I push myself to my limit, weaving through the crowds to reach my friend. His voice booms in the background, and ice fills my veins as she whispers, "Hurry, Quinn."

After calling Bruno and getting thoroughly yelled at, I hung up and tried to call Tina back but there was no answer. Dread roils in my stomach for the last few minutes it takes me to reach the building. I don't see Sam or Eric, which doesn't help the fear, but I don't have time to search for them. Thankfully someone steps off the elevator as I reach the doors, so I jump in and jam the button for the top floor.

The stairs would talk me longer, otherwise I'd just run them too.

Me:

Couldn't see Sam or Eric. Might need a medic. Or Rob.

I hit send on the message to Bruno, knowing that he'll get the right people here. I know reinforcements are on the way, but I can't just leave Tina to Matthew's mercy until they get here. If something happens to her and I know I just stood around waiting for backup, I'd never forgive myself.

I've been her.

I understand that fear.

Each time Trent found me, I felt it; the sickening twist of my stomach, the phantom pains of each hit, each assault on my body... I can't leave her alone with that.

Not if I can help.

And really, I don't know what I can do. I've been training, but I don't have a weapon. I have no idea what Matthew looks like, if I'm even strong enough to disable him, but I'll be fucked if I don't try to help my friend.

Impatience zips under my skin like fire as I wait for the elevator to reach the top floor. Once the ding sounds, I'm moving, heart in my throat when I hear his shouts from the hall. The door to the apartment is ajar and I take a deep breath before quietly pushing it open and entering the space.

He's not in the main room, but he calls out to Tina again.

Good, he hasn't found her. But he's close. He's in the bedroom.

My hands shake as I take a deep breath and try to creep

across the room. Thank fuck I learned where all the creaky boards were when I lived here incase this exact thing happened to me with Trent.

I make my way across the room, hearing him taunting her makes my blood boil, but I try my best to keep my cool. Bruno should be here with backup soon. If I can just distract him from her long enough…

Pausing, I realize I should draw him out of the bedroom, so I head back to the kitchen, grab a glass from the cupboard, and launch it at the wall.

His egotistical bullshit tirade stops at the sound and I duck down behind the island.

"Where are you Tina? Is this some fucking new game? Cat and mouse? I knew you loved it, baby. I'll chase you wherever you go."

A shiver runs down my spine as I try not to gag. My skin feels like I'm covered in slime from his words.

He's so much like Trent that it makes me want to physically be sick.

You can do this, Quinn. It isn't Trent, but you're stronger now. You're stronger than him. Than this. You can do this. For Tina.

He doesn't bother to mask his footsteps as he stomps into the room and the bedroom door swings so hard I hear it slam off the wall, wincing at the sound.

I really hope Tina stays hidden. I don't know why she

didn't answer her phone, but as long as she's alive and safe, that's what I care about.

My phone buzzes in my pocket but I ignore it, trying to focus on the threat in the room. I just hope it's Bruno or the guys letting me know they're here.

Matthew comes closer as he moves away from the broken glass. "Come out, little mouse. This cat is hungry. This chase has me all kinds of wanting."

Fuck me, he is so fucking gross.

I realize the cavalry isn't going to get here before he finds me, so I take a deep breath and steel myself to face him.

One.

Two.

Three.

I jump up, causing him to startle, and his eyes darken as the smile on his face twists. "And what a pretty little mouse you are. Did Tina bring me a toy to play with?"

"You fucking wish, asshole." The vitriol in my voice would make Tommy proud. "You picked the wrong people to mess with. Tina is my person now. You should leave."

He laughs, and I swear it's like standing in front of Trent. A vision of him flashes in front of me, but then I'm back, still facing off with Matthew.

"Oh she's feisty. I do love to break my toys."

I roll my eyes, maneuvering myself to put the island

between us as he slowly approaches. This is a game I know. He'll move slowly, then pounce.

The upside of spending my life with monsters? I know how they work.

He twists at a noise outside and I see the gun tucked in the back of his pants. Fuck, I hope that noise was Bruno. Or just anyone coming to help. I am not equipped to handle this asshole with a gun.

Coming here alone was stupid, but what else could I have done?

The guys are going to kill me if I survive this.

When no further sound distracts him, he turns back to me, but I've already cleared the room, my back to the bedroom door. If I can keep myself between him and Tina until help arrives, then that's a win for me.

Just as long as he doesn't consider me a threat enough to pull that fucking gun.

"Oh, you are a pretty little toy," he croons, grabbing his crotch.

I audibly gag and his face turns thunderous. "Abusive assholes don't do it for me."

"Sounds like you need teaching some fucking manners," he growls as he crosses the room toward me. I brace myself for the hit that's likely coming, but he grabs me by the throat instead of hitting me.

That I wasn't expecting.

He doesn't squeeze, just holds me, his eyes lighting up like he's enjoying the power play of knowing he could cut off my air. I try to slow the panic raging through me and remember what Hunter taught me.

This close, I can do some damage. So I step into him, which he wasn't expecting. His grip falters and I punch him as hard as I can in the throat. He releases me, grasping his throat, and bends forward. Using the movement to my advantage, I step forward and lift my knee as hard as I can into his nose.

The crunching sound gives me brief satisfaction as he stumbles, and without even thinking, I pull the gun from his waistband before he stumbles away from me.

It's nothing fancy, and not a gun I've handled before, but I flick off the safety and level it at him. "You should leave."

My voice is cold, flat, steady, like I'm not fucking terrified.

Let's not play the hero again, Quinn.

"You shouldn't aim a gun if you aren't willing to use it," he spits as he straightens, blood still pouring from his nose.

"Who said I'm not willing to use it?" I quirk a brow and tilt my head. He doesn't know me, and yet he still underestimates me. What the actual fuck is wrong with men? I have a gun pointed at him and he still thinks he can win.

His face twists with anger and he clenches his fists. "Stupid little bitch."

He dives for me, and without a second thought I pull the trigger.

Once.

Twice.

Three times.

Seconds later, Bruno and Rory burst through the door and find me still pulling the trigger on an empty gun pointed at the man bleeding out on the floor.

NINETEEN

RORY

"What the fuck do you mean she ran off?" Fear and rage spike through me as I grab the keys to the truck and run out the door.

"She called saying Tina was in trouble, her ex was there and that there wasn't time to waste, but she needed backup."

The engine roars to life and I slam the stick into gear before pushing my foot on the pedal like it's made of lead. The tires screech as I pull away from the curb and head from the club toward the apartment building. "Why the fuck weren't you with her in the first place?"

"She was eating, I was grabbing a sandwich. I was gone for less than ten minutes, across the street with a clear line of sight. I saw her leave the restaurant and start running, but I didn't catch her in time. She's fucking fast. So I jumped in the car the second she called. I can't be far behind her, but I lost her in the traffic."

A growl rips through me at the thought of Quinn being in danger.

A-fucking-gain.

Tearing through the streets, I barely pay attention to the other traffic, my sole focus on getting to her before something goes wrong.

"Shit," Eddie curses through the line, the phone still on speaker.

"What?"

"She texted. Eric and Sam are MIA, she's heading up to the apartment."

"Fucking woman," I hiss, grabbing my phone and typing out a message to her telling her not to enter that fucking apartment alone.

Slamming the brakes as someone pulls out in front of me, I see red. Taking a deep breath, I push the rage down, saving it for whatever I find when I get to her.

Once I'm moving again, I hit send on the message. "Did you call the others?"

"Not yet, I knew you'd be closest."

"Call Hunter. I'll call Meyer." I tell him before ending the call and dialing Meyer.

It rings a few times before he picks up. I don't give him the chance to speak before I do. "Quinn's in trouble. Grab Rob, meet me at the apartment building."

"Wait, what?" he asks. I can hear him already moving.

"Tina called Quinn, she was in trouble, her ex showed up. Bruno was across the street, Quinn ran off to help her. She's there alone. Sam and Eric are both missing. So move your ass and get Rob. I have no idea what we're walking into."

"We won't be long," he says before ending the call.

I drop the phone and focus on the last few blocks of the journey. It doesn't take long, but it feels like an age before I'm pulling up to the apartment building. Giving zero fucks that I shouldn't park here, I jump from the car, finding Eddie already in the foyer.

"You been up?"

He shakes his head. "I just got here."

"Let's go." I say, starting for the stairs.

"I called the elevator already," he says as the doors open. I consider the stairs again, but that's a lot of flights and, despite being in shape, the elevator will be faster.

"Let's go."

The ascent is torture, not knowing what's going on up there. I try not to let my mind go to the worst-case scenario, but after what happened with Trent... this shit was supposed to be over. She was supposed to be safe, for fuck sake.

The elevator opens to the sound of gunshots. Without thinking, I'm moving, gun drawn, and burst through the door to the apartment, finding Quinn holding a gun, the hollow click of an empty magazine echoing through the now-quiet space, and the guy I assume is Tina's ex lying on the floor, twitching as he bleeds out.

I holster my gun and cross the space, taking the gun from Quinn before wrapping her in my arms. "You're okay." Murmuring the words to her until she relaxes, I just hold her. Bruno secures the room and checks the body on the floor. I glance back and he shakes his head before moving into the bedroom, returning with a wide-eyed, tear-stained, shaking-like-a-fucking-leaf Tina.

"She okay?"

Bruno nods and moves her to the kitchen, avoiding the now-dead asshole behind me.

Moments later, Hunter, Meyer, and Rob enter the room, guns drawn. "Cavalry arrived," I joke, and Quinn laughs, but it's hollow.

"Looks like the cavalry wasn't needed," Hunter says as he approaches. I hand Quinn off to him and he moves her into the kitchen with Eddie and Tina.

"What happened?" Meyer asks when he and Rob reach me.

"No idea yet, I got here to find him on the floor, Quinn with a gun, and well, you arrived not long after. Any sign of Eric or Sam?"

"Luca is looking for them now," Meyer says before

turning to Rob. "Head down and help him, they might need you."

"On it," Rob says with a nod and leaves the room.

"What a fucking mess," Meyer grumbles, running a hand down his face. "You good to deal with this while I go make sure no one called the police over the gunshots?"

"Yeah, I got it." I pull my phone from my pocket and dial Tonio.

"What's up?"

"I need you to grab cleaning supplies and meet me at Quinn's old apartment. Leave Shae at home, make sure she's watched, and get your ass here."

He answers without hesitation. "On it. Any specific clean up method required?"

I let out a sigh and rub a hand over my head, the short hair grazing my hand. "We're going to need new carpet in here, but that's for later. Disposal first."

"Got it," he responds before ending the call.

Running over the shit we need to get aligned to ensure this doesn't come back on Quinn, I make a mental checklist. Disposal first, Meyer is dealing with P.D., then just making sure no one in this asshole's life comes looking for him. After that, we make sure the apartment is cleared. Nothing I haven't done a million times before, but knowing it's to protect Quinn has me triple checking that mental list.

Glancing over at her as I crouch beside the body, I

notice she's talking to Hunter and Tina. It's not hard to hear what she's saying. He attacked her, she fought back.

That's my girl.

A strange feeling of pride fills my chest. I taught her how to defend herself and that saved her. She might be a little traumatized from killing the guy, but that's better than her being the body on the ground. Her therapist can fix trauma, but she's not a necromancer.

Just the thought has my jaw clenching.

I roll the douchebag onto his back, noting his broken nose and smile.

She really nailed him.

Good girl.

I look over to her again and find her watching me. Watching him. I turn my stare to Hunter, who gets my silent message and takes the girls out of the apartment. She doesn't need to be here. Not for this.

She did her part, and now I'm going to make sure it doesn't come back on her. I might not have much to offer her, but this? This I can do.

After the clean up with Tonio, I headed home, knowing Meyer and Hunter brought the girls back here earlier. I haven't heard from them, but they knew I was busy and I knew they had our girl covered.

We have a lot to catch up on, especially after my morning with Trent, but first, I want to see Quinn. See with my own eyes that she's okay, in one piece and not falling apart.

Making my way to Meyer's office first, assuming that's where they'll be, I find him and Hunter sitting in silence, sipping what I assume is whiskey.

"Where is she?" I ask when I don't see her or Tina.

"Sleeping," Hunter answers.

"Her and Tina are in her room," Meyer informs me. "Eddie has gone home for the night, but I figured we didn't need him tonight anyway."

I clench my jaw, still pissed that he left her alone. "Did you deal with him?"

"Didn't need to," Meyer answers before finishing his drink. "He's beating himself up plenty. Quinn also went to bat for him, and I don't want anyone else watching her. We trust him, but more importantly, she trusts him."

I don't have to like it, but I nod. Part of me still wants to go up and check on her, but I also don't want to wake her. As if reading my mind, Meyer spins his laptop around, showing me a live feed of Quinn's room, showing the two of them curled up in bed, asleep.

"That's new."

"Put it in there tonight. She knows it's there, only

objected for an hour rather than six, so I guess she appreciates us watching out for her too." His smirk tells me that he enjoyed her submission to being watched, but I get the feeling Hunter is going to be the happiest about a camera in her room. He spins the laptop back around and finishes his drink.

Pushing the thought from my mind, I move to the bar, grabbing Meyer's glass on the way. I pour myself a drink, knock it back, then pour another for myself and one of Meyer before sitting in the chair next to Hunter, opposite Meyer at his desk, and slide his glass over to him.

"So I think we're done with Trent. He isn't giving up anyone else. There's too much joy in it for him. I think it's time to dispose of him and move on to other methods. Harper doesn't seem to know any more than she told you, Meyer, so we need to decide what to do with her too."

"Can we afford to let her go?" Hunter asks, and I shrug. Because really, probably not, but if she betrayed us once, she can do it again. If she was bitter before this, she's going to be even more so after. But, it's also not my decision, even if I would just put a bullet between her eyes and be done with it.

I turn my attention to Meyer, who is pinching the bridge of his nose. Yeah, he's overly stressed. Like, maybe needs to get some of it out before he has a heart attack stressed, but I get the feeling that me suggesting it would likely just stress him out more.

What a tangled web we weave.

"We get rid of them both. Loose ends aren't what we want right now. You handle Harper." A wicked smile appears on his face before he swallows down the drink I got for him. "I've got an idea for Trent."

"Care to share?" Hunter asks, but Meyer shakes his head.

"Not yet."

Hunter shrugs and leans back in his seat again. "Okay, is there any other business we need to deal with, since we're already all here?"

Meyer barks out a laugh and groans. "You mean other than the fact that Quinn killed someone today and we have no idea what his ties were?"

"I'll handle that," Hunter offers, and I thank him in my head. Rather him than me. I've still got shit to sort. "The gun run went fine, smooth handoff, Johnny is a happy boy, so I'm pretty freed up again."

"Johnny is never a happy boy," I snort before also finishing my drink.

Meyer nods, agreeing. "Just keep an ear out for shit with him, but yeah if you want to handle this shit from today, feel free. I need to call Edward Riley next week, and work out what the fuck is going on with the deal he had with Tommy. There was nothing at his place to even remotely hint at it, so we're fucked."

Hunter opens his mouth like he's going to speak, but closes it again, as if he thought better of whatever he was going to say.

Curious.

I tuck that away to question him about later, but for now, I stand and let out a yawn. "If that's all, I'm heading to bed."

No one says anything so I leave the office and head to my room, pulling up the surveillance feeds on my phone as I do. I find the one of Quinn and leave it playing on my phone as I get ready for bed, putting it on the pillow next to mine when I climb in.

If anything happens, I'll hear her, and this way, I can make sure I'm actually there for her before everything goes to Hell.

I hope.

TWENTY

QUINN

I wake up sweating and disoriented. It takes me a minute to work out that I'm in my room. Something hits me and I groan, realizing that Tina is thrashing around next to me, whimpering in her sleep.

Two guesses what woke me up.

I shake her gently, calling her name, and she startles awake, sitting up, shouting "No!"

The door to my room bursts open and Rory flies in half dressed and half asleep, making her scream even louder.

"What happened?" he demands, gaze bouncing around the room.

Tina shakes beside me, burying herself back beneath the blankets.

"Just a bad dream," I tell Rory as I climb out of bed and move toward him. "Are you okay?"

He double checks the room before relaxing and looking

down at me. "I couldn't sleep so I camped outside your door. Guess I must've eventually dropped off and then woke up to shouting. Sorry."

I quirk a brow at him and press my lips together while taking a breath so as not to laugh. "You slept out there in just a pair of jeans?"

He shrugs before pulling me against him and kissing the top of my head. "I got hot, then cold, and this is how I ended up."

"Fair enough," I say softly, giggling against his chest. My stomach growls and it occurs to me I haven't eaten since lunch time yesterday.

Oops.

"You want to go get dressed and I'll meet you in the kitchen?" I offer as I pull back from his embrace.

He frowns when he hears my stomach, though I'm not sure if it's from that or me basically dismissing him so I can make sure Tina is okay. His face softens when I point at the bed and my hiding friend. "Sure, I'll get Carlos to start cooking. What do you guys want?"

"Omelet, like normal," I answer.

A muffled, "Sounds good," comes from beneath the blankets and I stifle my laughter again.

"Got it," Rory says, kissing me quickly before leaving as abruptly as he entered.

Once the door is closed I turn back to the bed. "Coast

is clear," I tell Tina, who groans again.

A moment later, she sits up, blankets pulled up to her chest still, even as she fidgets. "Sorry. About everything. Waking you. Nightmares. Everything that happened yesterday. I…" She falters and I move back to the bed, taking her hand as I do.

"Nothing to apologize for. Trust me, I've had my fair share of nightmares."

She looks down into her lap, unable to meet my gaze. "If you'd never have met me—"

"Then I wouldn't have an awesome friend."

"Then you wouldn't have killed someone."

I take a deep breath, because I haven't quite processed that part yet, but I also wouldn't have done anything differently. Maybe that's why there isn't an extra weight on me today like I thought there would be.

"I don't regret it." I tell her honestly. "And if it got out, well, I'd claim self defense, but I have a feeling the guys have already dealt with it, and nobody's going to think anything other than he's fallen off the face of the Earth, like so many scumbags do."

God knows no one seems to have come looking for Trent, and if the boy wonder of Reddale isn't being looked for, I doubt anyone is looking for Matthew.

"But—" she starts and I cut her off again.

"No buts. It's done, I don't regret it. You're alive. That's what is important here." Part of me wants to ask why she called me, not the police, but I've been her. I already know why she didn't call them.

"What happens now?" she asks, wide-eyed. Sometimes I forget that she's so much younger than me. That bit more innocent. The only upside is she didn't suffer for as long.

"Now, we go have breakfast, find out from Rory if there's anything we need to know, but other than that, it's life like normal." The words sound far more confident and resolute than I thought they would, like I actually know what the fuck I'm doing right now. But winging it is all I've got and she needs me to be strong.

For her, that's something I can absolutely do.

Major crisis, I'm the one you want on your side.

Mild inconvenience, you'll find me rocking in a corner.

Please and thank you.

She just watches me like I spoke to her in Japanese, but I bounce off of bed and into my bathroom. Once I've showered and brushed my teeth I shoo her inside then start getting dressed. By the time my hair is dry, she's out, so I find her some clothes and we head down to the kitchen where the guys are already waiting for us.

Tina pauses at the threshold so I grab her hand and bring her into the room. "Morning."

The guys look up at my greeting and I sit Tina next to Hunter before moving to the coffee machine. Moments later, Shae, Tonio, and Bruno all walk into the kitchen and I let out a sigh of relief. I was kinda worried about Bruno, cause Meyer was real mad that I ran off and he wasn't with me. I had to go to bat for him pretty hard, but I was hoping I'd won.

Looks like I did.

Shae is her usual hurricane but it gets everyone talking about something that wasn't yesterday and by the time I hand over a coffee to Tina and sit down next to Meyer, she's smiling, everyone else is laughing, and it really is just like a normal day.

Thank you, Shae, for not making me a liar.

Once breakfast is over, Shae declares she's going shopping and Tonio's grumbling keeps everyone laughing until they leave.

The lightness Shae brought in leaves with her and I watch as Tina mentally crawls back inside herself.

Shit.

Before she spirals too deeply, I open my mouth, hoping to get things put to rights. "Anything we need to know about yesterday?"

The three guys stare at me like I have two heads, but Tina keeps her gaze on her coffee cup in her hands.

"All wrapped up," Rory tells me, like he gets it. "Nothing for you, either of you, to worry about."

Hunter and Meyer seem to catch on quick enough and

murmur their agreement. "Is there anyone who would miss him?" Hunter asks Tina. "A steady job? Roommate?"

"Nothing like that," she replies quietly, shaking her head. "He stayed at my old apartment, but I haven't paid rent there since I moved, so he was probably kicked out. A job isn't something he's ever held outside of dealing. He doesn't have any family, and his friends... they're not real friends."

"Okay, good." He nods, winks at me, then smiles at Tina again. "Means there's nothing else to be done. You get to move forward and get on with your life now."

"Does that mean I need to leave the apartment? Get a new job?" she asks, quickly glancing around at them before staring back at her hands. It hurts my heart to see her so timid again.

"Who said anything about that?" Meyer asks, staring at her until she looks up at him. "You're Quinn's friend, which means you're our people. The apartment and the job are yours for as long as you want them."

"Plus, if you leave right now, Yen will literally cut off my balls," Hunter jokes, drawing a laugh from Tina.

Jeez, I love that man.

"Thank you," she says quietly.

"Not needed," Meyer says before Hunter starts talking about some insanity for Thanksgiving.

Tina's eyes go wide at the change of subject, but I smile

at her, grab her coffee cup, and head over to the machine to make us another one.

Maybe I should feel worse about what happened yesterday, maybe I should worry about murder being so very nonchalant in my new life... but just maybe, this ease and acceptance and love is everything I've ever hoped for.

"I can't believe it's freaking December." I complain for the umpteenth time as Shae drags me around store after store to shop for gifts. After the whirlwind of November and Thanksgiving, eating way too much food, everyone just jumped into Christmas like it's their favorite time of year. Which it actually seems to be, but still.

It's been party this, decorate that, shopping this, wrap that and I swear, I'm almost over it already. I feel like the joy of Christmas is for kids and I missed out on that. We don't have any small humans around—and I don't intend on there being any anytime soon, either—so it's a little less sparkle than it should be. That magic isn't quite hitting the way I thought it would.

"You've said," Shae deadpans as she walks through the department store like she owns the place.

Knowing her, she actually might, but fucked if I know.

"You think Carlos would like this?" she asks, waving

at an air fryer. "Or do you think he'd be offended."

"It's Carlos," I answer, trying not to laugh. "Of course he'd be offended."

"You're right," she sighs. "I swear, him and my mom are the hardest people to shop for."

"You got the guys sorted?"

"Pfft, no! They're impossible, but I was thinking of buying you lingerie and gifting it to them." She winks at me and I burst out laughing.

"Even your brother?"

She shudders and I laugh again. "So gross, but yes, even him. Easiest gift I could think of. I get them chocolate and booze every year too. I swear, Teo is the only easy one to shop for. That boy's obsession with gaming is almost unrivaled."

"Is he coming home?" I ask. We haven't seen him since the trip to Tommy's. Angela was pretty sad when he wasn't home for Thanksgiving, and I felt awful because I'm fairly certain I'm why he's staying away, even if Meyer told me I'm being ridiculous.

Shae nods then moves out of the home section and into the clothing section. Shopping with her here feels weird. She usually drags me around boutiques; I did not expect a department store to be on the list of places to visit today. "Yeah, Meyer lost his shit on Teo after Thanksgiving and basically told him to get home or be cut off. I don't think

I've ever see him that angry."

Well, I had no freaking idea. I swear, sometimes I feel like I live in a world of my own, but I can't tell if it's on me for not paying attention, or just how awful those three can be at communicating in general.

"Don't pull that face. Do you have any idea how much shit I never know about? And I've been around my entire life. Their little boys' club is almost impossible to crack the secret code for. Even when you're in, they forget to tell you stuff. Why do you think they do like, daily debriefs? Cause otherwise they'd even forget to tell each other shit."

I unwrinkle my brow, not having realized I'd scrunched up my face, and stick my tongue out at her. "You think I'll ever make it to the inner circle?"

"You're already in. They just still want to protect you so they'll keep stuff from you without even realizing they're doing it. They're cavemen.." She bangs her fists on her chest and I laugh. "We men, you princess. We protect, grrrrrr."

I laugh even harder when I see Bruno and Tonio trying not to laugh as they trail behind us.

"Pretty accurate." I giggle and she laughs too.

Looping her arm with mine, she drags me toward the exit. "I thought so. Okay, this place is a bust. Coffee, lunch, or more shopping?"

"Coffee, please," I beg.

"You should eat," Bruno pipes up, and I roll my eyes, hearing the high five between him and Tonio. "Please let us eat."

"Fine…" Shae drags out the word, glancing back at them. "What do you want to eat?"

"We get to pick?" Tonio asks, sounding shocked.

Shae stops and we turn to face them as we exit into the main mall. "Well, it is the holiday season."

"Be still my beating heart, the generosity."

The teasing between the two of them is so much like siblings, it's fun to watch. It also occurs to me that I need to get Bruno a present, so I unlatch my arm from Shae, letting Tonio lead her to wherever we're eating, and walk with him.

"What is your Christmas wish, Br—Eddie?" Using his real name is still so weird.

He chuckles at me and shakes his head. "You can call me Bruno, Quinn. But my Christmas wish... is for my girls. They all have such big dreams for next year. The twins want ivy leagues and Ella wants Julliard. I don't remember when they grew up and got such big, expensive goals."

"How likely is it?" I ask, chewing on my lip because that was kinda rude.

He shrugs, but smiles. "We'll do what we can."

I tuck it away but ask him again anyway. "Okay, but what about you and your... boyfriend? Husband?"

"Husband," he chuckles. "Bruno, yes his *actual* name is Bruno, he and I, we don't want for much. A vacation would be nice. We haven't gone anywhere since the girls were little, but once they're away at college, who knows? He is going to shit a brick when he realizes how empty the house is going to be. He's going to want me to quit or something nuts."

"Would you?" I ask pensively.

He nods, patting my hand as I loop it through his arm. "If he really wanted it, I'd do it in a heartbeat. You do what you can for the people you love."

The lights on the tree are twinkling, music plays softly in the background, and the entire gang is here. The presents beneath the tree are spilling out into the whole room, and despite there being no small humans, the magic of Christmas is truly alive.

Mama Meyer is overjoyed at having all of her children here. Tina, Yen, and Tonio are all here too. Bruno would have been but I demanded he take the day off. Even Carlos took the day off to be with his family.

"Merry Christmas, Kitten," Meyer murmurs as he sneaks in behind me, wrapping his arms around my waist as he rests his chin on my shoulder. "I hope Santa brought you something you asked for."

"I didn't ask for anything," I tell him with a smile. "I already have everything I could possibly want.

"Well, I still owe you a present from your birthday, which, if it's okay with you, is going to be a Christmas present, but I do have a replacement gift from your birthday."

"You didn't have to replace—"

"Shhhhh," he says, cutting me off. He stands up, his arms disappear from my waist before coming over my head moments later and I catch a glint of something shiny before I feel something cold on my throat. "A beautiful woman deserves beautiful adornments. This is just a little something, so I am always close to your thoughts."

"Like you leave them." I laugh and move my hair to the side so he can latch the clasp. Once he's done, I press my fingers against my throat before turning to face him. "Thank you."

"You haven't even seen it," he says, chuckling.

"I don't need to, I already know I'll love it. Just like I know I love you."

"I love you too, Kitten," he whispers against my neck before kissing me.

Shae makes a gagging noise from behind us and I break the kiss, laughing. "Enough of that shit already. Let's do presents!"

TWENTY ONE

MEYER

"Why are we back here?" Quinn asks as I pull the car to a stop outside the warehouse. She didn't know who else was here when I brought her to see Harper, but today, she finds out.

"You know that birthday present that wasn't quite ready, so we agreed to bump it to Christmas?" She nods and fingers the chain around her neck, but still looks entirely confused. "Well, this is it."

Without another word, I climb from the car, move around it to open her door, and offer her a hand to climb out.

"I still don't understand."

I smirk as I kiss her hand. "Oh, I know."

Leading her inside, a slither of doubt creeps in that maybe this was a terrible idea, but after everything, I thought that this should be her choice.

The door to the warehouse opens before we reach it and Rob walks out.

"Okay, so now I'm really confused." I chuckle at her again and shake my head before turning to Rob.

"All good?" I ask and he nods, tapping his bag.

"Everything removed, kept steady for you till now. Let me know if you need anything else." He smiles at Quinn once he's finished then leaves without another word.

Also, not what he signed up for when he agreed to be my private doctor, but my friend has long since stopped questioning much of anything. I guess being friends with me for this long will do that to a guy.

"Thank you," I call out as he reaches his car before turning my attention back to the woman beside me. This might be the only thing I've questioned this much about her since she arrived; if this is the right move.

I don't remember ever feeling so... nervous.

Though not about her.

Never her.

Just at her reaction to me when she sees what's inside the warehouse.

"Ready?" I ask her, holding out my hand to her, thankful for its steadiness as she places her palm on mine.

She smiles and I swear, all of the heavy shit in my life falls away and it's just me and her. Nothing else exists, nothing else matters.

Not when she looks at me like that.

Like I hung not just the stars and the moon, but the entire fucking universe.

She makes me feel invincible. Like nothing is impossible. Breathing life and light back into me when, before her, I thought I'd never feel this. I accepted that that was my life. My karma.

But then she arrived and turned everything I thought I knew upside down.

Placing my hand on the door latch, I look down at her again. "If you don't like your gift, we can leave. There is zero pressure."

She barks out a laugh, her eyes dancing with joy. "I don't know whether to be scared or really fucking excited after an introduction like that. Your mind is a beautiful and twisted place, Meyer Marino. Now show me my present!"

I chastely press my lips to hers, not allowing myself any more... yet.

Opening the door, I motion for her to enter. "Ladies first."

Her giggle sounds again as she shakes her head. "We both know I'm no lady. Female yes, and I can absolutely pretend to be a lady if the situation calls for it..."

She trails off, poking her tongue out at me as she walks by, so I swat her ass, enjoying the squeak it pulls from her. I follow along behind her as she retraces the hall I walked her down when we came to see Harper, but she pauses at the end, looking back to me before turning right like we did last time.

"This way." Taking her hand, I lead her left, to where the monster who I know still haunts her nightmares is waiting for us.

"Why do I feel like I'm going to vomit?" she asks, her voice quiet as we reach the door to the warehouse. Thankfully, the soundproofing means even if he's awake and making noise, she has no idea what's on the other side of the door.

Pausing, I turn her to face me and cup her chin. "What waits for you on the other side of the door is a choice. If you decide to not accept it, that's okay. If you choose to accept it, that's also totally okay. This is a choice that no one is going to take from you, but regardless of what happens, you are still loved, you are still worthy, and you still deserve the world."

Tears fill her eyes and she blinks them back, her hands clasping my forearm where I have a hold on her chin. She squeezes my arm and takes a deep breath. "Thank you." The words are quiet, almost like a prayer, so I kiss her and show her that my words are more than words. I pour every ounce of truth, love, adoration, and outright fucking obsession I have for her into it. Her hands move from my arm to my chest, where she clutches to me like I'm her lifeline in a storm, activating that primal, caveman part of me that really fucking enjoys her bending to my will.

"Okay," I murmur, breathless. "We need to stop. Otherwise, we're not making it to the other side of that door." She pouts up at me, and I laugh once. "Oh, Kitten, we will definitely be finishing what we started, we're just pushing pause."

I kiss her again and she nips at my lips. "Naughty little kitten. Playing with fire."

Her eyes dance with delight and I take a deep breath, trying to will away the hard on that's very much on show. "Come on, present time."

Opening the door, I step into the warehouse first, knowing she's behind me from the sound of her footsteps. She steps around me and I know she sees him when her breath hitches.

"Trent?"

He's hanging from the beam by metal chains that are attached to the cuffs on his wrists. The ones Rory said he used on her, his own version of poetic justice.

She looks back at me, questions in her eyes. "This is your gift, Quinn. We have gotten the info we could from him, but Rory says he's done talking. We could have dealt with it, but after everything, I wanted to give you the option to do it yourself. To own the downfall and eradication of that monster, both in reality and in your head."

Trent splutters a laugh from across the room. "She won't do it. She's weak. She'll fail at your test like she's failed at everything her entire life. Then you won't want her, the way no one else has ever wanted her. Except me. I loved her and look where it got me."

Rage courses through my veins but I keep my gaze on the blonde before me. Emotions flicker over her face, but I watch as she works through it, takes a breath, and then there's peace.

"Thank you," she says to me, holding out her hand. I pull the gun from my waistband and hand it to her, keeping a grip on it while ignoring the laughter that still comes from Trent, despite him being half dead already. He's only alive because Rob put him on a feeding tube and IV. It takes a lot not to just shut him up myself, but she deserves this kill.

To quiet that voice in her head.

Sometimes the only way to quiet something is to know that it is truly gone and never coming back.

"You don't have to do this, but all that bullshit he spewed was exactly that. Bullshit. You can do this, but if you don't want to, we can just go home and someone else will deal with the issue for us."

"Give me the gun, Meyer." Her voice is low but her conviction is unwavering so I release my hold on it.

"I meant it when I said no one wanted you." Trent's

words make me clench my fists. "Even after your parents took you, they realized they fucked up. You know they're not your actual parents, right? They kidnapped you, wanted the ransom money for their next hit, but even your birth parents didn't want you. Wouldn't pay up. Unwanted by all except me. And you ran from me. YOU RAN FROM ME!"

What the actual fuck is he talking about? She was taken? I watch her, but it's like she can't hear his words. Like she's lost in her head.

"YOU DON'T GET TO RUN FROM ME." Trent shouts, and a shot goes off, my ears ringing in the aftermath.

Watching her stand there, gun in hand, facing down the man who has tormented her most of her adult life, brings out the animal in me. This might not be the first life she's taken, but it's the first intentional one.

Except her hand doesn't shake, even though she's hesitating to pull the trigger for a second time. The first shot hit his thigh and he screamed like a bitch, but now he's silent again, his jaw clenched, and it's taking everything I have to stay rooted to the spot. To not make him hurt some more for everything he's done to her.

She tilts her head while she observes him. He's already

broken and bleeding, a few weeks at Rory's mercy will do that to a man, but he still looks at her like he thinks she won't do it.

Like she's not strong enough.

He's always underestimated her, but that's his problem.

He has no idea how strong my girl is.

"Quinn?" I call out her name to pull her from the racing thoughts I can see running through her mind as they play out in her eyes. "I know I gifted him to you, but if you don't want to do this, you don't have to."

Her hand remains trained on him—apparently Rory has taught her well in their sessions—while she turns her gaze to face me. "I know I don't have to. But he has taken so much from me. A bullet feels too quick. Too kind."

A laugh falls from me as I grin at her. "That's my girl. It doesn't have to be quick, depends where you put the bullet. But as you can see, Rory's had plenty of fun with him too."

A grin spreads on her face. "Oh, I can see."

She turns that slightly sadistic smile back to Trent, whose eyes widen when he takes in the sight of her. I imagine he's finally seeing who she's truly become.

"I knew you were like me," he grunts and her smile widens.

"Oh, sweetie, I'm nothing like you. The demons that live inside of me were created, not born. They were raised by many monsters, so my demons... they're worse than you could ever imagine."

He laughs, spluttering a cough in the middle of it. "Even if you kill me, I'll still be with you Quinn. You'll never be rid of me because those demons will always haunt you and I helped create them."

"That's where you're wrong." She tilts her head again, raising her hand so the gun is in line with his head rather than his heart. "Once you're gone, you'll fade to nothing but a whisper of the past that will be forgotten. I've wasted enough of my life, my energy, on you. Life is for the living, and you? You're not worth another moment of my time."

She pulls the trigger, her body taking the brunt of the recoil like a pro, despite the gun being too big for her. The bullet enters his head, the back of his skull exploding from the caliber of the bullet as it exits, but she's close enough for the spatter to coat her.

"I thought a bullet was too quick?" I ask her, half teasing, half trying to gauge her.

Turning to me, she's still as calm as a placid lake, despite the blood running down her cheek.

The sight of it has me hard as a fucking rock. Probably shows just how fucked up I am, but who gives a shit?

"It was, but I didn't want to give him another second of my time." She walks over to me and hands me the gun, which I put down on the metal tray behind me before grabbing her cheeks, kissing her with every ounce of need coursing through my veins. She grips the front of my shirt, no doubt smearing blood on the white material, but somehow that makes me want her more.

"Are you okay?" I ask once I can bring myself to pull back from the kiss. Her grip doesn't loosen as she looks up at me, my own passion reflected back at me on her face.

"I am more than okay," she responds, unbuttoning my shirt. "But I could definitely be better."

"Don't have to tell me twice." I stroke my thumb through the blood on her face and the animal inside of me takes over.

I bring my finger to her bottom lip and, without taking her eyes from mine, she sucks my thumb into her mouth and licks up every drop of blood that I'd wiped off.

Is it sanitary? Probably not. Do I care? Not even a little bit because the lust coursing through my veins is boiling hot and my dick is hard enough to cause real pain.

As the corners of her lips tick up in a smile that resembles Rory's psychotic one, I realize that she has a piece of us, all three of us, inside of her and it only makes me love her more.

As my finger slides out with an intended pop, my body reacts on instinct.

Our shoes kicked off.

Her pants gone.

My fly unzipped.

Her shirt sliced open and hanging freely.

My dick out.

Her panties ripped off.

When I have her exactly as I want her—all lusty-eyed and panting—I grip her hips and slam her on the metal table that's usually reserved for some fucked up shit. Neither one of us cares at this moment.

We don't care that we're about to fuck with a dead man tied to a chair, head back from the blunt force of the bullet to his forehead.

We don't care that we're covered in his blood.

We don't care that her thigh is resting next to the gun that ended a life.

The only thing we care about is easing this itch that's consuming our bodies, our veins, our very essence and nerve endings.

If I don't fuck Quinn, right here and right now, I may just implode and we both know it.

Thighs spread with her pussy already leaving a wet spot on the shiny metal, I hook my arms under her knees and bring her pussy to mouth. I don't eat her cunt, that would be too gentlemanly. No, I fucking demolish it with my lips and tongue and teeth.

With every suck and lick and bite, she moans louder and louder until her thighs squeeze my face hard enough that I'm fantasizing the possibility of dying by pussy suffocation.

I figure it's the best way to go, so I don't relent. In fact, I devour her even more to test the strength in her legs. I fuck her pussy with my mouth to see who goes first. To see if she comes before she kills me with her lust.

Just as my tongue is coated with the onslaught of her cum, I wrap my lips around her clit and suck her deep, deep, deep until her screams—my name over and over again—bounce around the four walls of this death bunker. Until my ears are ringing with the pleasure I fucking gave her. Until her throat is sore from it all.

I made that possible.

My gift to her. My tongue. My lips. I did this because she's fucking mine now and always will be.

I'm not just claiming her, I'm tattooing her orgasm into the very fabric of my soul and making sure it's locked down tighter than the fucking pearly gates.

"Oh, God! Yes, fuck, yes!"

At her words, my hands pull at her knees, freeing my head from her death lock and looking up at her with narrowed eyes and a snarl on my mouth.

"Not God. Not anyone but me. You fucking say my name when you come on my tongue." Her eyes snap open and, for a second, we stare at each other, understanding dawning on her.

"Make me come, Meyer." I grin and it's closer to something Rory would do than Hunter. More psycho than fun and loving.

"Your wish, Princess."

My face is back to her pussy and my lips are back to sucking on her clit as her head falls back—hair touching the metal table—as she squirms and moans and thrust her hips impossibly harder so I can eat her like a starved animal.

I leave imprints on her thighs, nails digging into her skin and hoping to fucking God that they break the surface. That they make her bleed. That she feels the pain associated with her unwavering pleasure.

"Fuck, Meyer! Yes, yes, yes, don't ever stop!"

Much better.

With a flick of my tongue, I press hard against her clit and watch as she beautifully falls apart on my face. Thrashing, screaming, jerking her entire body on that flimsy metal table.

That's right, Baby, give it all to me. Only me. Always me.

Those thoughts run in a never-ending loop in my mind as I drink down her cum like it's water replenishing my battered body after a good workout.

Only once her body slumps from exhaustion and sated relief do I unlatch her thighs from around my face and lock eyes with her. Mine hungry, hers hooded and drunk on pleasure.

"My turn." Those two innocent words come out like a warning—like an omen—as I grab the open sides of her tattered shirt and pull her to me until her pretty, little soaked cunt is right on the edge of the table. In an instant, her eyes go wide. She's no longer the contented little kitten from before. Now, Quinn is on high alert. Every one of her muscles is rigid, like she's standing on a tightrope and one wrong move will send her tumbling down into a pit of starving alligators. It's not fear, exactly, it's anticipation and hyper-awareness.

I can smell her lust thickening at the thought of me destroying her all over again. I can feel the trembling of her flesh at the idea of me marking her entire body with my sexual rage and animalistic desire to rip her apart just so I can put her back together again with a pretty little bow to boot.

"In my world, nice and gentle don't exist. I'm not Hunter. There's no deprived need to watch you almost die under me, either. I'm not Rory. But Quinn…" I bring her mouth to mine but don't kiss her. "Your fear turns me on. Your flight instincts make me want to paint this room with my cum." I speak against her mouth, our lips brushing ever so often and our breaths dancing to the most fucked up music she's ever heard.

Quinn gasps when she sees me palm my dick and take a step back. "I'll give you twenty seconds before I come for you, and when I catch you, I'll come in you so hard you'll taste me in your mouth."

I grin—the sadistic and wolfish one she loves so much—as I take hard, unapologetic pulls on my cock and back away to leave her enough room.

Biting my bottom lip and closing my eyes, I take in a deep breath and savor the scents all around me.

The tangy scent of her cunt still plastered all over my face.

The metallic smell of blood mixing with the early tell-tale odors of death.

The potent onslaught of bleach that we use over and over again in this place after Rory has his fun.

It's all mixed together and creating this need to chase my prey.

"Run, little lamb."

It only takes her a moment to realize I'm not fucking kidding.

Jumping off the table, she looks around the room, keeping me in her periphery at all times, before her eyes narrow on the exit door.

I've locked it, not that she noticed earlier since her focus was on my well-presented present.

The shake of her head, like she's calculating the waste

of time it would be to run there only to be greeted with disappointment, makes me smile.

My smart little lamb.

There's only one way she can leave here and that's by taking the key to the door that's in my pocket, but I'm not telling her that.

What would be the fun in that?

"There's no way for me to win here." Her words are exhaled with a rough jerk of her head toward the door. "I bet that's locked and you've got the key on you."

I grin, this time wider. I love that her brain is as sexy as her tight little cunt.

"Fifteen seconds." Is all I have as a response.

Quinn's eyes flick all around as she begins to run in a controlled circle. She's frantic, her breaths coming in hard and shallow. Fuck, it turns me on like nothing else can.

"Ten seconds."

I walk further away from her, giving her the space to think clearly yet knowing my mere presence makes her irrational.

After all, the longer the chase, the harder the orgasm.

"This is so fucking unfair!" she cries out, her feet slipping on that fucker's blood, and for a second my protective half wants to run to her but my primal half holds me back.

"Five seconds."

She grunts out a huff of frustration as she tries the second door that only leads to a supply closet with no way to lock her in.

Hell, I'd happily fuck her in there against the wall like a wolf that's been denied its nature for way too fucking long.

"Four."

She stands at the far wall, her back flat against the surface with only Trent between us.

I don't move. Yet.

"Three."

Her eyes dart all around, measuring time and space to see her best options.

"Two."

My fucking dick is leaking precum at the anticipation of running for her and catching her and fucking the flight instinct right the fuck out of her.

"One."

With a grin, I let go of my steel-hard dick and zip up my pants.

"Here I come." Soon, baby, soon.

Without a hint of hurry in my steps, I casually walk around Trent's dead body as blood seeps out of his wound and adds to the puddle that's growing by the minute.

Quinn matches my steps as she slides along the wall with side steps, her eyes dancing all over me. Her fear is a palpable, living thing that crawls up my body and seeps through my skin.

"It's not fair, you know." Her words only make my heart happy.

"Never said it would be."

"But I don't have a chance, Meyer." Frustration evident in every word, I remember that Quinn hates to lose. Well, so do I, which is why I always create situations that have me as the victor.

"No, little lamb. You sure as fuck do not." Then I jump two steps forward, like the insane predator I am, just to see her pulse beat harder on the column of her neck.

Fuck, I'm so turned on, it's bordering on lethal.

"Meyer, let's just—" I don't give her the time to finish that phrase because she knows that the chase is my appetizer and her pussy is my three-course meal.

In less than two seconds, I'm close enough to smell her fear. Quinn scrambles, slipping again on the growing pool of blood and this time falling to her knees. Using her hands, she pushes back up to her full height and runs as quickly as she can, sliding across the room as she constantly checks behind her to know where I am at all times.

Good girl.

She's covered in blood that isn't hers. Blood that she spilled. Blood that she owns with her revenge and it's fucking intoxicating.

"Meyer." Panting and frantic, Quinn tries to negotiate with her eyes but I'm too focused on catching her now. My dick can't wait and my patience at my own little game is wearing thin.

"Run, Quinn, because when I catch you... fuck, I can't wait to make you cry."

Ah, there's that vein on the side of her neck pulsing a mile a second as she searches for a way out.

Suddenly, she stops and that action throws me off.

Her shoulders square and her chin lifts in defiance as she turns to face me completely.

"What are you doing?" I raise a brow, reminding her that the game is still on.

"Winning." A laugh erupts from my lungs as my head falls back.

"Keep telling yourself that, little lamb." Instead of running as my feet push off the floor to reach her, she walks to me—eyes fixed only on me.

"Quinn." Her name comes out in a growl and I have to unzip my pants to alleviate the throbbing pain of my steel-hard dick.

"Meyer." My name is all breathy and soft, just like her tits when I suck on her peaked nipples.

Fuck this.

I pounce on her, one hand in her hair, the other on said nipple as I slam my mouth to hers and back her up against the nearest wall. She's slick all over the place; from her wet, needy cunt to her blood covered body. Her mouth is hot and demanding as my tongue roams and plunders and takes everything she has to give me.

As her back hits the wall and my chest connects with her bouncing titis, I push my pants down and impale her without a second's thought.

We both gasp, our bodies trembling from the complete and utter consumption of this savage lust.

Fucking her mouth and her pussy at the same time is cathartic, it makes my rage and fear and lust and hunger all balance out into something sane.

Well, as sane as someone like me can be.

Quinn moans and I swallow the needy sound, savoring it in my very bloodstream.

I fuck her so hard I'm curious to know if we leave a dent in the drywall. Still, it's not enough. My hands hold her ass as I thrust harder and harder inside her.

Not fucking enough.

With a grunt, I pull out and, with my hand in her hair, I turn her around and lower her to the floor.

Somewhere in the back of my mind, I realize we're lying in blood, but my beast has consumed me and I can't seem to give a single tiny little fuck.

Spreading her legs wide, I push my pants, which are lying right beside us, away a few inches so I can lay myself over her completely.

Her hips are searching me out, her pussy eager to be filled by my cock, just as desperate as I am to return to her hot little hole and fuck it like it's our last goodbye.

"When you run, I'll catch you. Always." I follow my words with a deep, animalistic thrust, freezing as we both savor the feeling for a blissful second.

In that second, I forget all the shit happening to us. I forget the blood, the death, the killings. I forget her pain and her past suffering.

All of it is just a blip as my dick fills her completely. Owns her cunt like I own her soul.

When I start to pound her flesh, her eyes snap open and she meets me thrust for thrust. Her blood-soaked hands come up to frame my face, and in all the savagery of this moment, her tenderness undoes me.

Her love for me destroys all of my demons and sends them away with a whispered word.

"Meyer. Do you feel that?"

I fuck her harder. Slamming my hips against her groin, the sounds of skin meeting harshly with skin like a philharmonic orchestra playing in my mind.

This entire moment is perfect. She's perfect.

And for a brief moment in time, I'm perfect.

For her, for me. For us.

"Give it to me, Meyer. Fill me up with your cum."

Gone is the scared little lamb trying to run from me. Here, beneath my beastly thrusts and my uncontrolled kisses and bites and sucking of her tits, I see a warrior. A true queen who is afraid of no one.

That thought makes me lose all semblance of control.

"You first."

Her pupils dilating to the point of hiding the true color of her eyes, she wraps her legs around my waist and locks her ankles at the small of my back. With pure adrenaline, she lifts her hips just as I bury myself impossibly deeper inside of her and explodes all over my dick. I don't even pretend to hold back.

My cum spills inside her like a hose that's been held back by a pinch. It's rushed and it's violent but it's everything that is us.

Panting and lust-crazed, I carefully fall onto her and breathe her name into her ear.

"Quinn."

"I know. I know."

I close my eyes as she rolls us so that she's straddling me, my hands loosely caressing her sticky body.

In an instant, she's off of me and the heat of her body feels like it's miles away.

"What the fuck, Quinn?"

When I sit up, I see her at the door, unlocking it, before she turns to me with keys dangling from her fingers.

"I win."

This fucking girl.

TWENTY TWO

QUINN

Sometimes I wonder if being around monsters my whole life has made me one. I never used to think I was, but in the four days since I took Trent's life, I have felt lighter than I ever remember feeling.

That's not to say I haven't been twisting and turning over if he was lying about what he said about my parents, but a weight that's been with me my entire adult life is gone.

Partially replaced by the bullshit about my parents, but I've been... happy.

That said, Meyer said he called Denton to look into my potential kidnapping. I don't know that I believe it, but I also don't see what Trent would have gotten out of lying about it. Not at that point. I'm more confused about him not having used it against me before now. It seems like something he'd have held over me before now, but I don't know what to think.

So I've tried not to.

Instead, I've been attempting to continue on with real life. I've been at the club, helping Yen with management shit since Harper isn't around to do it. I've been talking to Shae about the charity boards she sits on to see if there's anything I can do to help.

I've been training with Bruno, the bruise on my thigh and the ache in my shoulders is testament to him not taking it easy on me like he promised.

I even tried getting Carlos to teach me how to cook his delightful spicy chicken pasta, but despite our new truce of love and adoration, it turns out Carlos is not a good teacher. Hunter watching and laughing the entire time probably didn't help, but I've decided that cooking flamboyant and extravagant dishes probably isn't a strength of mine.

Not that it's a skill I need living here, and a part of me keeps thinking that this might just be what forever looks like, but despite knowing the guys want me here, there's still that voice in my head that tells me it won't last.

That they don't love me.

That nothing is forever.

Oh, how I love that voice. *Not.*

I shake off the negative thoughts and draw my attention back to the laptop screen in front of me.

Have I been looking into kidnappings from the year

I was born? Obviously. But if I was kidnapped, is my birthday even my birthday? How does my birth certificate even exist? None of it makes sense.

I rub my temples, trying to expel the headache that's been threatening for the last few hours, closing my eyes in hope that it helps.

"You still staring at that screen?"

I look up and find Rory watching me, brow raised, shoulders tense, despite his nonchalant demeanor, and nod. "Yeah, not that it's been useful."

"I thought Meyer told you that Denton was looking into it?" His gaze runs over my body and his brow furrows, so I sit up straight and pain registers in my spine.

Oops.

"He did," I reply as I stand and stretch out. Apparently, sitting cross legged and hunched for the last few hours isn't good for me. I hadn't even registered that I was hurting anywhere but my shoulders. "But I was bored, so I figured I'd go down the rabbit hole myself, Alice style."

I wiggle my toes at him and he laughs at my fuzzy, thigh high, Mad Hatter socks. Another pair courtesy of Hunter. I still haven't gone through the extreme number of fuzzy socks he got me for Christmas, but they have their own special drawer in my dresser now, so I pick a new pair at random each morning, reveling in the childlike joy of a new discovery.

I meant it when I told him Christmas morning that that present would be like a new gift each morning. So far, I've proved myself to not have been lying.

Pressing my hand against my throat, I trace the chain from Meyer, thinking about everything they've given me, outside of Christmas.

Rory's gift isn't one I have on me right now, but the sword is a work of beauty. I just need to learn how to wield it. Not that I have plans to, but I think it'll be a cool feather to have in my hat.

"What brought you down here anyway?" I ask, knowing that it's rare for anyone to be in the family room, which is exactly why I holed up in here after I got chased out of the kitchen by Carlos after we had lunch earlier.

He shrugs before walking toward me and wrapping his arms around me. Shock flickers through me at the unexpected hug, but I hold him, squeezing tight for a few seconds, then rest my head on his chest. "You okay?"

"I am now," he murmurs before kissing my hair and resting his chin atop my head.

Sometimes I worry that he holds too much in, but I also know that, one, talking about the things in your head is harder than people make out, and two, guys are taught that emotions are weakness so they're even more reluctant to talk. So instead of pushing, I just say, "You know you can talk to me about stuff if you want to. You don't have to, but

I'm here. I love you, and anything you tell me isn't going to change that. I won't judge you or think any differently of you."

He holds me tighter, so I do the same in response.

"You love me?" His words are more of a whisper, but his hold is so tight that I can't move, so instead I whisper back to him.

"I do. I think I have for a long time, and I probably should have told you before. But I love you, Rory Beeston. Every single part of you."

He shudders beneath my touch and I smile to myself. "I love you too, Quinn."

The new year is well and truly here, and with it came a fresh slate.

Trent is dead.

My guys are here and I love them. They love me.

I have friends that are actually my friends, not fake fair-weather ones.

My life is unrecognizable. If the girl who ran from Trent those years ago, terrified out of her mind, was told this would be our life, she wouldn't have believed it.

Yet here I am.

Living. Thriving.

But still, the past has its claws in me. It's been almost a month since I took Trent's life. Since he told me about my supposed childhood kidnapping, and well... I still can't stop thinking about it. Though, hopefully after the next couple days, I'll have more peace.

I'll have truth.

Closure.

Something.

I close my eyes as the plane descends, my hand in Hunter's, clinging to him like a lifeline.

Who I am today might be leaps and bounds from the girl I was then, but that doesn't mean this entire trip doesn't have me twisted up.

Denton's search came up inconclusive. There was a girl kidnapped around the area I lived in as a child, but without more details it's kind of hard to confirm. We have no idea if I was supposedly taken from this area, or somewhere else. When it would've happened. Anything.

I probably should have asked Trent before I shot him, but that would've been another thing for him to hold over me and I don't believe he'd have told me anyway.

So after realizing that we had too little information to really figure anything out, I told Meyer I wanted to go and see my parents. See if they would give me answers.

I'm aware it's highly unlikely, my parents have never really given a fuck about me, but maybe, just maybe, they'll actually not disappoint me for once in my life.

The plane bounces onto the runway and I swear every person on the plane expels a breath. The flight has been rocky at best.

"Never flying commercial again," Hunter grumbles. Meyer wanted to send us on the jet, but it felt a little extravagant to fly that way when there are flights multiple times a day already in place across the country.

I giggle at him and roll my eyes as I release the death grip I have on his hand. "And here was me thinking I was the princess in this pair."

"Oh you absolutely are, but this heathen has fine taste, and flying commercial isn't something we're doing again. Definitely not economy." He fakes a shudder, making me laugh again. Thankfully, the third seat in our row is empty, so we had a bit more space, but that didn't stop him complaining about the lack of legroom or his ass going numb.

He is definitely a princess.

"If you say so." I remove my belt once the light goes off, and everyone jumps to their feet the minute the plane stops, starting to try and get their luggage, despite the fact that we're probably going to be stuck here for at least another ten minutes. Not that I've flown commercially before. Hell, my time on the jet was my first time flying at all, but I've seen enough tv and movies to know that departing a plane takes forever.

"You ready for tomorrow?" he asks while I stare out of the window into the inky nothingness that is the dead of night outside.

I nod once, still staring out, mostly seeing my own reflection. "I think so. Seeing my parents isn't something I thought I'd do again, but knowing the truth would be nice. I don't have high hopes for them being honest, mind you. Do you think people might ask me about Trent?"

It's the one thing that's been playing on my mind since Hunter suggested this trip. Coming back here, to where the old version of me existed, seeing the people who knew me then... knowing they have no idea who Trent really is, that they might ask where I went or where he is…

"I don't think so," he tells me again. "I told you when you asked the first time that no one has been looking for him. There was a suspension on his file at the station, but it was mostly redacted. I don't know what he got up to before he went looking for you, but whatever it was, I get the feeling his hero helmet was removed."

Nodding, I chew the inside of my cheek as people finally start leaving the plane. He did already tell me that but it's almost impossible to think that someone finally saw the truth about him. Maybe people won't ask about him. Maybe I'll manage to not see anyone who used to know me, or maybe I'll hear what happened here for no one to be looking for him…

The plane is almost empty before Hunter stands and grabs our carry-on luggage. He takes my hand and leads me from the plane. We get through the airport quickly thanks to not having more bags, and before I've even really had a chance to look around, Hunter's got us a cab and is ushering me into it.

The drive to the hotel takes just over an hour. It's more of a motel, really, just on the outskirts of town. By the time we arrive, I'm exhausted. I let out a yawn as we open the door to our room, trying to stifle it because we still haven't eaten.

"Food," I tell him when he looks at me like he's about to demand I sleep. "Then sleep."

"Never would've thought I'd be telling you to sleep when I got you alone in a hotel room, but I guess stranger things could happen." I laugh at him as he drops the two duffel bags onto the bed. "Where are we eating?"

"There's a twenty-four-hour diner about a ten minute walk from here," I tell him. "As long as it hasn't closed down since I left."

I yawn again and he looks a little concerned. "You've been really tired this last week, maybe you should start training and working out less. Sleeping more."

"Pfft," I hiss. "If I take it any easier I'll be dead. It's just been a long day. Apparently, flying takes it out of me."

He quirks a brow at me, but seems to decide to drop it when my stomach grumbles. "Fine, food first, then sleep. I'll play with you delightfully in the morning instead of tonight."

I grin at him, reaching up on tiptoe and kissing his cheek. "Oh, such charming words you weave me. However will my heart cope with such adoration and wonder." Heading out of the room, he swats my ass, laughing when I squeak at the contact.

"Oh, Angel, words aren't the only ways this tongue can charm you. Just you wait."

My hands shake as we pull up beside my childhood house. We picked up my old car from Trent's garage earlier. The upside to his place having been in the middle of nowhere was no one seeing me arrive, use the key under the bush to get inside, or to watch me take my car and leave.

Upside, we have transportation.

Downside, I went back to that house and it's haunted me the entire drive here.

Albeit that's like, forty-five minutes, but it feels a hell of a lot longer.

And now I'm here, where my nightmares began, and I feel about seven years old again. Like I'm going to be in trouble when I walk through that door and the beating might be one that I don't survive. Even though all I ever wanted was love.

To be loved.

To be seen.

To just be happy.

"You ready?" Hunter asks as he shuts off the engine to my crappy old car.

I take a deep breath and open my door. "No, but let's do this anyway." Climbing from the car before I can change my mind, I round the car and walk down the broken path to the front door. Hunter is a step behind me, his hand on my hip as I lift my own to knock on the door.

I hear the shouting before my hand is even back at my side and I wince. All the therapy in the world couldn't have prepared me for coming back here, having this conversation.

The door is wrenched open and I find my dad snarling down at me. His skin is pale, eyes sunken. He looks like he's dying. "What the fuck do you want?"

Hunter tenses beside me, tucking me into his side, protecting me from the man before us.

"Good to see you too," I sigh. "We need to talk."

"Who is it?" I hear my mom screech before she appears behind him. "Oh, it's you."

"We have nothing to say to you," my dad says before

eyeing up Hunter, as if finally realizing he's there.

Hunter straightens and puts a hand on the door as my dad tries to close it. "She said we need to talk, so you're going to invite us in, sit the fuck down, and answer her questions."

My dad startles, like he's not used to anyone speaking to him like that—and I guess he probably isn't. He visibly gulps before shrugging like he's unbothered and walks away from us. My mom is still just standing to the side, watching us.

"You too," Hunter growls at her and she scuttles along after my dad.

Watching them now, it's hard to picture them as they were. So terrifying. The people who were supposed to love me but tormented me instead. The monsters in my nightmares.

It's hard to see them this way and not wonder how I found them so scary, but I know that small me saw them very differently.

They were different.

I guess all of the substance abuse is finally showing on them.

Once we're inside, Hunter closes the door while I look around the sitting room. It hasn't changed. Even the couch is the same threadbare, beat up brown monstrosity that was here the day I left.

"Sit," Hunter barks, and the two of them startle before sitting. He looks over at me, warmth flooding back into his eyes, and I let out a breath. It's the first time I remember feeling entirely safe when someone is noticeably angry. Because I know he's not angry at me. He makes me feel safe.

And that is *everything.*

I pull strength from knowing that he loves me and start with my questions.

"Are you my parents?"

They both look at me like I've lost my mind, then start laughing.

Hunter moves to my side, not blocking me this time, just adding his presence to mine, letting me lean on him. "She asked you a fucking question."

"Pay us," my dad says boldly, jutting out his chin. "I see your fancy clothes. You want answers, we want money."

"Done," Hunter snaps and my mom starts laughing again. "If you don't shut off that fucking barking, I'll break your goddamn jaw. Now answer her."

My mom stops laughing instantly and snarls at me. "No we're not, and thank the fucking lord for that."

Her vitriol is so thick, I swear all of the oxygen is taken from the air. It takes me a second to recover from her truth, but then I ask, "So why do I think you're my parents?"

"Because it was the only way we stayed out of jail,"

my dad says, his hands shaking. I can't tell if it's fear, anger, or withdrawal.

"Explain," Hunter says when I stay quiet, trying to process what that could even mean.

My mom rolls her eyes and stands. "You don't need us both for this."

Hunter glares at her and she stills. "Sit the fuck down or I'll break your legs so you can't stand again."

She drops back to the couch, glaring at me like a petulant toddler having a tantrum.

My dad rubs his hands together, the joy on his face at the thought of getting money obvious enough ro make my stomach roll. "We took you. Your mom had money, we needed money. Except she fell when we were getting out of the house. We ran and didn't look back. When we tried to contact her to give you back and get the money, we were told she died in the fall." My dad pauses, glancing at Hunter before turning his attention back to me. "We were going to just leave you at the station, you were only a small thing, but the sheriff caught us. He worked out what we did and told us the only way to stay out of jail was to get clean and raise you as our own. He checked in almost daily at first, so we had to. He got us your birth certificate, a good fake, good enough to pass, and he made sure we stuck to our part of the deal.

"By the time he passed away, it was too late to just

leave you somewhere, you were older, people knew you were ours, and the sheriff said he'd told someone else what we'd done, that they'd uphold his half of the deal if we didn't keep up with ours. We never knew who, but after he passed, the threat was enough to keep us playing it safe. Then, when we realized whoever knew wasn't coming to check on you, well... the fear was gone. But you were valuable by then. Do you know how many people paid us to watch you just sleep? It's amazing what people will pay for."

My stomach twists and I want to vomit.

I had no idea they did that.

What the actual fuck?

"Then when you got older, you left anyway. When you came back, Trent was with you, and he knew the truth. But he paid us to stay quiet, to leave you alone. Ignore you. Which wasn't exactly hard. We never wanted you here in the first place."

Hunter is practically vibrating with rage beside me, but I have more questions to ask, so I take his hand and open my mouth. "What was my mother's name?"

"Kate something," my mom answers. Disappointment flickers through me, but I push it down, along with every other emotion threatening me right now. Being numb is the only way I'm going to survive this. "Is that it?"

"Do you have the original birth certificate?" Hunter

asks, his voice lower than usual. I guess the anger he's holding back is to blame.

"No," she answers, folding her arms over her chest.

"Where did you take her from?" Hunter continues questioning them while I check out a little.

"A city a few hours from here," she answers.

"No real answers, no fucking money," Hunter snaps at them.

"Fine, fine." My dad answers, but I shut out the rest. I can't do this anymore.

Hunter moving startles me back to reality, and I have no fucking idea what happened but he has my dad by the throat, dangling in the air, and a gun pulled on the woman I thought was my mom.

"Parasites like you don't deserve to have a daughter like her, let alone to keep breathing." His growl is followed by a gunshot and my mom drops to the ground. My dad claws at Hunter's arm, but in his frailty, he's no match for my blond god of a man.

Part of me knows I should be horrified, should react somehow to what's happening. But I don't.

I have nothing but numbness.

They let people watch me while I slept.

"Did you let them do anything but watch?" I croak.

Hunter loosens his grip just enough that my dad can suck in air to answer me. "You'll never know."

His eyes light up with such delight at the thought that that might haunt me, and I'm sure it will, but I know he won't tell me.

"End it," I say to Hunter, my voice empty and hollow.

Another shot echoes before a thud as my dad's body hits the floor too.

Another chapter closed.

For good.

TWENTY THREE

HUNTER

I can't say I pictured disposing of the bodies of the parents of my girl to have ever been a thing I'd do, and yet... here I am at the ass crack of dawn, loading two bodies into the back of their beat up fucking car.

My rage from last night is still simmering beneath the surface, but after everything, my main concern is Quinn. I mean, she's always my main concern, but hearing the shit they told her yesterday…

I slam the trunk closed and tilt my head back. Yeah, they deserved the end they got. If anything, the ending they received was too kind.

Heading back inside the rundown house, trying to push down the anger, I find Quinn in what I assume was her childhood room. It's stark, cold, and everything she isn't. The small bed pushed into one corner of the room. The falling apart dresser beside it, topped with a broken lamp.

"I'm surprised they kept it," she says quietly from where she's sitting on the bed, a stuffed bear with one eye in her hands.

"The bear?"

She laughs once, shaking her head. "The room. The bear. Any of it. You heard them. They didn't want me, they had no choice but to keep me. It's not even surprising that my childhood was so shitty, because they literally didn't give a fuck. I was an extra mouth to feed, a liability that they only kept around so they didn't go to jail... and then to know that Trent basically bought me. Paid them to not ask questions, to disappear... that they didn't give a fuck about why he would do that—"

"They were shitty humans, Quinn, but they weren't your parents. They said they took you from your birth mother, and that she died, that's why they didn't get money from her. That they didn't know who your dad was, but that someone in the local PD worked out who you were and said they needed to raise you right otherwise he'd put them in prison. Whoever that was probably thought they were doing right by you, giving you a family outside of the system." I crouch in front of her, wiping away the tear that spills down her cheek, wanting to wage war for her, despite the fact that all of the people who are responsible for her pain are now dead. "They fucked up, but it sounds like your mom loved you, and would have loved you your whole life if she'd survived. We have a name now, so we can research. Let's get out of here, and when you're ready, we can look into it all. But for now, don't let them take anything else. Not one more day of your life."

"You're right," she says with a sniffle and wipes at her face. I stand up and offer her a hand, which she takes, sucking in a deep breath, then releasing it. When she does, it's like she released more than the breath, she stands taller, head high, more like the Quinn I arrived here with than the one who had her entire life dismantled. Again. "They don't get to take anything else from me. Let's go."

I follow behind her, watching the phoenix rise from the ashes of her life, and I know that I'll follow her anywhere. Once she's outside, I grab the gas cans and walk back through the house, dousing it thoroughly, knowing it's the best way to get rid of it all.

"You take your car back to the hotel, I'll deal with everything else," I tell her once I'm back outside and offer her the pack of matches. "You want to do it?"

She shakes her head and opens the car door. "No, I've already destroyed this place once. You do it."

She gets in and closes the door, not looking back at me once before starting the engine and driving off. Once she turns the corner at the end of the street, I light one of the matches, use it to spark the entire pack, then throw it inside the house, closing the door with my shoe. Once the flames start licking underneath the front door, I start the car and leave, watching the house burn in my rearview.

One thing down. Two more to go.

I didn't want to let Quinn go back to the hotel alone, but there wasn't anyone close enough to here to deal with the cleanup for today so I had little choice. There's already an itch beneath my skin at being separated from her.

Taking a deep breath, I turn the corner and head in the opposite direction than the one Quinn had left in. Now, just to make a call and find the nearest friendly crematorium.

Then I can head back to my girl and make sure she's really okay, because she might be strong, but what she went through today would be an overload for even the strongest of people.

If I could take it all away for her, carry those burdens myself, I'd do it in a heartbeat. Instead, all I can offer her is to be there for her whenever she needs to break, to help her reignite the embers when it's time to revive from the ashes again, and I will.

I'll be anything and everything she ever needs.

Even if it means sacrificing myself.

The drive back home has been pretty quiet. We ended up trading in her car halfway through day one because it crapped out on us. Thankfully, car dealerships are everywhere, and now I got to gift her a new shiny. Even if she didn't want to drive it today. It's day six of the trip back and I'm not surprised she didn't want to drive. It's been a long ass trip and it's obvious she's processing everything that just happened. Finding out the truth, then disposing of the people who not only kidnapped her but then tormented her, her entire childhood... it's a lot to deal with.

I've been trying to give her time to work through it, though her body count is definitely growing these last few weeks. Meyer's Christmas present to her this year was definitely an eye opener, but I also get the feeling that she'd have ended up on this path with or without us eventually.

Though maybe not. Either way, I wouldn't change one thing about her.

Her hand on my thigh steals my attention and I look over at her, finding her watching me as she bites her lip.

"You keep biting that lip and I'm going to pull this car over," I tease, but she trails her fingers up my thigh and her eyes light up.

"Maybe that's what I had in mind."

"Oh, Angel, if you want taking care of, all you have to do is ask." I murmur, scouting out the traffic around us, checking where we are and just how much risk there is if I pull off.

"Maybe I want to take care of you," she responds,

licking her lips, and just like that, I'm hard as a fucking rock. Her fingers trace up to the button of my jeans, popping it open before she slides down my zipper. "I wonder how well you can focus if I do this?"

Her voice is playful and teasing and I am so here for it. Plus, the thought of people being able to see us messing around just does it for me. Always has. The thought takes me back to the first time I had her in that elevator, knowing Rory was watching the camera feed. It just does shit to me that I refuse to ever question.

"I guess we can find out," I moan as she strokes my dick. The upside to rarely wearing underwear. Less barriers for my girl. "Fuck, that feels good."

Her touch is like a whisper against my skin to start with and a shiver runs down my spine.

As her fingers wrap tightly around my dick, I grit my teeth, willing my eyes to stay focused on the road. I'm driving fast and the more she touches me, the harder my foot presses on the accelerator.

Darting my eyes to Quinn, I smirk at her smug grin, like she's got me exactly where she wants me.

"Less posturing, more sucking." I wink when she gasps in mock offense then relax against the seat as her head fits perfectly between my dick and the steering wheel. "That's right, Angel. Make sure I can hear you gagging and keep your ass in the air."

"You're a pervert." She teases but does exactly as I instruct her to do.

"And that's why you love me." I almost run off the road as she moans around my dick, her hot, wet mouth taking me in all the way and bumping against the back of her throat.

My teeth clamp down on my bottom lip as I weave around some two-hundred-year-old grandpa driving forty miles below the speed limit. Yeah, yeah, it's all exaggerated but my brain is uber focused on one thing only: Making Quinn gag on my cock. These fuckwits on the road are only getting in the way of my goal.

Thank fuck they're few and far between.

"Come on, Angel. I know you can do better than that. Take it. Fucking swallow it down, baby girl." Her ass shakes on the seat, making my hand itch to slap it as a little incentive.

And well, I'm not very good with self-control when it comes to Quinn so I reach over, sliding my palm over her spine and landing a quick, hard slap to her right cheek.

The effect is immediate. As Quinn reacts to her spanking, her head jolts forward and my dick pushes just a couple of inches further into her throat.

I barely manage to stay on the road, swerving left then right, both hands on the wheel and my teeth clenched so hard I almost break one.

"Fucking Christ, Angel."

Then she flips me off since her mouth is too full to sass me.

"Awful daring for someone who's choking on a whole lotta cock." Grabbing her hand, I suck her middle finger then bite the tip just as she takes my entire length and makes a gagging sound around my root.

Holy mother of Christ, she was trying to fucking kill us.

Yeah, I'm all about road head but I'd rather survive it. Plus... my turn.

Pulling over on the side of the road, I drive down far enough to be half hidden by the corn stalks but open enough that the danger of being spotted is still there.

Coming to an abrupt stop, I slam my head on the back of the seat as dust and tiny rocks fly all around the car.

When I look down, she's still going to town like we didn't just almost die out there.

But that's fine. We're all good now and before I have my way with her, I want to feel her just one more time.

With one hand on the wheel, I take the other and push her head down all the way, almost losing my ever-loving mind as her saliva drips onto my groin and the tip of my cock chases the deepest recess of her throat.

"Goddamn, Angel. Your mouth is unholy." My fingers curl around her luscious locks as I begin pulling her off.

I'm not fucking coming like this. Quinn always goes first, no matter what.

"Up you go." When she finally faces me again, my dick grows impossibly harder at the sight of her. Hair a tangled mess, mascara running black down her cheeks, and lips so swollen they beg for me to kiss them.

Again, self-control isn't my strong point.

Slamming my lips to hers, I devour her mouth, licking and biting at her until we're both a frenzied mess of lustful arms and legs in the confines of the car.

"Out." Is all I can say once I realize that I love her mouth but I need the taste of her cunt on my tongue and I need it right the fuck now.

"Ooooh, are we being naughty outside?" This girl. Christ, what did I ever do to deserve her? Any of us, really?

"I'm hungry and your pussy is gonna hit the spot." Her uncharacteristic giggle makes my dick twitch again but I ignore it, hellbent on getting her naked on the hood of my car.

I'm in no way delicate with her. Placing her on the hot metal, I bring her mouth to mine and kiss the sass right out of her, all the while unbuttoning her jeans and pushing the offensive material off of her.

"You are not allowed to wear anything but a skirt or a dress. I need easier access than this shit." She laughs and I want to hear that sound for the rest of my life.

I freeze when I reach for her panties.

Pulling back, my eyes drop to the apex of her thighs and my entire body hums with satisfaction.

"Correction. You can only wear skirts and dresses and no more panties." The fact she's gone commando, like I do on most days, fills me with some kind of possessive bug that travels all around my bloodstream. Yeah, the idea of easy access, anytime, anywhere, any way I want is better than any drug invented by man or nature.

She's my favorite addiction and I never want to go to rehab.

Licking my lips, I push Quinn back on my hood and bring my undivided attention to the wet slit between her thighs. I love how she gets herself all worked up by pleasuring me.

Giving me head makes her cunt nice and soaked. What a fucking gift she is to us.

With her legs spread, her heels on the bumper and her elbows propped up so she can watch me, Quinn moans long and hard as I bend down and lick a slow, torturous line from her asshole to the top of her slit and around her clit.

"Fucking delicious. All you, Angel. All fucking you."

Hooking the back of her knees over the inside of my forearms, I lift as high as I can and bury my face in her pussy.

The slurping and moaning and long, drawn out groans are the only sounds around beside the occasional car passing by on the nearby road.

I hope they see me. I hope they know I'm making my girl soar with pleasure. I hope they realize that I'm the luckiest bastard on this fucking planet.

Quinn pulls me in closer as her orgasm begins to build. No longer capable of holding herself up, she lies all the way down, her head against the windshield.

I can't imagine she's all that comfortable but that's a problem for another time because right here and right now, neither one of us gives a shit.

The only important thing is making her come.

And scream.

And lose her goddamn mind.

My nose is pressed against her mound as my tongue searches out every ounce of her cum, seeking out that magical moment where she gets lost to the moment.

"Oh, fuck, Hunter. God, yes. Please, please, please don't sto—"

Pushing two fingers into her tight little cunt as I suck on her clit with one goal in mind, I grin into her as she screams her release. Legs shaking, hips thrusting up, seeking more, wanting everything I can possibly give her, she quickly collapses onto the hood again and gasps for every breath she can get.

Meanwhile, I take my time lapping her up. A languid tongue licking one side, then the other, sucking on her lips and her clit before cleaning up her inner thighs with my tongue.

"Mmm, five star Michelin." Winking at her, I place a tender kiss on her mound and bring my wet fingers to her mouth, silently demanding that she have a taste.

Mouth open, eyes still drunk on her orgasm, she sucks on her fingers and moans like she's eating grade-A Belgian chocolate.

That's how good her pussy tastes.

"That looks painful. We should take care of it." My eyes follow her line of sight and I grin.

"Let's."

Looking around, I think about where I want to fuck her and my gaze lands on an old wooden carriage you'd typically see in a Western movie. With a grin, I carry her to it, loving the fact that from this spot, people driving by can see my ass thrusting, know that I'm fucking like a king, but she'd be protected by me.

Fucking perfect.

Reaching back, I pull my t-shirt up and over my head before placing it on the dusty wood surface. It's not much but it's enough to protect her ass as I pummel her cunt until I come inside her.

The carriage is covered, just like the ones in the

nineteenth century, and when she moans at my fingers prepping her, I hear a faint echo.

Fucking hell, Quinn's orgasm will be in surround sound. What could possibly be better than that?

"I'm getting some interesting role-play ideas right now but I'm too eager to bury my dick inside you to actually play them out." My voice is a deep rumble of want and desire and impatience.

"No time. Just fuck me, already." I flash her a feral grin as I spread her legs wide and in one smooth, unguarded thrust, I bury my cock so deep inside her cunt, I can feel her womb.

"Oh, shit!" I hope people in the next town heard her. Hell, I hope the whole goddamn state heard her. Because I did this. I'm doing this to her, over and over again.

Quinn grabs on to my shoulder with one hand as the other holds her steady at her back, head thrown in lusty abandon, eyes shut and mouth dropped wide open. Every time I bottom out, she expels a gust of breath as though she's no longer in control of her own body.

With nails digging into my skin, I revel in the bite of pain she's gifting me. I wish she'd dig deeper, make me bleed from her pleasure.

"Fucking give it to me, Quinn." I pound her pussy in a brutal rhythm, in and out, slamming her across the surface as she scrambles to keep up with my need.

"I... oh, God... I…" I love hearing her barely coherent. Fuck, what am I saying? She can't line up two words and that thought makes me the happiest I've been.

Reaching out, I grab her roughly by the hair and slam my mouth against her, lips and teeth colliding as I continue to fuck the breath right out of her.

The movements of my tongue match those of my dick; powerful thrusts that say everything I can't with words.

You're gorgeous.

You're mine.

You're every fucking thing in this world.

Mostly, they say, "Come for me, Angel."

Just as I bottom out and grind my root against her soaked little cunt, she explodes all over again. Her cries bounce off the hard surfaces of the carriage, piercing through the ringing in my ears caused by my own damn orgasm.

I come so hard, I can feel every spurt as it fills her up, threatening to spill out as I continue fucking her, unable to stop. Not wanting to stop... ever.

"Hunter…" My name is just a breath but it says everything I've ever wanted to hear.

"Me too, Angel."

We've been back on the road for a few hours now, and my girl is asleep in the back of the car. I've got one earbud in so that she can sleep while I listen to music, but I can still hear her if she needs anything.

My phone rings, and when I see Meyer's name on the screen, I answer, double checking it goes straight to my earbud. "What's up, Meyer?"

"How is she?" he asks, and the echo lets me know I'm on loud speaker. I'm guessing Rory is with him. I know neither of them wanted to stay behind, but since Meyer got the call from Edward Riley about us and the Knights, he had to stay back, and it made sense for Rory to go with him.

"She's... devastated but she's okay. This is going to take a minute to come back from, but she will." I explain almost everything that's happened since we got here, ignoring the litany of curses that spew from them both. "There's something else... I don't think she noticed, so I haven't said anything. But I think... you remember Tommy's sister, Katherine? How she died?"

"Hard to forget a mom breaking her neck trying to save her kid," Meyer utters.

I glance in the back, making sure she's still asleep. I haven't said anything because I didn't want to let her know until we can confirm it, but my stomach has been in knots for days keeping it from her. "Yeah, well, I think... I think

Quinn might have been that kid."

"What?" They shout down the phone, and I explain further.

"Let's just try and look into it, and keep it to ourselves until we know."

"Fuck," Meyer grunts.

"I know…" I pause because she groans in the backseat, and I hope to God she's actually asleep still. Wanting to change the subject just in case, I ask, "What happened with Edward?"

"He won't agree to whatever terms Tommy had in place. They want this city, and they want it bad." Meyer grunts, his dissatisfaction at how their meeting went is palpable. "His terms are basically shit or get off the pot."

"So why don't we?" I ask, smiling to myself. "I thought that a few months back, when he first showed up."

"What do you mean?" Meyer asks and I roll my eyes.

"I mean, why are we still doing this? We have money, we have more of it than we could ever need. We have houses and investments and well, we have a lot. But most importantly, we have Quinn now. Why don't we cut our ties, hand it over, and get the fuck out. Why would we keep risking ourselves, our family, risking her, if we have an option?"

Silence meets me when I finish speaking, but I know he's processing. His family built this life for us over the course of generations. It's all any of us have ever really known.

"We could keep HellScape, have something legit, but hand over the rest. Do you really want to keep living this life? Have your kids live this life?"

"I hadn't really ever thought of it. There wasn't any other option." Meyer's tone is thoughtful, like he might actually be considering my idea.

Who would've thought it? Maybe I am an ideas guy after all.

"Well, maybe there is now," Rory says, but I can't tell if he thinks it's a good idea or not.

Quinn stirs in the back seat and I glance back at her before looking back to the road. "I think Quinn is waking up, so I'm going to go. We'll be back tonight, so talk it out more then?"

"Sure thing," Meyer says and I end the call just as I see her stretching out in the back seat.

"Morning sunshine," I coo with a grin and she yawns before sitting up and leaning forward between the front seats.

"Wow, I've been asleep a while."

"Yeah, but what can I say? I exhausted you." The grin on my face is wide as I think back to being inside of her just a few hours ago.

"So full of yourself," she mutters.

"I think it was you that was full of me," I tease, and my heart does that pitter patter thing when she laughs.

It's the second laugh I've heard since the day with her parents, the first was mid-teasing, so it didn't count. I was starting to worry. But this laugh, this is my Quinn. My angel. My phoenix.

"How long till we're home?" she asks as she climbs through to the front seat like a feral little gremlin. I tut as she gets comfy before pulling her seatbelt on.

"A few hours, and don't do that again," I demand, and she sticks her tongue out.

"Yes sir," she says with a salute. "You sound like Meyer."

"Well maybe you sass him less," I tease and she grins, shaking her head.

"Not a chance."

Her stomach growls and my smile drops to a frown. "I need to feed you."

"I'm fine," she argues, but I shake my head.

"You need to eat, so you're going to eat. Pull up the maps and find the nearest diner." She does as she's told and puts the location into my phone, rerouting the GPS. "There's a good girl."

I wink at her and her cheeks spill red.

Oh yeah, that's a look I love on her.

And one I intend on seeing again and again.

TWENTY FOUR

QUINN
NINE MONTHS LATER

Life being this way was something I never thought possible. When I look back over the last few years of my life, I realize Tommy saved me, time and time again. He continues to save me every single day. And that's exactly why I'm adding this ink to my skin.

This buzz of the tattoo gun as I lie back and let the artist paint on my skin is something I've missed. When I first started decorating my body, it was to hide the parts of my past I didn't want people to see. I remember Tommy's disapproving gaze when I told him my why. He didn't think I should hide the parts that made me who I was, but he never stopped me. He even helped me pick out a few designs that I tweaked to make more me.

Then it turned into a sort of therapy. The scratch of the needle a nice kind of pain that helped not only hide my past, but quieted my thoughts.

It's been too long since my last, and I'm fairly certain that the guys are a little miffed that Tommy will grace my skin permanently before they do, but I also know they understand.

The sword wrapped in sunflowers that will grace my thigh is everything Tommy is to me: the strength, the hope, the loyalty, the resilience. All things he gave me, all things he just was. And he'd probably call me soppy if he knew what I was doing, but he'd also have that light of pride in his eyes.

If I close mine, I can see that look clearly and it makes me smile.

A smile that, a few months ago, I didn't know if I'd have again.

After everything with Trent and the people I thought were my parents, I broke. The pain of losing Tommy hit me like a ton of bricks all over again, because he was the best dad I could have ever hoped for, and Trent took that from me. Just like the people who called themselves my parents took my mom from me.

They took Tommy from me too.

Finding that out stole the breath from my lungs.

He was my uncle.

Truly my blood.

I actually had family who cared for me, even if I didn't

know it in the time we had together. Hell I didn't even know he had a sister, but I guess I understand why he didn't talk about his family. Losing people, reliving that... it hurts.

Even when you talk about the good times. It still hurts, just in that bittersweet kind of way.

I've seen pictures now, Rory helped me go through the storage container we discovered Tommy had... in my freaking name. The little sneak. But it was full of so much stuff that reminded me of him, and so much more that taught me things about him I never knew.

And the photo albums…

So. Many. Photos. The man was a hoarder, he just hid it well, apparently.

"Alright, darlin', you're all done. Go take a look in the mirror then we'll wrap it up." The guy's southern drawl reminds me of Denton, that poor sweet baby angel of a lawyer. Which reminds me, I owe him a drink... and a free pass for him and his buddy to the basement.

Might just ask Hunter about that, I already know Meyer is not the man to ask. Especially since HellScape is his last true business baby now. The Knights... well, I'm still a little fuzzy on all of the details, but the guys are, mostly, legit now. It's been a bit of an adjustment for them all, and it's not like we don't still basically have an army back at the compound... but it's a smaller army. Meyer insisted that they still have enemies, so security is still a must. Plus, it's not like they haven't dived into a dozen other ventures still.

Turns out I'm not the only one who gets bored of sitting around.

I hop off the table and head over to the mirror. The smile stretching my face almost hurts as I take in the beauty of the new ink on my leg.

Tommy.

I contemplated adding his name to the hilt, but I can visualize his eye roll, which is why I decided against it.

The guy washes down the skin to get rid of the rest of the trace, then wraps it and sends me on my way. The spring afternoon is cold, but the sun is shining and there isn't a cloud in sight.

"All done?" Bruno asks, and I hug him tight. He's kinda gotten used to my pounce hugs lately. I was never really a hugger before, but lately... well, life is too short and you never know what's around the corner. So now I am totally a hugger... well, sometimes.

"All done," I say, my grin still wide when I release him. "Let's go home and get ready for this party. The thought of the guys in suits for karaoke, it's giving me life."

"I still don't know how you persuaded them to do it." I wink at him and he barks out a laugh. "Actually, I don't want to know. But I am glad we got out of the house today.

Shae was in party planner nightmare mode. Tonio has been bitching in my ear about it all afternoon."

I let out a cackle as he opens the car door for me. "You and me both, buddy. Why do you think I booked my tattoo for today? I knew Hurricane Shae would show up. I almost feel bad for volunteering Tina, Yen, and the girls to help her."

"I knew there was a reason I liked you," he teases before closing the door and climbing into the driver's seat.

"Eddie." I stop him with a hand on his shoulder before he can start the car and he must hear the seriousness in my voice because he doesn't even try to ignore me, just turns as far as he can in his seat and waits for me to continue.

"I've spent a lot of time thinking about Tommy lately, the ink today is probably proof enough of that, but I've wanted to do something to carry on his legacy, you know? Keep saving people from futures they might not have a say in."

I lick my lips, suddenly nervous as his stare bores into me, then rush through the rest of my words before I can chicken out and do it via text or something lame. "I set up a trust fund for your girls as soon as they got their acceptance letters. Tuition and housing will be paid in full as long as they maintain their grades. They deserve a brighter future and just because they don't need saving from monsters doesn't mean they don't deserve help with achieving their dreams."

The shock that flashes across his face is almost as shocking to me as the news must have been to him. But then his eyes glass over and I can see the tears collecting in their ducts.

"Oh, don't cry, Bruno. If you cry then I'm gonna cry and we won't get *anything* done."

He clears his throat and wipes away the single tear that manages to escape.

"Thank you, Quinn. I think Tommy would be proud of the way you've managed to keep your heart with you through everything. You're too good for this world."

I smile and nod, brushing away my own tears as he turns around and starts the car, pulling away from the curb and into traffic.

"So, is now a good time to tell you that I also bought you and Other Bruno a twelve-day cruise in the Bahamas and got your time off approved by Meyer?"

We almost sideswipe the car next to us when he whips his head around to glare at me.

"Eyes on the road, big guy! You can yell at me when we get home!"

Oh yeah, these last few years might have been a lot to overcome, but now I'm looking forward, and I know the fun is only just about to begin.

The house is almost unrecognizable as I stare out over the bannister into the abyss of party land. There are balloons and streamers and just stuff everywhere. It seems the entire Marino clan was invited, despite the fact I've hardly met any of these people, and the last time everyone was here... well, just no. Not going there. Not today.

The bass from what I think is a DJ set up in the family room makes my heart almost vibrate as I descend into the party madness.

My shimmering black mermaid dress, a gift from Meyer, clings to my body like a second skin. Between that, the red soled shoes from Hunter, and the choker from Rory that hugs my throat and trails down my back, I feel like a princess.

"Stunning," Rory groans in my ear as he presses up against my back. I swear, I don't even startle these days. I'm almost used to them just randomly pouncing on me in the house. He pulls me up against him, his hardness pressing into my ass, and I bite my lip.

Tipping my head back to rest on his shoulder, I kiss his neck, nipping at him just to tease him right back. "This is going to be a long night if you're starting this right now," I murmur, and his hands tighten their grip on my hips as he lets out a soft groan.

"Oh yeah, one very long night. Unless I can steal you away now."

A zip of thrill runs down my spine, but before I can agree to his temptation, I hear my name being called.

"Quinn Summers, don't you dare do what I think you're going to do!" Shae's voice reaches me seconds before she does, and then she's pulling me from Rory's grasp. She turns to him and wags her finger. "Absolutely not, little lion. My mama wants a dance, and well, you're not kidnapping the birthday girl. Not yet anyway. There are people to see, gifts to open, music to be danced to, and songs to sing."

He pouts at her and a giggle falls from my lips. "Do not call me little lion, you freaking nightmare. And don't steal her all night. I want at least one dance."

"I won't be that selfish," Shae retorts, sticking out her tongue at him before tugging on my hand that she's not yet released and pulling me into the family room. I get a glimpse of the dining room, where there's a full bar set up, the DJ, and tables of food galore.

In the family room, there's another bar, a dozen speakers, and a gift table that makes my eyes water. "That's not all for me right?"

"You are the biggest joy kill ever. It's your birthday, people love you, let them freaking show that," she chastises, but then hugs me. "We love you, this is how we love. You're going to have to get used to it one day, because I don't know if you've noticed, but not one of those boys is ever going to let you go."

I follow where she motions to and see all three of my guys standing together by the bar. Meyer in a full tux, bowtie and all—be still my beating heart. Hunter is in a suit, with a tie that he's already fucking around with, so I'll be amazed if it lasts even an hour, and Rory in his shirt and dress pants.

It's enough to make a girl pant.

But she's right, I might have noticed that they're kind of attached to me. Which is good, considering I'm kind of attached to the goofballs too. I'm not sure how the four of us will work in the long run, but I'm willing to find out. Love isn't something I thought I'd ever experience, but those three show me each and every day just what love is.

"Okay, enough of the soppy shit. Time for cocktails, shots, and dancing. And if you think I'm not getting you on the karaoke machine tonight, you, my friend, are delusional."

I groan at the giant smile on her face, but it's half-hearted. I love that I have Shae too. Having a friend like her, a sister, is more than I ever pictured. She always shows up for me and I'm grateful for her every day. Even if she is trying to get me a hangover for my birthday.

We head to the bigger bar, away from my guys, and find Tina, Yen, and the girls already waiting, cocktails in hand and a tray of shots already poured for us.

I guess I'm doing this.

I take the shots offered, throw them back, my face scrunching up from the sour lemon liquor, then take the cocktail, relieved by the fruity goodness. I have no idea what it is, but it tastes just like juice. This shit is going to be dangerous.

The night passes in a blur of dancing, laughing, singing so terribly I'm pretty sure the DJ turned off my mic, and welcoming in the next chapter of my life surrounded by love and joy.

I'm not sure I ever dared to dream that this would be how my life looked, but I'm going to cling to it with both hands.

"You can run away now," Shae murmurs as I droop against the bar. She motions to my guys, who I've seen on and off all night, and I grin. "Happy Birthday, Quinny."

"Thank you Shae, for the best birthday a girl could have asked for." I kiss her cheek, hug her, then almost sprint away from her, which is no feat in these heels. Her laughter follows along behind me as I fall into Hunter, who is waiting to catch me.

This might just have been the best birthday I've ever had. Not that the Halloween party vibes last year weren't awesome, but today was my big 3-0, and everyone went all out. I don't think watching Meyer croon some Michael Bublé while in a tux, his bowtie undone and a drink in his hand, is something I will ever forget.

But now... now I want them to myself. All of them.

I lean forward, the heels giving me height enough that I can whisper straight into his ear. "Let's get out of here."

When we reach Meyer's office, the music finally dampened, voices trail through the halls as Shae gets everyone out to the cars to be taken either home or to their hotels.

I close the door behind me, watching the three of them as they cross the room, and smile softly.

This really is the best birthday ever. Now... if I can just…

Toeing off my heels, I pull my hair around my neck and call out, "Will someone please unzip me?"

I feel all three sets of eyes on me and I don't know if it's the copious amount of bubbles I've drank tonight, general frivolity, or just me being playful and greedy, but the words fall from my lips regardless. "Then how about one last gift to me?"

Hunter is on me first, his lips graze the nape of my neck before his hands clasp my waist. "If we can give it,

Angel, it's yours."

He handles my zipper like a pro, lowering it until he hisses as the top of my lacy black thong appears.

"What is your request, Kitten?" Meyer asks, his voice low and rough. I turn my head to look at him over my shoulder, my bare back still on show. His eyes darken as he takes in the freshly-inked skin—yet another gift—and a smile tugs at my lips.

I glance at Rory, but I already know he and Hunter will be on board. Meyer is the one who may require... finesse. Locking my gaze back on the man in question, I lick my lips before biting down on the lower one and letting my dress fall to my feet.

"All of you."

"So in," Hunter practically whoops, and I can't help the small laugh that falls from me. Rory stays quiet, but Meyer watches me like a predator assessing his prey.

"All of us?" he asks, his voice a low growl that sends a shiver down my spine. His watching gaze is so intense that I feel like I might shatter from that alone. "You think you could handle that?"

I nod once, laid bare before them in his office, the fire crackling the only noise in the room as I practically hold my breath, waiting to see if I'll be denied.

Meyer releases me from his gaze and looks to Rory, who nods, and my heart picks up speed.

This might actually happen.

It's something I've thought about. Often. But Meyer has always kept me to himself. Never joined in the fun with the others.

Which is totally fine, and if he doesn't want to, then we tap out. Totally fine.

But the thought of being manhandled by all three of them.

At once.

Fuck me, I am so wet just thinking about it.

Again.

He turns his attention back to me and starts to unbutton his shirt. "Well then, I guess your birthday request is to be granted."

My mouth drops open and my nipples tingle with anticipation as his answer begins to sink in.

I barely register Hunter's "Fuck yeah" that whispers across my neck right before he plants a kiss to my pulse point.

"But I have conditions." And... reality slaps me in the face.

"Of course you do." The sass comes from Rory, who's already chucking off his suit jacket and popping off two buttons from his crisp white shirt.

Maybe I'm pushing him too far. Maybe he's not into this. Maybe I should just forget about it. After all, it's not like my body isn't being beautifully slaughtered on the regular.

"We don't have to if you don't—" My words are cut off by Hunter's sudden fist in my hair and his lips at my ear.

"Don't do that. Don't sound defeated, or worse... insecure. Let the man lay out his conditions." He chuckles as he takes my earlobe into his mouth and bites hard enough to make the walls of my pussy clench in immediate reaction. "I have a feeling this is going to be interesting."

It's no surprise that Hunter is all for it. Hell, he's probably hard as a rock just thinking about watching us, watching me getting my pussy pounded like the precious whore I want to be in the bedroom.

"One: I'm in charge." At Meyer's commanding voice, I roll my eyes just as Rory pipes up.

"Shocker."

Hunter laughs at Rory's word, probably because we're all thinking it.

When my eyes dart to Meyer, I smirk at the narrowed glare he sends his best friend, who's kicking off his shoes as he stands near the crackling fireplace.

"Two: for every one of our orgasms, she gets two." Meyers throws me a pointed stare, a smug smirk firmly planted on his lips.

"But that's impossible!" I mean... it could happen?

Maybe? But only if they come once each.

Meyer just ignores my protest and continues.

"Three: no sass from you." I almost roll my eyes again but catch myself at the last second. I'd hate for this to end before it even begins just because I can't follow instructions.

"Done, done, and done. Let's get naked." I giggle at Rory, who's practically naked save for his slacks that he's unzipped with his hard-as-fuck cock peeking out of his boxer shorts. Jesus, he's motivated.

"I have a request." This comes from Hunter, who is now unbuttoning his shirt with his heated gaze piercing me.

"Oh, for fuck's sake. Can't we all just fuck and leave the talking for the pillow later?" Again, Rory.

Hunter ignores him and just continues. "I want to watch you both fuck her first. Get myself nice and ready for the grand finale." I frown at his words, turning to face him and not bothering to hide my practically-naked form.

"Grand finale? What am I, a circus show?" There's absolutely no venom behind my words but I think I'm getting all my sass out before we begin and, technically, it's aimed at Hunter so I don't think that counts.

"Ah ah... the man said no attitude and it's barely been five seconds, Angel." Hunter's wink only makes me chuckle, but when my eyes dart to Meyer, the heat that flares in his irises has my skin heating instantly.

So here we are in varying states of undress as Meyer takes a seat on one of the big chairs, Rory standing by the fireplace, with Hunter making himself comfortable on the other chair.

"Rory. Get our girl nice and ready for our cocks."

And so it begins.

"My pleasure." Rory doesn't walk over to me, he stalks me. His eyes are consumed with lust, hooded and bright, nostrils flaring as he runs his tongue from one corner of his mouth to the other before sinking his teeth into the plump flesh. "I do love first dibs."

These guys with their stupid metaphors. All thoughts fly out of my mind as his arm flies out and his hand wraps around my throat, pulling me close to his face.

He doesn't kiss me right away, his breath fanning across my nose and mouth as the pads of his fingers squeeze just a tad more.

It's only when Meyer speaks that I realize why he's just standing there.

"Kiss her." Meyer's words are calculated, almost detached, but when I slice a glance to the side, I see him getting comfortable on the chair, his legs spread wide and his jaw clenched tight. The perfect vision of control.

I don't have time to analyze anything else because Rory's mouth is suddenly on mine, his tongue invading every inch as he takes his time scrambling my brain with his talent.

When I reach out to bury my hands in his hair, his hand squeezes even tighter, his hard cock pressing against my belly.

The rustling of fabric is a distant sound but I'm guessing Hunter or Meyer or, hell, both are getting rid of one or more layers of clothing. Rory continues his assault on my mouth and we're all teeth and tongue and sucking lips as he briefly cuts off my air supply until I sense my consciousness beginning to wane.

Just when I think I'm going to pass out, he releases my throat, never stopping his all-consuming kiss throughout my gasp and need to inhale oxygen. It's like he doesn't even notice, which isn't even possible.

"Stop." At Meyer's command, Rory groans out his protest but ends the kiss with a scrape of his teeth over my bottom lip. "Kitten. Sit on the coffee table and show me how wet you are." I blink at his command but do as he says, taking the two steps to the other side of the table and sitting as I face both Meyer and Hunter while Rory stays planted right behind me.

"Spread." Again, I follow Meyer's command, my eyes dissecting his every reaction. I think on some level I'm afraid he's not going to enjoy this, that he's going to stop everything because the thought of sharing me drives him to the wrong side of sanity. Except, when his eyes drop to my pussy, his tongue darts out and his lips curl at the corners. "My pretty little kitten is soaked." Meyer lifts his gaze from my panty-clad pussy and looks behind me at Rory. "Eat her cunt. I want her dripping."

The familiar jolt of lust that whips through my body at his words has my thighs aching to close so I can get a little relief. At Meyer's clicking tongue, I know he's two steps ahead of me and I have a feeling he wouldn't be disappointed to dole out a little punishment with my orgasms.

With my eyes fixed on Meyer, I lean back on the coffee table enough to give Rory the space he needs to carry out Meyer's commands.

"You seeing this, Hunter? Just the thought of my mouth on her has her primed for a good fucking." My smile is automatic at Rory's crude words. In another lifetime, I would have been offended by his nonchalance, but being with these men has taught me a lot about myself. Namely, this. I fucking love being the center of their lustful fantasies and knowing they will always come true.

"Yeah, I see it, but what I don't see is you tongue fucking her yet." Hunter winks at me and I stifle a laugh as Rory raises his middle finger at Hunter, eyes on me the whole time, before taking said finger and pushing it slowly inside my pussy.

Lowering his head, he flicks out his tongue and teases my clit, all the while turning his finger, fucking me slowly as he gets my blood roaring with need.

My hips are searching out the more he won't give me. The more I seek him out, the less he gives and the more I want. It's a vicious game they play, and although I always lose the battle, the ultimate goal is to win the fucking war. And that, I do... every single time I come.

From the corner of my eye I see Hunter readjusting himself then spreading the lapels of his slacks before palming his cock from root to tip, his thumb circling the slit. My mouth waters at the sight but the sudden pinch at my clit brings my attention fully back to Rory.

"Eyes on me, baby." It takes effort to drag my gaze away from the perfection that is Hunter but Rory won't stop at just biting down on my clit. Besides, I begged for this so I need to evenly distribute my attention to the three of them.

When Rory's tongue licks down my swollen lips all the way to the rosebud of my ass, a shiver runs across every nerve ending in my body.

My eyes fall shut, my mouth pops open and my muscles give out just enough to help me relax into this oddly comfortable position.

Without much thought, I extend my hand, wanting to grab on to Rory and maybe grind my pussy harder into his mouth when I feel a prickle of awareness a half second before lips capture my own. My hand falls back to my side as my entire body melts into the new touch.

It's an upside down kiss, not unlike Spiderman, except for the fist in my hair and the sharp nip of teeth into my bottom lip.

I don't need to open my eyes to know it's Meyer. His scent was the easiest clue I could get.

The crackling sounds from the fireplace are fused with the erotic sounds of sucking and moaning. The fact I'm getting tongue fucked at both ends of my body is making me burn from the inside out.

What the fuck is going to happen when Hunter joins in?

Meyer's fingers tighten in my hair, forcing me to concentrate on him, on them.

The sensation has my body tensing with the familiar feelings of an impending orgasm.

I'm chasing it, riding Rory's face like my life depends on it, needing that extra push to get me to the other side. When Rory thrusts two thick fingers inside me, it's like he's reading my mind. And when he sucks on my clit just as his fingers curl inward and rub against that sweet, sweet spot, I lose all pretense of control.

Screaming, I realize my sounds are muted and remember Meyer is still kissing me, now swallowing every sound that Rory is forcing out of me.

"How wet is she?" Meyer's lips are brushing against mine as he speaks, his breath fanning across my entire face and cooling my burning skin.

"Enough that I can drink her up." Rory's eyes are fixed on me as he answers, his face wet from my cum and lips swollen from relentlessly sucking on me.

"Suck on his fingers, Quinn, like a good little kitten." I'm panting, my lids heavy from what just tore through my body, but I obey, letting my mouth drop open for Rory.

"That's it." Rory's not gentle as he roughly pushes his fingers inside my mouth while Meyer continues to hold my head, his face above me, looking down like the god of chaos. Closing my lips around Rory's fingers, I keep my gaze locked on Meyer as I curl my tongue around those two digits, following his orders. Irises swimming in lust so unhinged dart between my mouth and my eyes and I don't know how he's keeping his control under wraps.

"Hunter, come here and hold her head." In this position, all I can see is Meyer looming over me, but seconds later, Hunter is by my side, kneeling, with his lips to my cheek and his fingers replacing Meyer's. "Open wide, Kitten. Time to suck my dick with the taste of your pussy on your tongue."

I barely have time to register this twist of events before Hunter pulls hard at the back of my head, and from the other side, Meyer buries his cock in my mouth.

"You look majestic with your mouth full of cock, Angel. So, so pretty," Hunter coos in my ear while I'm trying really hard not to choke on Meyer, whose thrusts are nothing if not brutal.

With my eyes wide open, I keep my hazy, watery gaze on Meyer's larger-than-life frame.

He always commands a room, but right here, standing tall above me with his cock going deeper and deeper inside my throat, he's just more... Larger than anything I know.

I'm so consumed by his presence that I don't realize until it's too late that Rory's not sitting back watching. He's been preparing, waiting for the perfect timing, calculating the exact moment that would…

"Oh, fuck yeah!" Meyer's cock pushes all the way down to the entrance of my throat as Rory thrusts his cock deep inside my pussy. I'm not sure who's moaning at this point— I'm too concentrated on not suffocating—but I know Rory has just vocalized his pleasure.

"Breathe through your nose, Angel." Hunter speaks to me but it's Meyer I'm watching. It's like he's trying his best not to hurt me all the while wanting to destroy every inch of me.

One breath.

Tears fall at the corners of my eyes but Hunter catches the ones on his side with the tip of his tongue.

Two breaths.

Rory is pounding my pussy like he's trying to open the gates of Hell and claim the throne.

Three breaths.

Meyers places one hand on the top of my head, the other at my chin, and pushes his cock impossibly deeper until my nose is buried in his groin and all I can smell is the male alpha that he is. Primal and commanding. And all fucking mine.

"Gooddamn, Angel, watching you being used like this, knowing you're loving every fucking second of it? Fuck." I can't see Hunter but his breaths at my ear are getting choppier, the tell-tale sound of his hand on his cock is like music, one of three instruments in this erotic symphony we're creating.

It's too much. Too much pain and too much pleasure. Too much physical and emotional stimulation and my body is primed just like they knew it would be.

The power behind my orgasm takes me by surprise. Choking and gagging, I thrash against someone's hand on my stomach keeping me still as I lose my ability to breathe, to see, to move. It only heightens the sensations barreling through my body as Rory continues to fuck all sense out of me and Meyer cuts off all means for me to take in air.

Just when I think I'm about to pass the fuck out, something uncontrollable happens and I'm almost mortified thinking I've lost control of my bodily functions. But then Rory has his mouth back at my pussy, drinking me in like I'm his first drop of water after a marathon in a desert.

"Fucking hell, that's... fuck, I'm gonna come." Somewhere in the haze of it all, I hear Hunter speak just before hot, thick spurts of liquid fall on my stomach and my tits as hands rub and squeeze and pinch at my nipples.

Meyer pulls out just the slightest before he comes straight down my throat, his spurts hitting the back of my mouth with every grunt.

"Motherfucker, that was too hot to resist." Rory calls out before he buries himself back inside and comes long and hard.

I cough, all the while trying to gulp in as much air as possible, when Hunter helps to lift me back up to a complete sitting position.

"You were absolutely gorgeous." I look to Rory and frown.

"Did I just..?" Looking pointedly at my pussy then back up at him.

"Oh, pretty baby, you squirted for me and it was fucking epic."

Well, hell yes... we can definitely do that again.

TWENTY FIVE

MEYER

Never in a million years did I think I'd be capable of watching the woman I love being touched and fucked and cared for by anyone other than me. It's one thing to know I'm sharing her outside of my bedroom, it's a completely different monster to witness it.

Except watching her at the height of her pleasure is nothing less than extraordinary and, in any case, I cannot deny her a damn thing.

So, here I am, watching her lose her fucking mind from not only me slamming my dick down her throat, but from Rory pressing down on her lower abdomen and making sure she squirts right into his mouth.

It was impossible not to come. More than that, I didn't want to hold back. As it stands, my little kitten has our cum on her and in her and, to my utter surprise, that thought keeps me hard as a fucking two-by-four.

"Hunter, move the table and set us up in front of the fireplace. Blankets and pillows are in the hall closet." Hunter doesn't hesitate at my words as Rory places a tender bite onto Quinn's inner thigh like he's marking his territory, earning him a growl from me. His responding chuckle only makes me want to punch him in the throat, but this is about Quinn, not me.

Lifting her into my arms, I cradle her naked body into my chest and kiss her on the top of her head, murmuring, "You're such a good girl, Kitten. So pliable and responsive. You please us every time you come for us." She mewls, the tiny sound penetrating the titanium wall I have surrounding my heart. Only she can affect me like this. Only Quinn.

Rory has dropped all pretenses, ridding himself of every stitch of clothing as Hunter returns with arms full of blankets and pillows he's arranging around the fire. Not too close that we burn but not far enough for the cold to touch us.

"Come, little kitten, let's see how many more orgasms we can pull from you."

As I take the three steps to our makeshift bed, Hunter shucks off his own clothing and lies down on the comforter, arms wide open and ready for Quinn. There's a moment of hesitation for me. A slight second where I don't want to hand her over, my mind screaming *mine, mine, mine*. Until I remember that this isn't about me. This is what she wants.

Kneeling with her in my arms, I settle her down with Hunter and watch as Rory licks his lips like the calculating psychopath he is. Eyes dart from Quinn to the fire and back to Quinn as his hand goes back to his cock, and just like that, this motherfucker is hard all over again.

I'm almost afraid to ask what's going through his mind.

"I don't think I like that look on your face, Rory." I sit on the big chair facing the fire and spread my legs as Quinn's color returns to her cheeks and her body begins to rub up against Hunter's naked form. He's kissing her neck and collarbone, his hands roaming up and down her back and ass, pausing only to dip his fingers into her pussy before roaming back up to her long dark hair.

Fuck, I'm so hard.

"Quinn. Come here, Kitten. Crawl to me." Fuck, she doesn't even hesitate, her body following my orders like I'm the master pulling her strings and she's my good little puppet.

When she reaches me, I pat my lap and turn her around so she's facing the others, her pussy sliding down my cock like it's finally coming home.

"Now, I think Rory and Hunter need their cocks sucked." Kneeling in a reverse cowgirl position, her folded legs aligned with my thighs, I hold her steady as she reaches out and takes both their cocks in her hands.

I lead the rhythm, pulling her up and down my dick

and watching her press both their cocks together, licking the tip and moaning at the taste of them.

I'm surprised by how fucking hot I find it. Her pleasing other men but still belonging to me, taking pleasure from me. Allowing me to own her body while she pleases my best friends.

Fuck, her pussy is like velvet, warm and wet, taking me so deep every time I bottom out.

Rory's hand goes to her head, his fingers digging into her scalp as he guides her, pushing her to take him deeper into her mouth.

"My turn." Hunter's cock is now in her mouth and she's moaning around his length while her hand is jacking off Rory's dick.

"Fuck, she feels so goddamn good," comes from Hunter, who locks eyes with me and I can see he's about to come again.

I reach around and pinch Quinn's little clit, my arm a tight band around her waist as I start to pound harder and harder into her.

The guys pull out of her mouth, she's unable to suck their cocks at this point and it's time for her to come so we can take this to the next level.

"Come on, little Angel, show us how beautiful you are when you come." Hunter and Rory kneel at her feet, hands and mouths at her tits, driving her insane while ripping another orgasm right out of her.

Pulling her down onto my cock, I tighten my hold on her as her head falls back onto my shoulder and her cries of pleasure drown out the crackling of the fire and the heavy sounds of our breaths.

"Fuck yeah." Rory's two words are reverent, like watching her come undone is the most fascinating thing he's ever seen. And it is. Quinn letting go is never less than majestic.

"Get the lube." I call out as I get up and bring Quinn with me to the bed area.

I don't have to tell Rory twice. He's up and heading for the desk where we always keep a bottle and to-go packets—just in case—before he joins us on the floor.

"You think you can handle us, Kitten? All of us?" I've got the bottle in hand, popping the top as we get into position.

We each take turns lubing her up, rubbing the thick oily matter all over her cunt, her ass, her tits, and our cocks. For what I have planned, there is no such thing as too much lubrication.

Once I'm satisfied that she's as slippery as she'll ever be, I lay her down on top of me, my cock easily sliding inside her cunt, her tits full and ready for my mouth.

Rory and Hunter kneel behind her, their legs straddling mine as they begin to push their fingers inside her, stretching her ass to fit them.

Her mouth comes down onto mine, kissing me with energy I didn't think she could still have in her, but my little kitten has resources to spare and we're the lucky bastards that get to take advantage of it.

"Fuck, she's tight." Quinn moans at Hunter's words while I slowly fuck her pussy in and out, adding her cum to the lubricant we'd spread all over her.

We're all slippery and sliding skin-on-skin as Hunter pushes his cock inside her ass, earning us all a groan. She's suddenly so tight it's bordering on painful. She's lucky I have a high tolerance for it.

"Goddamn, she's sucking my cock inside her, fuck." I can feel Hunter pulling out, relieving some of the tightness as Rory walks around, eager to get his dick wet with her mouth.

The fire bathes us in its heat, adding sweat to our already slippery bodies as I pinch and bite her nipples. My dick bottoms out every time Hunter pulls out until we find a rhythm that has her writhing in our grasps.

When Rory wraps his hand around her throat and presses hard enough on her pulse points to have her choke on a moan, I can feel her cunt squeezing my dick to almost painful degrees.

"Fuuuuuuuuuck." Hunter's head falls back and I know he's feeling her muscles contracting, too.

"Be a good little girl and suck my dick, baby." Rory slides his hand to the back of her neck and pushes her mouth onto his cock, fucking her face in time with our thrusts.

It's all wet sounds and grunts, the thick scent of sex enveloping us like an erotic blanket as we continue fucking her into oblivion.

I'm close, so fucking close, but I refuse to come first.

Quinn's inner muscles contract once more and I know Hunter's about to lose his fucking mind when he moans like he's in physical pain.

"Switch." I look to Rory and he doesn't need to be reminded of who's in charge here. Pulling Quinn's head off his cock, he brings her mouth to his and kisses her like he's punishing her for the pleasure she just gave him.

"I fucking love your mouth, baby." Hunter pulls out too, his jaw clenched and his nostrils flaring. I know that look, he's trying to hold back.

Quinn gets on all fours where Rory redirects her mouth to his cock once more and I slam back into her cunt like I'm starved for it.

In this position, I don't hold back.

With every thrust of my hips, I hit her sweet spot over and over again until she's screaming around Rory's dick, making his eyes roll to the back of his head.

I'm almost at the edge of my control when Hunter

walks back in, his cock clean and ready to fuck her pussy.

We move once more and Quinn is almost a rag doll by now, but that permanent grin on her face is an image I'll never forget and the knowledge that I helped put it there only drives me to give her more.

More of me.

More of us.

More of this.

Moving back to my chair, Quinn kneels at my feet as she takes my balls into her hand and my cock in her mouth.

Behind her, Hunter and Rory add more lube to her pussy and, like they've practiced this a million times, take turns fucking her.

Her mouth is basically a tight vessel for my cock. I'm the one controlling her movements because, with everything happening, she's completely lost in the sensations of it all.

"You like this, Kitten? Getting your pussy and ass pounded by the three of us? Me using your mouth like a good little whore? Huh? You want to swallow up their cocks, beautiful? Take them both?" I'm just rambling at this point, getting her wetter and wetter, enough so that she can take them both at once.

I know the exact moment they both enter her because her entire body goes still. She's barely breathing, my cock stuffed inside her mouth, her hand clutching my balls with a finger pressing against my taint.

Fuck me, I'm going to lose it before any of them.

Once she's adjusted, she relaxes again, her mouth more pliant, her finger rubbing my sensitive skin to the point that I doubt my abilities to hold back.

"Make her come, Rory. Fucking now!"

Rory reaches up with both hands and wraps his fingers around her throat as Hunter circles her waist until he finds her clit.

My cock is deep, so deep I know I'm in her throat as she coughs and gags around it while Rory takes her ability to breathe away long enough to bring panic into her beautiful eyes.

She looks up at me, love and appreciation swimming in her irises as I mouth, "I love you" to her.

She loses it.

Just as her body begins to convulse, Rory lets go of her throat and they both begin pounding her pussy like it's the fucking promised land while I make her swallow my entire length.

I think we all come at the same time. The wet, slapping sounds of their bodies and the gurgled gagging coming from Quinn as she swallows my cum all happen at the exact same moment.

It feels like we come for an eternity. Rory and Hunter's heads are both thrown back in ecstasy while mine is resting against the chair, looking down at my little kitten as she laps me up like I'm her favorite milk.

When the guys pull out, Quinn relaxes, her mouth sliding up my spent cock and her lips placing a chaste kiss on the slit where another drop of cum beads just for her.

The greedy tip of her tongue takes it into her mouth before she climbs up my body and curls into a little ball on my lap.

"Happy birthday, Kitten. It's going to be hard to top this next year."

I wake up, back stiff, and realize I'm still on the floor of my office, wrapped in Quinn and blankets.

Well shit. I am way too old for this.

Rory and Hunter are MIA, so I'm guessing they woke up and were sensible enough to find an actual bed.

Holding in my groan as I extract my arm from under Quinn, I push myself to sit up, rubbing a hand down my face. It's fucking freezing in here. The fire must have died overnight and these blankets are not enough to stay warm.

Watching the blonde beauty sleeping is enough to distract me from the cold and pain, but when her eyes flicker open, she stretches, winces, then shivers and I call time on my personal little peep show.

"Come on, Sleeping Beauty, let's go shower, warm up,

loosen up and then I have another surprise for you."

She blinks at me, yawning as she stretches again, her face scrunching up as she does. "We're too old for sleeping on the floor."

I laugh at her parroting my earlier thoughts. "Unfortunately, we are, so let's scratch camping off of any bucket lists. I think real beds are necessary."

Her laughter is enough to push the thoughts of cold and aches away as I stand, offering her a hand as I do. She grabs the blankets, throwing one at me before wrapping one around her shoulders. "Real beds and hot showers. Now come on, I happen to know your shower is way better than mine."

She winks at me before high tailing it from my office, so I grab my clothes from the floor and chase behind her, my blood pumping at the thrill of watching her run from me, even if it is all just a tease. I let her keep ahead, watching her ass bounce where the blanket doesn't quite drop low enough is more than a good enough reason to lose this race.

She dips into my room and I follow behind, closing the door behind me as I hear her turn on the shower in my bathroom.

Not exactly how I pictured our morning going, but you won't find me complaining.

Except my phone rings right as I go to step toward

the bathroom. "I'll be in in a minute," I call out to her, frowning harder when I see the name on the screen of my phone.

"What do you want, Edward?" I grunt down the phone. I have nothing to say to this asshole, so there's no reason to call. We wrapped up the shit with the Ghosts and the Demons before handing over everything to the Knights. Not that they gave us much choice, but since our goals aligned, we accepted their terms. The bikers are their problem now, and good luck to them. That is one headache I don't fucking miss. Childish, inflated ego, assholes that they are.

"That's no way to greet a friend, Meyer. So good to talk to you. I just wanted to check in, make sure you're playing along to the rules of our agreement."

I clench my jaw, trying to keep my rage bottled. Yes, we agreed to give these assholes basically everything, to play by their rules, but the threats they made about Quinn if we didn't... yeah, it still pisses me off. "You already know we are."

"Glad to hear it," he purrs. I swear I can see that stupid ass smile on his face. I'd love to beat it from him. "We have some new... opportunities coming up. I wondered if you and your family would be interested."

"I told you we were out and I meant it. Your rules aren't hard to follow because we don't want to be a part of that shit anymore, so you can keep your opportunities and leave us the hell alone." The silent threat hangs in the air between us. I wasn't exactly subtle after his threats to Quinn, but I wasn't bluffing then either.

The Knights might be powerful and far reaching, but you touch the things I love and I will burn you and everything you hold dear to nothing but ashes.

"Oh, I remember." I pinch the bridge of my nose and contemplate changing my fucking number, not that I think it will help, but it might make me feel better. "Anyway, that was all, just checking in. I'm sure we'll speak again soon."

"Lets not," I grunt and end the call.

I won't say there aren't parts of that life I miss, but for the most part, I'm happy with the exchange we made. That doesn't mean I'm not still waiting for the other shoe to drop at some point.

People like Edward Riley never really let you go once they have their claws in you, not unless it's to let you bleed out slowly. So slowly you don't even notice it.

Letting out a breath, I drop my phone onto the bed and enter the bathroom to find Quinn already showered and wrapped in towels. "I was cold and now I'm hungry. We can play later."

She pats my cheek before ducking away, but I swat her ass as she runs. I grab a quick shower, dressing once I'm done while she dries her hair.

I clear out my emails while I wait for her, excited about her last gift, but also curious as to how she'll react.

"Food?" she asks as she shuts off the hair dryer, and I can't help but laugh. I do love her appetite.

"Let's get food," I agree.

Carlos cooks up a storm for breakfast, it's basically a breakfast buffet in my kitchen, but since he wasn't here yesterday, I guess this is his version of birthday breakfast for Quinn. I do love how they still bicker like they hate each other when it's so obvious how much they don't.

The guys are already chowing down, and I know it'll be hours until Shae makes an appearance. Mama will have already been up and out for the day. I got my early-bird trait from her, that's for sure.

I sit and enjoy my coffee while enjoying watching her eat. It's only when she leans back, groaning and rubbing her tummy, that I pull the envelope from my back pocket.

Her eyes go wide as I slide it across the table to her. "What is this?"

"The surprise I said about," I tell her with a wink.

"I thought breakfast was my surprise. You already got me so much, you give me so much every—"

"Open the freaking envelope, Quinn," Hunter says, cutting her off. I know she's still not used to being loved, and especially not in the potentially over-the-top ways we go about it, but this is how we love. And it's never going to change.

She carefully opens the envelope and her eyes go wide as she reads the paper inside. "Snow?"

"Yes, there will be snow," I chuckle. "At least, there better be. Can't really go snowboarding without it. We have a cabin on the lake, not far from the main resort."

The way her entire face lights up is exactly why I got us this trip. I remember her telling me how much she missed snow last Christmas, that she'd never got to play in it as a kid, but whenever it snowed, she could hide and pretend that she was in a land far, far away. Admittedly, this is only Canada—I wanted to take her to Austria, but Shae thought a closer trip would be a better idea for our first actual vacation together—but there will still be plenty of snow for her to pretend she's back in her fantasy land.

"Thank you, Meyer," she gasps, flinging herself from her chair and into my lap. "Thank you."

"Happy birthday, Kitten. Here's to the many more that we get to spend together."

EPILOGUE

QUINN
TWO YEARS LATER

It's funny to think of how I thought my life would go. Because being here, tidying up after today's baby shower, really isn't something I pictured. Surrounded by friends and family, celebrating Shae's pregnancy.

Freaking wild,

It took a lot to get here.

Pain.

Heartbreak.

Betrayal.

But also, love.

So. Much. Love.

Being out of "the life" has been hard for the guys, especially when they seem to keep getting dragged back in, but now with a lot less power than they had before. I try not to worry, but since Denton moved out here and is almost a permanent fixture here at the moment, sometimes it's hard not to.

Times like when they disappear for days on end and tell me the shit going on after it's happened. It doesn't seem to matter how much I yell at them that I can handle knowing before, they always seem to think it's safer for me to worry like crazy and know later.

I love them but my God, they're still giant assholes.

Except, they're starting to gray, and it's funny teasing them about it.

"Earth to Quinn," Shae teases, rubbing her rounded belly, and I smile wide. She is glowing.

Not long after we found out about Tommy being my uncle, she came with me to find more of his... *my* family. Which is when she met Rosie. The love of her freaking life.

Who just happens to be my second cousin.

They started the whole baby making thing about six months after meeting, and well, now we're here, joining our two families.

Some people might think it's a little weird, I'd maybe call it unconventional, but also, love is love. The universe works in mysterious ways, and I've learned not to question it too much.

"Are you okay?" I ask her when she winces.

"Yeah, this little guy just seems to think he's training

for a soccer team or something." She groans as she rubs her stomach again, then Rosie appears like a ball of sunshine and Shae is smiling instantly. "I'm hungry," Shae whines, and I laugh right along with my cousin.

"My love," Rosie coos. "You are always hungry. I'm convinced you've just got a black hole in there, not our kid."

They continue to tease each other as they head to the buffet tables that are still laden with food as I finish bagging up all of the discarded wrapping paper from where they opened the gifts before most people started to leave. Tonio watches over them fervently, like he always does. I swear, that kid is going to have more protective "uncles" than it knows what to do with.

Lucky for him, I'm totally prepared to be the fun, wild, rebel-against-them all, crazy aunt.

Looking around, I smile again. So much love came from something so dark, and I can't help but wonder if that's what the universe had planned all along. I never used to think much about fate, but maybe I had to go through what I did, to meet these people, to end up here.

I tie a knot in the final trash bag and look around for someone to help me get rid of it all. I think Angela is with Meyer and the guys in the kitchen, Yen and Luca disappeared, so they probably made a mad dash to leave, and Tina... I have no idea where she got to.

"Want some help with that?" Bruno asks, popping up, scaring the crap out of me like the silent ninja that he is. He chuckles when I squeak and does a fist pump. "Still got it."

"You're an ass," I say with a chuckle. "But yes, please. Who would've thought there'd be this much trash from one baby shower?"

He grabs most of the bags before quirking a brow at me. "Have you met the Marino clan?"

"Yeah, yeah. I know." Turns out the Miller clan are just as bad. Which has made birthdays and Christmases insane. But it's fun to be surrounded by so much love, so while it's still a little weird to me, I've learned to embrace the fact that our families have merged the way they have, and just roll with the crazy.

I find Tina sitting on the front steps, crying on the phone. Frowning, Bruno takes my bags from me and nods toward her. "Thank you," I mouth to him and move to sit by my friend, who leans her head on my shoulder while she finishes her call.

Once she hangs up, she quietly cries beside me, so I sit with her, arm wrapped around her, for as long as she needs.

"Sorry," she hiccups as she sits up and wipes at her face. "That was James. It's over."

"He ended it over the phone?" I swear to God, that man better hope I don't see him any time soon. He's an ass and Tina deserves way better than him, but she's also my friend, so I've been here for her through their whole eighteen month, on again, off again, maybe is, maybe isn't relationship.

"It's for the best," she says before letting out a deep sigh. "He's a great guy underneath all his pain, he's just not a great guy for me. I can see that now. And whether he realizes it or not, and no matter how much it hurts right now, I know that this is the best thing for me. He says I deserve better, and he's right. Maybe if he'd actually taken the time to work on his shit like I have been doing, like I encouraged him to, things would be different, but he wasn't ready. And that's okay. I think it's going to be good for me to be alone for a while, focus on me."

I wrap my friend in a tight hug. "I am so freaking proud of you." Not one lie falls from my lips. I know how hard it is to come to that realization, to understand that the hurt is only temporary, but also necessary.

"Everything okay out here?" Turning, I find Meyer standing in the doorway, concern written all over his handsome face. The salt and pepper in his hair really does suit him, even if I tease him about it every now and then.

"Just fine," I tell him, smiling wide at him.

"I should go," Tina says, releasing me before standing. "Thank you for today, it was great. Tell Shae and Rosie I said bye?"

"I will," I nod to her, noticing O'Connor hovering in

the distance. I wave to him as I stand and he strides across the front yard, keys in hand, and Tina moves to him before they walk to his car.

Hmmmm, I wonder.

"Don't you start matchmaking," Meyer murmurs as he wraps his arms around me from behind. "Today has me thinking we should keep trying for the small humans."

I let out a laugh as his stubble grazes my cheek while he kisses the edge of my jaw. "I thought we'd agreed no small humans?"

"We did, but maybe we should talk it out again? Family meeting?" His arms tighten as I lean my head back against his shoulder.

"Family meeting," I agree, my heart full of joy. We talked about it before, but we weren't all ready. One thing we did decide... if we decided to go ahead, if we had a boy, his name would be Tommy. A girl would be Kate. And yes, I cried for at least a whole day.

Maybe now is a better time. Who knows?

All I know for sure, is that this life is full of surprises and you never really know what's in your next chapter.

SIGN UP FOR MY NEWSLETTER TO HEAR ABOUT UPCOMING RELEASES

ABOUT THE AUTHOR

Lily is a writer, dreamer, fur mom and serial killer, crime documentary addict.

She loves to write dark, reverse harem romance and characters who will shatter your heart. Characters who enjoy stomping on the pieces and then laugh before putting you back together again. And she definitely doesn't enjoy readers tears. Nope. Not even a little.

Visit her website at http://www.lilywildhart.com to sign up for the newsletter or find her on social media through the links below.

ALSO BY LILY WILDHART

THE KNIGHTS OF ECHOES COVE

(Dark, Bully, High School Reverse Harem Romance)

Tormented Royal

Lost Royal

Caged Royal

Forever Royal

THE SAINTS OF SERENTIY FALLS

(Dark, Bully, Step Brother, College, Reverse Harem Romance)

A Burn so Deep

A Revenge So Sweet

A Taste of Forever

THE SECRETS WE KEEP

(Dark, Mafia, Reverse Harem Romance, Duet)

The Secrets We Keep

The Truths We Seek

THE SHADOW WALKERS SAGA

(Dark, Paranormal/Fantasy Why Choose Romance)

The Ruin of Souls

The Birth of Chaos

The Secret of Pain

The Misery of Shadows
The Reaping of Envy
The Rise of Dawn

THE SHADOW LEGACIES I

(MF, Rejected/Fated Mates, Paranormal Romance)
Luna Rising
Alpha Bound
Alpha Born